W9-BZS-350

Under the INFLUENCE
ELIZABETH TRAVIS

W☉RLDWIDE.

TORONTO • NEW YORK • LONDON
AMSTERDAM • PARIS • SYDNEY • HAMBURG
STOCKHOLM • ATHENS • TOKYO • MILAN
MADRID • WARSAW • BUDAPEST • AUCKLAND

UNDER THE INFLUENCE

A Worldwide Mystery/March 1992

First published by St. Martin's Press Incorporated.

ISBN 0-373-26092-X

---------------- ★ ----------------

FROM THE CROOK OF THE ARM THAT RESTED ON HIS CHEST, THE HANDLE OF A KNIFE PROTRUDED...

Carrie grasped the back of the chair and stood swaying, rocking the chair on its feet. She could not stop looking, though the smell she had traced hung about her now in an invisible, choking cloud. Or was it her horrified recognition of the corpse that had closed her throat so she could not breathe?

For, deny it all she might, only one man had eyes with such long, dark lashes; only one a head of brown hair so youthfully streaked with blond; only one man besides Ben wore blue jeans streaked with paint. It was Greg Dillon who lay there stabbed to death on the floor of Ben's office.

---------------- ★ ----------------

"With deft strokes, Travis reveals the psychological motivation of the crime; the denouement is a complete surprise."
—*Publishers Weekly*

A Forthcoming Worldwide Mystery by
ELIZABETH TRAVIS

FINDERS KEEPERS

To Elizabeth Murray,
without whom it would have been
a very different story.

ONE

Friday, June 13 Evening

THE RIVERVALE RAMBLERS launched one of their heavy-handed attempts at rock and roll, clearing the floor in minutes of all dancers but those too drunk or too tone-deaf to notice the switch—and Gregory Dillon and Carrie Porter, who continued moving smoothly about the floor in time with some inner music of their own.

They were, of course, conspicuous, dancing against the thrust of the music, still pressed close together as they turned and swayed in graceful contrast to those who followed the jarring rock beat. They had been conspicuous before the music changed, would have caused heads to turn in any setting, they were such a well-matched couple: both tall and slim, both with the shining, blond-streaked hair and tanned skin of teenagers, although they were in their thirties. And both were unperturbed by the attention turned on them, Carrie because she was lost in the dream-like pleasure of dancing with Gregory Dillon, Greg because attention had become an accustomed gloss on his life, as necessary as the coat of varnish he applied to his finished paintings.

"Hey, everybody's out of step but us." Carrie smiled up at Greg, moving her body a fraction away from his with some regret.

"Who cares?"

There was a second's gleam of smiling brown eyes, the flash of white teeth, then Greg's warm cheek was pressed to Carrie's once again and the fraction of space between them eliminated. She felt his long legs striding, pausing, turning with hers in the effortless rhythm that distinguished Greg Dillon as a dancer, as an athlete, and, Carrie had thought more than once, probably as a lover.

She pushed away more firmly, and this time slowed her steps and dropped her arms. Still clasping his hand, she said, "It's always hard to stop, isn't it?"

"Impossible." He seized her again, but she slipped out of his grasp and drew him to the edge of the floor, toward the round tables where their friends—among them her husband and Greg's wife—sat over their after-dinner highballs.

Faces turned to watch their progress; certain ones had been focused on them for some time, Carrie was aware, and she held herself very straight and pushed her hair back from her flushed face as she and Greg approached her table. There she quickly scooped up her handbag, and instead of sitting down in the chair Greg held for her, excused herself and headed for the ladies' room to make repairs. Ben Porter, she had observed in her quick survey of the table, was apparently unaware of either her arrival or departure. He appeared totally absorbed in conversation with the good-looking, auburn-haired girl from Oyster Bay who had come to the party with the Dillons, but whom Jenny Dillon had had the good sense to seat at the Porters' table. Even so, Greg Dillon was at that very moment advancing to ask her to dance. Carrie could see him from the corner of her eye and could also see the girl, Jenny's cousin, she thought she was, looking up as he approached with a smile of welcome forming on her lips.

Carrie was smiling too as she entered the ladies' room. Would it be incestuous for Greg Dillon to sleep with his wife's cousin? And if so would Greg be deterred? The question was as laughable as was the possibility that the girl might turn him down.

The door swung shut behind her, and the throbbing din of the music was instantly replaced by another dissonance: the sound of female voices, some soft, some strident, rising from the women who politely bobbed and jostled in competition for a place before the mirror. Nimbly stepping into a momentary opening, Carrie gave her full attention to her reflection. Her fair skin was indeed flushed, she saw, but only slightly; her hair needed work, of course, lying flat against the side of her head that had been pressed to Greg's cheek, but a moment's work with her hairbrush took care of that.

Bending close to the glass, she saw that her makeup was in good shape; the long lashes that framed her blue eyes were still neatly mascaraed, her lipstick remained on her lips, not her teeth; all she repaired was a dash of powder and a squirt of cologne and she could return to the fray.

She smoothed her white linen sheath over her flat stomach, pleased by the way the starkly simple dress enhanced her figure. Be grateful, she often told herself at such moments; good looks were largely a matter of luck, she knew, and Carrie had been luckier than most.

A face appeared beside hers in the mirror, quite another kind of face than Carrie's, but, in its sharply defined contours and dramatic coloring, as distinctive.

"How are you, Carrie?" The voice was crisp, as direct as the clear, dark gaze reflected in the glass.

"Oh, fine, Enid; but what happened? I thought you and Garvin weren't coming."

Carrie stepped aside to give her place to another woman and waited while Enid Thorpe pulled a brush through her dark hair with firm, efficient strokes.

"I finished the paper I've been working on ahead of schedule, and Garvin seemed to want to come, so..." Carrie saw an expression of puzzlement flicker across the face in the mirror, as if a husband's desire for an evening of pleasure were some kind of strange aberration.

"Well, you deserved a night out, Enid; you work so hard."

Enid swung around, snapping her handbag shut, and, striding to the door, held it open for Carrie to precede her. The Ramblers had returned to their usual more melodic repertoire, and the dance floor was once more crowded with rhythmically gyrating couples.

Enid raised her voice to be heard above the music. "We ought to be leaving soon. Garvin's busiest day is Saturday."

They had reached the cluster of round tables, most of them deserted by the dancers, and, with their white tablecloths now wrinkled and spotted, their skimpy centerpieces of day lilies beginning to droop, looking less than inviting. With her lime-colored silk skirt swirling about her ankles Enid threaded her way purposefully between the tables, pushing chairs back into place as she went.

Carrie saw that her table was empty. Even Ben, who hated to dance, must have gone in pursuit of Jenny Dillon's beautiful cousin. Turning for a look at the dance floor, Carrie saw him, in fact, happily swinging the girl about and talking energetically into her ear.

He was probably persuading her to pose for him. Carrie sometimes teased that he had taken up painting only to gain entree with pretty girls, to which he would loftily reply that he didn't have to resort to such measures.

Greg Dillon, temporarily detached, was threading his way towards the edge of the floor. In a second he would spot her standing there, Carrie realized, and it would not do for them to dance together again so soon. Luckily she had paused near a table that was still partly occupied. She sank into the nearest chair and, drawing it close, began an animated conversation.

Too late she realized her mistake. The table she had chosen as refuge was the Dillons', and even as Jenny turned her smiling, pretty face in her direction Carrie felt a hand lightly brush her shoulder, and an instant later saw Greg Dillon slide his lithe body into the seat beside her.

"How's my girl?" His voice was husky, intimate, appallingly so to Carrie, until she saw, her glance having frozen on Jenny Dillon's face, that it was his wife Greg had addressed.

There was always a radiance about Jenny Dillon, but her husband's words set off such brilliance in her smile, such a glow in her eyes, that Carrie turned away. The devotion was too naked; it should not be so openly displayed—not for a man who deserved it as little as Greg Dillon.

Someone else apparently felt as Carrie did. Before Jenny could reply a man who had come up to the table said, "Come and dance, Jenny."

It was Garvin Thorpe who drew Jenny to her feet with the authority of long acquaintance, while she gave a small, helpless shrug, still directing that melting look of love at her husband, then pushed back her chair and rose to go with Garvin.

Carrie felt the touch of Greg's fingers on her arm, but at the same instant the man on her right, Bill Kingsley, seized her hand and pulled her out of her chair, and feeling a mixture of relief and disappointment, she went willingly along with him to the dance floor.

What ensued fell into a different category of experience from dancing with Greg Dillon. Following Bill's unpredictable steps called for all of Carrie's considerable expertise, and made her wonder if parties like that night's could possibly be sectioned off, with certain tables for dancers, others for conversationalists. And then what would you do with Bill Kingsley, who was neither? Leave him in the bar, where he would be most content? No, for much as he loved it, drinking wasn't Bill's forte either. His round face was red and perspiring; still he felt obliged to press it against Carrie's cheek—to show his friendliness, she supposed, or sexiness, or perhaps because he needed to lean on somebody at that point and she happened to be there.

The music stopped and Bill Kingsley released Carrie from his warm, damp embrace. Brightly they beamed at each other, grateful, it might appear, for having been granted a glimpse of heaven; then Bill escorted Carrie to her table, steering her with a firm grip of one arm back to where he had left his unfinished drink.

The group at the table was much reduced and, while Bill Kingsley seized his glass and beckoned to a waiter for a refill, most of the returning dancers paused only long enough to say good night, then began moving in the direction of the door.

Ben Porter patted the seat beside him, looking at Carrie with a quizzical expression that told her he knew exactly how much she had enjoyed the last dance. Jenny Dillon sat on his other side, looking as fresh in her daisy-printed silk dress as she had at the beginning of the evening. Carrie sank into her chair, feeling, in comparison, like a plow-hand returning from the fields.

"I've ordered you a drink," Ben said. "Hope you don't mind."

Carrie searched her handbag for her compact. "We ought to go, shouldn't we? What time is it?"

She felt Ben's knee pressing against hers and looked up to see him slide a meaningful glance at Jenny Dillon, whose smile, Carrie now realized, had taken on a sadly familiar bleakness.

That bastard! she said to herself, darting a quick, searching look around the nearly emptied room. Nowhere among the stragglers did she find the tall, attractive figure she sought; no head of blond-streaked, slightly tousled hair, no flash of laughing, deep brown eyes. Equally notable was the absence of another of the evening's more striking personalities: Jenny's beautiful, auburn-haired cousin from Oyster Bay.

The scenario for the next hour had been well rehearsed. Jenny Dillon would stay drinking and chatting with the Porters and the Kingsleys, her face growing pinched with strain, until the yawning waiters could no longer be ignored. Then, with a great show of reluctance and no mention of missing husbands or good-looking relatives, the group would get up and take their leave. Jenny would accept a ride home with the Kingsleys, who lived near her, and while they walked to their cars pretending to ignore the absence in the lot of Greg Dillon's brown Jaguar, the suggestion of a nightcap would be bandied and good-naturedly dropped.

Someone would remark on the beauty of the night and the size of the moon reflected on the shimmering river.

Voices calling good night would float briefly on the cool night air, car doors would slam, and the crunch of departing tires on the gravel would signal the end of the Boat Club's opening dance.

TWO

GARVIN THORPE CONDUCTED his psychiatric practice in an office wing he and Enid had added to their brick ranch house when they moved to Rivervale three years earlier. The zoning had been changed since, making the neighborhood strictly residential, so Garvin was careful not to offend. He provided a generous off-street parking area for his patients, with a high hedge to shield it from view, and had marked the entrance to his office with a discreet brass plaque beside the door.

The door opened on a small, windowless reception area that was carpeted in light beige and contained two small sofas upholstered in coral tweed and, in a clay pot on the floor between them, a three-foot plastic ficus tree from which Garvin shook the dust every morning on his way in. A bentwood coatrack stood in one corner, and a table beside it held current issues of *Psychology Today* and *Natural History* magazine.

The consulting room was also done in beige and was furnished with a full-size sofa and three chairs upholstered in the coral tweed. Garvin's bleached walnut desk stood before a wide window that looked out onto the Thorpes' neatly mowed lawn and hedge. The top of their neighbors' wooden swing set rose above the hedge, and since Garvin sat with his back to the window, his patients could sometimes see children climbing on the bars and hear the rhythmic creaking of the swings. Garvin sometimes speculated on whether the sight helped with their laborious quest to retrieve childhood memories.

When the doorbell rang that Saturday Garvin had already been at his desk for an hour. He needed a period of quiet each morning to review case histories and prepare himself, mentally and emotionally, to meet the demands of his patients. He knew almost nothing about this first one, he realized, as he went to the door, except that he lived in the nearby town of Springfield and was disturbed about his marriage.

At first glance Frank Lundy appeared to be in his forties, older than he had sounded on the telephone; but he moved with the springy, athletic step of a younger man as he entered and followed Garvin into the consulting room. He cast a quick glance of appraisal around the office, then turned the same cool, measuring regard on Thorpe himself. It was his manner that was old, Garvin decided; his pale, serious face looked so taut it might hurt to smile.

His clothes aged Frank Lundy too; he wore a gray business suit made of smooth, almost slick, wool gabardine, and a white shirt and navy blue tie. He adjusted the trousers as he sat down in the chair before Garvin's desk, apparently to preserve their sharp crease, then crossed his legs, folded his hands in his lap, and looked across the desk top with the guarded expression so many patients wore on the first visit.

Garvin's idea was to appear comfortably relaxed, the wise old family doc who could absorb all revelations with benevolent understanding. Knowing he was too young to look the part, he tried to compensate by wearing baggy corduroys and sweaters and a slightly shaggy haircut. He kept a pipe on his desk, though he never smoked, and a pair of spectacles that he put on and removed at intervals, if he thought of it.

The first few moments of the interview were taken up with Frank's personal history: his upbringing in a small town in western Connecticut, where his father had been a housepainter and his mother a teacher; his brother and sister, whom he rarely saw; his education at the University of Connecticut, which had led to an accounting degree and eventually to the opening of his own office in Springfield.

"I think that takes care of the vital statistics," Garvin said finally. He smiled across the desk and said, "How did you hear about me, Frank?"

"Called the hospital," Frank Lundy replied briskly. "I don't know anybody who uses a shrink."

"As far as you know." Garvin's smile became confiding.

"Right. As far as I know."

"And what made you decide to take the step?"

"My wife." Lundy's face was suddenly bleak. The pale skin seemed to draw tighter over his high cheekbones and the bridge of his nose. "She's sleeping around."

"Are you certain of that?" Garvin was no longer smiling, but he kept his voice low and gentle.

"Well, I haven't caught her in the sack, if that's what you mean, but hell yes, I'm sure." Lundy shifted in his seat, uncrossing his legs, gripping the arms of the chair as if he were about to spring out of it.

"Has she admitted that she is having an affair?" Garvin peered thoughtfully at Frank Lundy. "I guess I'm assuming that you have asked her, perhaps accused her. Have you?"

Lundy sank back, dropping his hands limply into his lap. "I suppose it's weird to admit it, but no, I haven't. I'm...I guess I'm afraid to." He swallowed hard and glanced away from Garvin's probing eyes.

"But you feel certain something is going on. Why?"

"Partly because I've caught her lying: saying she was on her way to the nightclub where she works and then not being there when I called. And she's changed, sort of clammed up around me. She's quiet; she doesn't have much to say. Her mind always seems to be somewhere else."

"I'll want to hear more about that, but first, what kind of work does she do in this nightclub?"

"She's a singer. Thinks she's big-time talent, I guess."

"What do you think? Do you like her singing?"

"I don't know a damn thing about music. I'm an accountant. I wouldn't let Maria sing in any nightclub, but this place belongs to her cousin, Joe DeLucca. She sure looks great up there, I'll say that.''

"Maria is a beauty, is she?"

"She's a knockout. That's the problem, I guess. You know that Italian coloring, the black eyes and shiny black hair? Plus Maria has great skin, sort of pink and white, and a super body. Did I tell you she also poses for a couple of artists in Rivervale?''

"No. How do you feel about her modeling?"

"The way any guy would feel. I hate it, even though she swears she never poses in the nude. Modeling and singing in nightclubs; I ask you, is that what a wife's supposed to be doing? I must be a wimp, letting her run around like that, showing herself off..."

"You feel you should be in charge of Maria? Tell her how to behave?''

"I sure as hell do. I want you to help me with that. I'm sick of lying awake waiting for her to come home, wondering what she's doing, thinking of all the guys sitting around drinking and ogling my wife.''

"That's hard for you." Garvin's voice had dropped to a near whisper; his brown eyes were soft with compassion as he waited for Lundy's response.

"Yes," Lundy muttered huskily, then quickly cleared his throat and sat up straighter in the chair.

"I gather you don't wait up for Maria to come in from her singing jobs?''

"I can't do it, running my own business. I've got to be in the office and on the ball at eight in the morning or forget it. There's plenty of CPAs out there. It's a damn competitive business.''

"What do you say when she comes to bed?"

"Sometimes I'm asleep; sometimes I pretend to be asleep just to avoid a hassle. Especially if she's been drinking.''

"Oh? Is Maria a heavy drinker?"

"No, but drinking goes with the territory. She says it relaxes her, makes her sing better. And she's a friendly type; likes to kid around with the customers.''

Garvin penciled a note on the pad he held open in his lap.

"How about your own drinking habits?"

"I can take it or leave it. Or I could. These days it's different. If I wake up and start wondering about Maria I have a few belts so I can get to sleep. I can't get by with three or four hours, the workload I'm carrying."

"How do you feel when you think of your marriage breaking up?"

"I feel terrible, sort of sick. I'll tell you something, Doctor; I even feel scared."

All at once Lundy looked young and vulnerable. His thin cheeks were tinged with pink, and Thorpe saw genuine alarm in his eyes.

He said gently, "You don't have to call me Doctor. I would like you to call me by my first name, Garvin. Now what is it that scares you? Can you say what it is?"

"I'm scared that I'll fall apart if she leaves me. I don't know what that would be like except bad, lost, helpless." The words came in a rush, and Lundy stopped abruptly, fighting for control.

"You are afraid of how you might feel."

"Yes, that's it." He paused, again struggling with his emotions, but his eyes had filled with tears. He said, "Oh God, I didn't think I'd break down like this."

"There is Kleenex on the table beside you," Garvin said. "You don't have to be ashamed here, Frank. This is the place to express your feelings."

"There's more to it than that." Lundy's voice was suddenly harsh. "I'm scared of what I might do."

"To Maria?"

"Yes. Or to the guy. Especially if it's who I think it is, one of the painters she poses for. He's got it coming, the bastard. But am I going to let him wreck my life?"

Garvin started to speak, but Lundy sprang to his feet and, planting his fists on the edge of the desk, demanded, "Should I let them push me into doing something that would get me in jail? That's just what they'd like, wouldn't they? Well, I'm not making it so easy, I tell you. He's the guy that ought to be locked up, not me!''

"Please sit down, Frank." Garvin spoke calmly, still comfortably slouched in his chair. He looked at his watch and said, "Our time is nearly up, I'm afraid, but I want you to come back soon. How about Tuesday at ten? Can you make that all right?"

Lundy stared at him for a moment, then groped behind him for the chair and slowly lowered himself into it. He said in a monotone, "I have an appointment Tuesday at ten."

"How about eight-thirty?"

"I can do that. Eight-thirty Tuesday. Okay."

"Meanwhile, I'm going to ask you to do something that often proves very helpful: Keep a record of your dreams, and bring it with you when you come in."

"My dreams? What is this? I thought you were a psychiatrist, not some kind of nut."

Garvin smiled. "Feelings of which you may be unaware are often expressed symbolically in dreams. Interpretation of these symbols can be a useful tool for the therapist."

"Well, I don't have time for that kind of crap."

"Just note down what you remember, as sketchily as you like. A line or two is often enough. I'd like you to try it once or twice anyway, Frank."

Shaking his head dubiously, Lundy got to his feet and adjusted his trousers, bending to straighten out the sharp crease. His voice was muffled as he said, "I'll think about it."

Garvin rose and came around from behind the desk. He said, "How would you feel about my having a talk with Maria?"

"Oh, I don't know about that, Doc. I don't want her to know I came in here. Not yet anyway."

"Very well. But later on if you should feel like it I think it might be productive to bring Maria into our discussions."

"Just don't push me, Doc, I warn you. Don't push me and we'll get along fine."

Saturday, June 14 Afternoon

WHEN THE TELEPHONE RANG Ben Porter did not stir. Carrie shaded her eyes from the noon sun as she watched him continue reading while the phone rang three more times, then she picked up the portable instrument and carried it into the house. She was smiling as she said, "Hello."

Ben's concentration meant that he was caught up in Sam Blake's new manuscript—a great relief, since Sam's last two hadn't passed the test, and if his fans grew tired of waiting and turned to other mystery writers they might find they could live without Sam Blake. That would be something of a disaster for the Porter Publishing Company.

"Carrie, it's Enid Thorpe. I hate to bother you on Saturday, but it's so hard to catch you at home during the week. I don't like to call you at the office."

"I know, Enid. Very thoughtful of you, but it's really okay. Did you have fun at the dance? You looked terrific."

"The dance? Oh yes, very pleasant. What I'm calling about, Carrie, is the Mental Health Committee. You asked me to serve again next fall."

"I do hope you're saying yes."

"Well, I feel a little guilty about it, but I'm going to beg off this time. It's been five years, you know, and I'm thinking about getting back to my own work."

"I can't blame you for that. We've been lucky to have a psychologist on the board this long. Are you going to practice with Garvin?"

"I'm not sure just how we'll set it up. I hope by September we'll have things figured out. Meanwhile, I assure you the committee is well able to carry on without me. Lots of good people—Jenny Dillon, in particular. She would make a fine chairman."

"I agree with you, if we can get her to take it on. You know, Enid, I think it would help if I could tell her you would serve as a sort of consultant. What would you say to that?"

"I thought you might want me to, but I wonder if you might be receptive to the idea of asking Garvin instead. He thinks it's time he gave something to the community, and actually I think Jenny will be more likely to take on the job if she knows Garvin will be the adviser. They're old friends, you know, from college."

"I didn't know that, no. And Enid, I really appreciate your taking the trouble. I mean, wasn't it hard to talk Garvin into this? He's so busy..."

"I think it might depend somewhat on Jenny's decision, to tell you the truth. We have a delicate balance here, Carrie. If we get one of them we'll probably have very little trouble getting the other."

"That's a wily psychologist talking. Thanks, Enid. I'll attack along those lines, and I hope you'll give me more advice if I need it."

"Any time; but I think you'll do fine on your own."

Carrie clicked off the phone and placed it on the recharging unit that stood on the table near the door to the deck. She slid open the screen door and stepped out into the sun. She could hear the children playing in their plastic pool on the side lawn. They sounded happy, and, glancing at her watch, she saw that it was just twelve-thirty. No use starting lunch until Brooke and Terry got bored or started fighting. Ben appeared not to have moved, but she saw that the stack of manuscript on the table beside his chair had grown higher, so he had been turning pages, at least.

"Hey!" She walked over and gently ruffled his gray-streaked brown hair. "Are you all right? You haven't moved for two hours."

He looked up at her, crinkling his eyes against the bright sun. "We've got a winner here. With a new opening, and a little tightening in the middle..."

"Oh boy. We need one. So does Sam, I should think."

"Yes, it's been a while." Ben placed the unread sheets on the deck, frowning while he looked around for something to anchor them down.

Carrie handed him the clay flowerpot that served as an outdoor ashtray. "We can get it on our spring list, I should think, if we can start on the editing right away."

"What else do we have for spring? I've forgotten."

"There's the Percy Morris spy story, a self-help by good old Agnes Mathison Sleighbury, two cookbooks, that vet's story: *Grooming Secrets of the Stars' Pets* . . ."

"I never thought we'd sink so low. And didn't we send Reynolds a contract for a first novel? The girl from Kansas who's been writing since she was four?"

"I remember that depressing lunch. She put lemon juice in her drinking water and brought her own granola." Carrie smiled, reflecting. "But we can have a great lunch with Sam. Let's call him right now and tell him the good news."

"Wait till I finish it. Sometimes he does funny things at the end." Ben leaned back, closed his eyes, and lifted his face to the sun. "I'm bushed. What time did we get home last night?"

"It was almost three. I think we've lost another sitter." Carrie sat down in a deck chair and carefully freed the *New York Times* from where she had pinned it down with one chair leg. She looked across at her husband and her face softened with affection. With his head thrown back and his skin ruddy with sunlight he looked like a healthy boy. His features were craggy, and unexpected small muscles moved when he talked. He had the most expressive face she had ever seen. "I'm glad you're not one of those pretty men," she said. "Like Greg Dillon. They never seem to get over their own gorgeousness."

"He looked good to you last night."

Carrie's glance sharpened, but Ben was still lying back looking completely relaxed.

"Well, he is an unbelievable dancer," Carrie said, "and last night he fixated on me for some reason."

"Probably because you're old and fat and ugly."

"Probably because you were monopolizing Jenny's gorgeous cousin at the time. I wasn't too occupied to notice the way you were drooling over her."

Ben grinned. "What a vulgar way to describe a man's friendly interest in an attractive and stimulating woman." He sat up and sighed. "And after exerting all that charm I lost her to Greg Dillon. That bastard. I suppose he convinced her that he's a better painter than I am."

"I wish I thought that's what he was up to. How can he do such things to Jenny, over and over again?"

"The real mystery is why Jenny stands for it. She's a beautiful woman herself, also intelligent and, I gather, well fixed financially. Why, you would have kicked that guy out years ago." Ben paused. "Wouldn't you?"

"I think so."

"You *think so!* My God, Carrie, if I so much as dance a lot with the same girl I hear about it. And Greg doesn't stop with dancing, you know that."

"The point is, I never would have married a Greg Dillon in the first place, so I can't exactly picture what I'd do in Jenny's situation. I was always drawn to another type, if you recall."

"I recall very well." He reached out and took her hand, and they smiled at each other, both remembering the fun and the surprise of falling in love.

They had met when Ben was hired by the publishing firm of Foote and Marshall, where Carrie worked at the time as a trade books editor. Ben's appearance had immediately caught the attention of the female employees, most of whom were young and single and too attractive for the sort of male editors Foote and Marshall generally employed. These were more apt to be endowed with flawless pedigrees than with anything that remotely could be perceived as sex appeal.

Ben, on the other hand, was tall and lean, with a lazy, athletic grace. His face was too casually thrown together to be called handsome, the brown eyes too deeply set, the nose a bit off center. Still, it was a face that perfectly conveyed Ben's most endearing quality: He was *interested.*

The look in his eyes suggested a mischievous nature held in check, a promise of laughter and naughty secrets to be shared. The word that he had been hired set off a flurry of lunch-hour hair stylings and shopping trips, but the competition did not last long, for Ben had fastened his attention on Carrie almost immediately, and within a year they were married. Four years later, when their son, Terry, was two and their daughter, Brooke, on the way, Ben and Carrie had left Foote and Marshall to start their own small publishing company in Rivervale.

Neither of them had ever regretted either step—the marriage or the business—even though the latter was, after four years, only beginning to show a profit. The marriage had yet to falter, though Carrie felt a twinge of guilt that morning when she remembered how much she had enjoyed having Greg Dillon's formidable charm focused for a while entirely on her. More than once he had suggested that they meet for lunch, and although to Carrie lunching with men was a routine part of her business life, she felt such an unaccustomed thrill at the thought of meeting Greg alone that she knew it was out of the question.

Ben said, "You're blushing."

"I'll bet I haven't blushed for ten years."

That was not true, for Carrie had the fine, fair skin that betrays emotion only too readily. A drawback, she thought; but aside from that debatable one there weren't many drawbacks to being Carrie Porter. Not only was she slim and tall and almost naturally blond, Carrie's children were attractive and reasonably well behaved, her charming converted farmhouse was cared for by the best cleaning woman in town, she was married to a man she loved and who made her laugh a lot, and she had a job she enjoyed—most of the time.

Ben had gotten to his feet and was peering fixedly into the distance, thinking about lunch.

"Chervil," he said. "I'll make a chervil dressing for the chicken in aspic. And maybe some popovers."

"And at least one Bloody Mary."

They started for the kitchen, Ben's arm lightly encircling Carrie's waist; but a wail rose from the play pool, mingled with an angry piping voice, and Carrie stopped in her tracks.

"Two peanut butter and jellies, please," she called as she started for the wooden steps of the deck. "Hold the chervil."

THREE

JENNY AND GREG DILLON lived in a white colonial house
on a road that bordered the village square. The house was
a local landmark, having been owned in the eighteenth
century by a Connecticut lawmaker who required prox-
imity to Litchfield as well as Hartford and found Rivervale, about halfway between, an attractive solution. He
and some of his more prosperous and discerning col-
leagues built themselves gracious, pilastered houses on
wide lawns and completely altered the character of what
had been a simple farming hamlet on the banks of a me-
andering river.

Two hundred years later, in the early twenties, the town
was changed even more when well-to-do New Yorkers
found that acreage was cheap and domestic help plentiful
in the hills and valleys of central Connecticut and began
buying and restoring the beautiful old mansions to use as
summer homes. Ten miles away the town of Springfield
provided rail transport and such amenities as libraries,
hospitals, and movie theaters, leaving Rivervale a residential oasis with only a few shops and offices to provide essential services.

The Dillon house was one of the largest, most valuable
properties in Rivervale, but when the townspeople got over
being impressed and became acquainted with Jenny Dillon, they found that affluence had not made a snob of her,
not in the slightest. Jenny quickly became known as one of
the kindest, friendliest young women in town, always
ready to help raise funds for charities, work on church
fairs, and help run the cooperative nursery school—and it

was observed that all these projects ran more smoothly when Jenny had a hand in them.

She was smart, for one thing; Phi Beta Kappa in college, actually, though she never made a big thing of it. And she was so pleasant and cheerful, and so pretty, with her wide brown eyes and fluff of shiny brown hair, that everyone loved working with her—almost as much as they enjoyed going to her parties.

The Dillons entertained rather more elegantly than most people in Rivervale, with interesting food, enough waiters to serve it attractively, and always the extra exciting dimension that most parties lacked: the unpredictable behavior of the host. Although to the unimaginative there might appear to be only two or three ways a husband could ruin his wife's parties, Greg Dillon's resources were apparently limitless. So that while a guest might look forward to a repeat of the time Greg ran off with one of the waitresses before dinner, he would not be disappointed if instead he pulled the president of the League of Women Voters into the pool, fully dressed, or persuaded one of the prettier young wives to climb a tree with him, taking along a bottle of champagne to enjoy among the branches.

The marvel was that none of this seemed to bother Jenny. "She's a saint," was a frequently voiced opinion, or "She's so self-confident she can handle it," or "She doesn't care as long as she knows he loves her." None of which was the truth.

Around eleven o'clock that morning Jenny called Greg at his studio to ask if he had a moment to talk. She had never appeared at the studio unannounced in the three years they had lived in Rivervale, though no one knew that, of course, but the two of them.

After she had put down the phone Jenny stood gazing thoughtfully out her bedroom window, which overlooked the wide back lawn. Her five-year-old son, Cabot, called Cabby, was playing on his swing set with Brooke Porter, the two children watched over by one of the corps of teenage baby-sitters whose names monopolized Jenny's telephone book.

Jenny turned to her dressing table mirror for a quick, appraising glance, pushed her curling brown hair up a bit on the sides, then went downstairs and through the kitchen to tell the sitter that she was going out for a few minutes.

Automatically she started for the garage, then turned instead and walked down the center hall of the house to the front door. Greg's studio was only four blocks away, after all. Its location had been a deciding factor in their move to Rivervale.

Stepping along the cracked sidewalk, Jenny recalled her parents' amazement when she had invited them to inspect the house she and Greg had found.

"Rivervale! Darling, it's miles from nowhere. The school system..."

"You're out of date, Mother. Now that the New York suburbs are so crowded Rivervale is the place to be. The schools are getting better all the time, and there is that nice lake, so we won't have to go away in the summer. Bill and Lou Preston are starting a boat club. Also, we can get twice as much house there."

"The taxes are bound to be lower than Greenwich." Jenny's father liked to think his daughter had inherited his business sense.

"And it's near enough Springfield so I can work there eventually, if I want to. That beats living in a completely suburban playground."

Jenny had a point there, the Cabots silently conceded. She had majored in social work at college, preparing for a career in New York. But then she fell in love with Greg Dillon, and it quickly became clear that New York was not the place for Greg—or at any rate, not the place where a wife could live happily with Greg.

She was too tactful, however, to stress the fact that it would be best if Greg didn't have a reason to commute. "A painter needs a studio and lots of peace and quiet," she had said. "That's why this town is so perfect. There's a cottage on the river just a few blocks from the house. Greg won't have to live by timetables; he won't even need a car to get to work. And there are plenty of artists in Rivervale. When he wants company he'll find his own sort, not a bunch of businessmen and golfers.''

Businessman-golfer Charles Cabot bridled at that, but managed to keep silent. He and Betty knew what effect their open disapproval would have, and although the effort required was heroic, they were determined to appear passive and agreeable in regard to Jenny's marriage. She saw through the facade, of course, but instead of feeling contempt for what might look like her parents' weakness, she saw their restraint for what it was: evidence of their love for her. She vowed to repay it by never letting them know if anything went wrong, and she was certain it wouldn't. She was smarter than all those girls Greg had gotten away from; she had covered all her bases. She could afford to; she had her own money. And she loved Greg far too much ever to let him go.

THE COTTAGE STUDIO that made life so agreeable for Greg Dillon was situated on the town's main street, not far from the start of a mile-long cluster of shops and offices that made up the commercial center, such as it was, of Rivervale. All but a few business enterprises were carried on in converted Victorian houses that were kept freshly painted (white with black shutters—no trendy pastels) and maintained with a fastidiousness that would have astonished their original owners.

Maple Street, where the Dillons lived, ran down a hill to meet Main Street a few hundred feet from the start of a tall privet hedge that surrounded, and largely concealed, the grounds of Greg's studio. A bumpy gravel drive intersected the hedge and led along a slope of lawn to a small, brown-shingled house on the bank of the river.

Jenny Dillon's expression as she walked purposefully down the drive would have startled her fellow committee members and probably have frightened her little boy to the point of tears. Her aspect had little effect on Greg Dillon, however, who pushed open the screen door when he heard her step, and waited there, leaning outward with a welcoming grin on his tanned face.

"Hi, darling." He bent to kiss her, but she turned her face away and brushed past him to enter the cottage.

The painting studio occupied most of it: a room about twenty-five feet square, with stairs leading to a loft at the near end, the remainder of the upper story having been cut away to accommodate a sloping glass window that admitted the desirable north light. On the left a narrow passageway led to a compact kitchen, then a bathroom, storeroom, and one small, dark bedroom. Jenny had not entered that passageway once in the last two years.

She strode to the center of the room and swung around to face her husband. He had followed her in, wearing a politely inquiring expression that would have been totally maddening had her attention not been diverted by the huge painting of a nude woman propped on the easel in front of her.

"You might at least have put that away. Why do you think I called first?" Jenny's normally merry brown eyes were like hard, glinting marbles.

"I wanted you to see it. You haven't looked at any of my work for some time, you know."

She shook her head in wonder, still holding his gaze. "Should I congratulate you on your improved technique? If so, in what area? Painting or lovemaking?" She turned her head stiffly toward the easel. "Obviously the latter, though I'd have no way of knowing first-hand."

She felt his warm breath on the back of her neck, though he did not touch her as he said softly, "Come with me to the back room, my darling, and we'll make up for lost time."

Jenny was trembling as she stepped away, then wheeled around to face him. "You would, wouldn't you? It makes no difference to you. One woman is just like another."

"Well, not entirely..."

"Greg, I've had it. I thought I could take this sort of thing, but I can't. You win—or lose, however you look at it. I'm getting a divorce."

"Oh, don't talk like that, sweetness." He stretched out his arms in appeal. "Come on, give me a hug. I'll behave myself, I promise."

She took another backward step, her face twisting with disgust, and felt her heel bump the leg of the easel.

"Watch out! That paint is wet!"

Greg sprang forward, reaching past her to steady the easel, and in the same instant Jenny spun around and swept her hand diagonally down the canvas from the right-hand corner. He seized her wrist and she stiffened her paint-smeared fingers, holding them before his eyes like a vengeful claw.

"That gets you, doesn't it! Oh, how good it feels to hurt you—to finally find a way. Here, let me finish . . ."

But he wrenched her away, his strong fingers biting into her arms, and while she thought, almost gleefully, that he was about to dash her to the floor, he hurled her into a chair instead—the chintz-covered wicker one that had once stood on her parents' porch.

He strode to the easel then and stood with his back to her, and she could hear his harsh, angry breathing as he studied the ruined painting. Seconds passed. He drew a long sigh, then slowly turned, and saw that all the anger was gone from his face. Only its pallor betrayed his emotion as he said, "I hope that made you feel better. Poor Jenny. It must be terrible to have so little control. Over yourself or anyone else. Because of course you can see that now I'll have to have more sittings with my beautiful model—many, many more. I imagine it will take all summer to do that painting over."

She felt the blood drain from her face as she listened. She was aware that her paint-smeared hand was staining the arm of the chair, but it didn't matter.

"And it will be a better picture when I do it again, because you got it wrong about my technique, Jenny. The lovemaking didn't need improvement; I've never gotten any complaints about that from you or anyone else. But that's a triviality. The important thing is that I'll be getting big money for my work, substantial money, if you know what I mean. And then I won't need you any more, or this little place, either. I'll let you know when I'm ready to leave—probably. Meanwhile I'm staying put. And I'm keeping the studio locked."

He stopped. He stood watching her calmly, totally composed.

"Now run along, will you, dear?" He glanced at his watch. "I have a lunch date. See you tonight."

Tuesday, June 17 Morning

GARVIN THORPE HAD installed a tape recorder in the end of his desk, concealing it in a space meant for a drawer so that his patients would not be inhibited in their revelations. Tapes provided an accurate record, not only of a patient's words, but often of the anger or sadness or elation he might have felt as he spoke them. Such a verbatim record might also serve to protect the therapist in cases of litigation, and was an excellent way to collect material for a clinical paper or book.

Garvin did not record every therapeutic session, but that morning, when he heard a car pull into his graveled parking area, he placed a fresh tape in the machine. A moment later the buzzer sounded, and he strode to the door to admit Frank Lundy.

The two men were equally grave as they shook hands in the reception area. To Garvin, Frank Lundy seemed more harried than on his first visit. He looked, in fact, utterly exhausted, and Garvin saw that his hands were shaking as he settled into the chair before the desk.

Wishing he had suggested it at their first meeting, when Frank Lundy had appeared to be in a more receptive mood, Garvin said, "Before we begin I would like to ask your permission to record our sessions together." Seeing Lundy's face stiffen in alarm, he went on, "I haven't turned the machine on, and I certainly won't if you object. But a taped record can be useful in recalling our talks in detail; and of course would be kept absolutely confidential."

"I don't know. I saw you taking notes before. You're a slow writer, huh?" Lundy forced a lame smile.

"I still take some notes, even when I'm taping, as I think of comments and questions, but a taped record is much more complete. On the other hand, if you have any negative feelings, we'll skip it."

"To tell you the truth, Doc, it would paralyze me. I have a tough enough time telling you all this garbage. With a machine on," he waved his hand wearily, "forget it. I wouldn't even show up."

"All right, Frank, we will forget it." Garvin opened the folder on his desk and picked up his pencil. He said, "Last time we talked you were having trouble sleeping. Has there been any improvement with that?"

"It's gotten worse." Lundy's gray eyes glowered accusingly, as if he blamed Thorpe for his fatigue. "I'm so tired all the time I go around like a zombie. Can't concentrate on my work. And when I do sleep I have wild dreams. I write them down the way you told me to, but it sure seems crazy. I hide the notebook so Maria won't see it."

Garvin did not smile. He said, "Does it seem less crazy if you think of dreams as messages from your unconscious? Messages that reveal feelings of which you are not consciously aware?"

"My feelings are pretty damn clear, it seems to me. I'm going nuts because my wife is screwing around, and if she doesn't quit somebody's going to get hurt." Lundy paused to catch his breath. His face was suddenly damp with perspiration, and he twisted angrily in his chair to pull a handkerchief from his pocket.

Garvin said, "You feel agitated today, don't you?"

"Yeah, and my head aches like hell. Has for a couple of days."

"Would you like an aspirin?"

"No, thanks, I took a couple when I got up." He finished wiping his face and began folding his handkerchief, avoiding Garvin's eyes. He said, "I'm wondering how much good I'm getting out of this, Thorpe. None, if you want my opinion. I'm more scared of losing control now than I was when I came in. It's only fair to tell you."

"Strangely enough, that could be a good sign, Frank." He paused. "Before we talk more about it, let's discuss your dreams."

Once more Lundy searched his pockets, this time extracting a crumpled piece of paper from which he smoothed the wrinkles before holding it up to the light.

"Okay," he began, darting a look of hostility across the desk. "I dreamed about a wild stallion trying to swim across a river, thrashing around and kicking while the water got deeper and deeper. I felt like I was the horse, only I was also watching from the bank. I tried to yell at him, to help, but I couldn't make any sound come out. It doesn't sound so bad, but I woke up sweating."

"It felt as if you were the horse struggling in the water?"

"Yes, but I was also myself trying to yell and I couldn't."

"And that frightened you?"

"Yeah, it was scary, like someone else was controlling me; I couldn't do anything for myself. I was helpless."

Garvin had been rapidly penciling in his notebook; now he closed it and swiveled his chair around so that he could look out the window. He swung back to face Lundy, and said, "The horse is often seen as a symbol of energy—inner, psychic energy—and if we look at it that way this dream seems encouraging. It says that you are working hard to direct your energies in the right way. There's a lot of turmoil—your anger, perhaps, symbolized by the turbulent water—but the horse is strong. A stallion, you say it was? A big one?"

"Big and powerful, yes. That's why I thought he'd make it."

"Ah, you felt he would get across the water eventually? That's excellent."

"Well, fine, but all this stuff seems like a holding action, that's all." Lundy squirmed with exasperation. "Maybe you'll keep me from going berserk. Maybe, that is. But what do I do about Maria? Just wait for her to get tired of the bastard?"

"Today you sound very certain that she is having an affair. Have you discussed your suspicions with her yet?"

"No, and I'm not going to. You know why? I finally figured it out." Lundy gripped the arms of his chair and leaned forward to thrust his pale face closer to Garvin's. "Because I can't compete with Greg Dillon. No way. The bastard has everything: looks, money, talent—and not only artistic talent, I gather from the way the women in this town can't wait to jump into his bed. On top of that he's got a rich wife who's apparently too nuts about him to kick him out." Lundy paused and for a moment there was no sound in the room but his labored breathing. Then he rushed on. "So what I figured out is I can't threaten Maria, right? Because if I do she'll pick him, right? So I have to hang on if I can. And that's where you come in."

While Lundy's words poured out Garvin Thorpe wrote steadily in a notebook on the desk before him. His pencil, moving without pause in firm, even strokes, recorded Frank's words almost as fast as he spoke them; when he stopped talking the pencil stopped also. But Thorpe did not look up.

Still keeping his eyes fixed on the notebook, he said, "Greg Dillon?"

"One of the painters Maria poses for. Remember I told you there were two of them? Well, I'm sure he's the guy; he's a famous womanizer, and I've never heard that about the other one, Ben Porter."

"And you say this Greg Dillon has what you perceive as formidable assets: his looks, his money.... I suppose he's said to be charming too?"

"All those things. The bastard's got it all."

"You feel the deck is stacked in his favor, is that right? Because of what you see as his strengths?"

"I sure do."

"Frank, you have strengths. What would you say they are?"

"My strong points? Oh, I'm good at figures, obviously, or I wouldn't be a CPA. And I'm neat and quiet and I'd say I have a good disposition."

Garvin smiled. "Are you proud of these qualities?"

"Not very. I'm just civilized, is the way I see it. A decent guy. I can't compete with a Greg Dillon."

"Do you see Dillon as a macho figure, if you know what I mean by the term?"

"I guess so."

"Frank, this question may anger you. Have you ever had any doubts about your sexual orientation?" Garvin's voice was gentle, almost a whisper, and he immediately looked away from Frank Lundy's shocked face and concentrated instead on a glass paperweight he had picked up from his desk top, turning it in his long, slim fingers while he waited for Lundy's reply.

"Orientation? You mean have I ever been afraid I was queer? Or gay, I guess I should say." Trying to order his thoughts, Lundy kept his eyes fixed on the piece of greenish glass in the therapist's hand. It was the figure of a plump frog, he saw.

"You use the word *afraid*. Do you feel afraid when you consider the possibility of being homosexual?" Thorpe's tone was mild; he continued to turn the smooth glass frog he held in his hands almost caressingly, as if the touch of it gave him pleasure.

"I don't know what you're getting at, Thorpe." Frank Lundy felt his pulse pounding in his ears, each beat sending a jolt of pain to his already aching head. "I've never worried about it, okay? Never had a problem that way in my life, so if you're suggesting that's why Maria... Well, you're nuts, that's all."

Garvin Thorpe's face remained expressionless. He carefully set the glass frog on his desk, placing it first on a corner of the blotter, then shifting the ornament to a spot beside the clock. He leaned back in his chair then, holding out the fingers of his left hand while he gazed critically at his nails. Finally he said, "I would like to see you again tomorrow, Frank. Can you come at the same time, eight-thirty?''

"I'm not so goddamn sure I want to unless you explain..."

"And meanwhile I want you to think very carefully about our discussion. And make careful note of your dreams. Will you do that, Frank?''

While Thorpe rose and walked around the desk to usher him out, Frank Lundy sat immobilized in his chair, incapable of action, unable to decide whether to push Thorpe for a satisfactory response or simply to get himself and his throbbing headache out of the office as quickly as possible.

When Thorpe reached his side he stood looking down at him with an expression of kindness and understanding that Lundy found almost unbearably moving. He felt tears filling his eyes as he pushed himself to his feet, and when Thorpe shook his hand and said softly, "Eight-thirty tomorrow?'' he could not answer, but only nod dumbly before he turned and hurried out the door.

FOUR

ON HER WAY DOWN the gravel drive, Maria Lundy stumbled on a loose stone and, catching her balance, saw the black mark it had made on her freshly cleaned white sandal. She wouldn't miss this part: finding an inconspicuous parking spot on a side street, then making her way to Greg's on foot, trying to look normal and businesslike in case someone saw her. Of course posing for an artist was a perfectly respectable profession, and that was what he paid her for, wasn't it? Her lips twisted at the thought of Greg Dillon having to pay for the other. That would be the day.

His door stood open behind the screen, so he was in. She could hear him softly whistling, in fact, some vague, madeup tune, as he often did when he was painting. She brushed her moist palms on her smooth-fitting gabardine pants, drew a deep breath, and knocked on the rattly wooden frame of the screen door.

The whistling stopped. Now she heard Greg's footsteps approaching. "Who is it?" he called out, and suddenly was there in the doorway, his face filled with surprise. Then a slow smile formed and his dark eyes softened with tenderness.

"Well, well. How nice. Did I forget something, or is this a special treat?"

He pushed the door open, bending to draw her into the cottage. She took his hand without resisting and when they were inside went into his embrace, will-less as a kitten.

When he released her she stepped back and smoothed her hair, but before she could speak he said, "It must be ESP. I needed to have you show up today; in fact, I was planning to call you. The new nude met with a mishap. We'll have to start pretty much from scratch, I'm afraid.''

They had moved into the studio, and in the clear light she saw the ruined canvas and sniffed the familiar odor of the turpentine he had been using to clean off the smeared paint. She felt a sharp sense of loss. It had been a splendid picture, masterfully executed and so alive with passion her heart beat faster when she looked at it. Its wreckage made a bizarrely appropriate setting for the speech she had rehearsed all week.

"Greg, I won't be posing for you anymore. I won't, won't be coming here at all.''

She forced herself to look away from his face. The intensity of his gaze was causing her to stumble over her words.

"I can't stand what I'm doing to Frank. He's so unhappy I can't bear it. I've either got to stop seeing you or leave him. And I know what that would mean.''

"That could mean a wonderful new life for us.'' His face was solemn; his voice throbbed with sincerity. He reached for her hands, but she moved away from him.

"Let's be honest, Greg. It might be wonderful for you, but I would be nowhere if I left Frank. Just hanging around on the outskirts of your life till you got tired of me and found someone else.''

"That day will never come, I swear it. No, wait.'' She had started to speak, but he gently pressed his finger against her lips. "I don't have to swear it any more than you do. Because you know that we're part of each other, blood and bones and spirit. The only thing that could ever come between us is that lively imagination of yours.''

"Then you want me to leave Frank? You really think I should?''

"Can you imagine loving him the way you love me?''

"And you're planning to divorce Jenny so that we can be married?''

"When the time is right, of course. But you must leave that to me, darling girl. I don't want to hurt Jenny any more than you want to hurt Frank. You see I'm just as capable of loyalty as you are. And there is a child to be considered.''

"I'd like to have a child."

"Our child. Oh Maria, I can see her now—a beautiful baby girl with your eyes, your smile . . .''

"Greg, sometimes I think you are a monster. How can you play on me like that? How can you tease me with visions of everything I want—just to keep me dangling, until what? Till you're ready for a new lover, or till your goddamn painting is finished?'' Her voice broke on the last words, and she felt hot tears pouring down her cheeks.

"Maria, darling, don't do this. Don't spoil the wonderful thing we've shared. It's too precious, too rare."

He was holding her tightly against him while she sobbed, stroking her back and murmuring softly in her ear as he gently propelled her into the dim passage that led to the bedroom.

She knew where they were headed, and she went unprotesting; but looking at his eager, beseeching face as he sat her on the bed and began worshipfully to unbutton her silk shirt, she thought, Well, anyway it's the last time; and then later she thought, Or anyway next to the last. And then she stopped thinking.

Friday, June 20 Morning

THE OFFICE DOOR SWUNG shut behind the departing figure of Frank Lundy, and Garvin Thorpe stood very still beside it, his ears cocked to hear the closing of the outer door, followed by the sound of Lundy's car starting up. It was very important, for some reason, to know that Lundy had left the premises, was not likely to plunge back into the office to unload more of the misery that Garvin was finding so contaminating. Their sessions were becoming pure torture for him. He knew why, and he could not face knowing why.

It was obvious that his tension had communicated itself to Lundy, although the man probably attributed it to his own unsolved problems. His face had relaxed in an almost comical look of relief when Thorpe had suggested a short break in therapy. Today's session had been their fourth, and Garvin told himself that he too should feel elated at the prospect of a weekend free of Frank Lundy's disturbing presence. Instead, he felt only a paralyzing dread of their next appointment, which was for the following Monday. He was appalled to find that his hand shook as he penciled it in his book.

Making an effort to emerge from his gloom, Thorpe went to one of his office windows and pushed it open. He leaned on the sill, feeling the warm air on his cheek and observing that in the intense sunlight the grass had turned the unreal green of movie grass and the picket fence a blinding white. Instead of lifting his spirits, however, the innocent, sunshiny brightness made him feel strangely sad. Such a beautiful day was meant for a happier, younger person than he; it was designed for the person he had been once—he tried to remember when.

Garvin sighed and moved back to his desk, where he studied the calendar. He had been glad to have a free hour following the session with Lundy; now, however, he would have welcomed the distraction of another patient. He observed the date, June 20, and at once recognized the cause of his nostalgia. There had been a time, years ago, when he had eagerly looked forward to that date, for it was graduation day for him and Enid, and for Jenny Dillon— then Jenny Cabot—as well.

Had Greg graduated with their class or the one behind? He hadn't seemed one of them, exactly, but of course Greg Dillon had never fit into any classifiable group and never would.

Now the sadness rose again, flowing into his awareness like the water of a brook undammed as Garvin recalled the painful days leading up to graduation, remembering how the time they had all anticipated with such excitement had become for him a time of loss amounting to bereavement. He had lost Jenny Cabot that June, had lost her irretrievably, he knew, even though his friends had assured him she would get over Greg Dillon, would see through him eventually; she was too smart not to, and too devoted to Garvin. He needed only to be patient, understanding, forgiving and, most of all, tenacious, for he'd be crazy to let a girl like Jenny get away. There would never be another like her.

They were right about that; there never had been. No other girl ever moved him as Jenny had, so that to suddenly glimpse her smiling at him in a roomful of people could bring a lump to his throat. She would laugh in her soft, throaty way, sliding him a mischievous glance as if they shared a secret, and he would feel a joy that made his eyes tingle with the threat of tears.

It had been such a surprise the first time, when at some beer party she had laughed that way at a remark of his, then had come to sit with him and laugh some more. He thought he had probably never recovered from the first shock of having Jenny Cabot single him out.

That miracle had happened in the fall of their junior year, and from then on that year stood forth from the calendar of his life in richly glowing dimensions. Not that he had been unhappy before, only not quite alive, it seemed when he looked back: a healthy, good-looking, intelligent boy who did what was expected of him in the way of sports and schoolwork, often feeling a disdain he was careful to conceal, though he couldn't have said why. He was waiting for something; it turned out to be Jenny.

They used to talk about it, sitting in her room at night, or on the long walks they took in the hilly countryside, both trying to analyze love, marveling at its effect on them: how they felt stronger, brighter, filled as never before with invention and promise. This would have amused any one of their friends, as both had long been looked upon as star achievers, Jenny more spectacularly then Garvin, who all his life was unaware of how highly his peers rated him. It was an endearing trait, this natural modesty; Jenny saw that immediately.

"You might have been a frog prince in a fairy tale," she said to him once after he had expounded on the total dreariness of pre-Jenny existence. "You just needed a

beautiful girl to kiss you and bring you out of your shell.''
She kissed him to demonstrate, and it was some time before the discussion was resumed.

"But I'll never understand why you thought so little of
yourself before," Jenny went on, sitting up and reaching
for her half-empty can of beer. "I mean, I feel great now
too, but I always did have a ball, I have to admit, and always enjoyed getting attention."

"It wasn't that I thought little of myself; I didn't think
about myself at all. Except to sort of check and make sure
I was doing okay. Now . . . God, now I could do anything.
It's as if having you makes me into a king."

"There's that royalty syndrome again."

Sharing their secret joke, they had both taken parts in
the drama club's production of Aristophanes' play, *The
Frogs,* and on opening night Jenny had given him the small
glass frog he kept on his desk.

Reaching for it, he tried to imagine Jenny's reaction if
she knew he still treasured that frog. She might be touched,
or amused, or she might not remember ever giving him the
glass frog or what it had symbolized.

What it symbolized for Garvin now was pain as much as
anything. Loss. Disillusion. An awakening quite different
from the one Jenny had in mind when she talked of a frog
prince: an awakening to bitter reality.

At the start of senior year Greg Dillon had come to
Cornell. He was said to have transferred from a smaller
college to pick up some needed credits, but no one knew
for sure if that was the case. It hardly mattered. There was
no way to fit Greg Dillon into any logical pattern of behavior. He was like some gloriously colored tropical bird
that had decided to go slumming in a farmyard. His presence stunned them; they didn't know what to do with him,
not so much because of his remarkable good looks, but
because he possessed a charm and self-assurance that
placed him light-years beyond them.

It quickly became obvious that Greg Dillon would select what he wanted from his new environment, the most
desirable quarters, the companions who appealed to him,

and the courses—only the required minimum—in subjects that interested him and whose teachers were considered entertaining. And for many it was an unhappy fact that his freedom of choice extended to the girls. Indeed, the prettiest and sexiest and smartest of them—the ones who had been accustomed to doing their own choosing—were the first to capitulate.

Except for Jenny Cabot.

Predictably, Jenny was one of the first girls to be asked out by Greg Dillon. She was also the first to refuse him, though not rudely and without any explanations about her attachment to Garvin. She simply said no, so Greg tried again, more than once, and in his disarming way never tried to conceal his bafflement at her refusal.

At parties he sought her out, and she appeared to enjoy his company as much as the others, perhaps more. She shared his gift for amusing banter, and wherever Jenny and Greg happened to get together soon became the desirable place to be. They also danced wonderfully, with the kind of concentration usually displayed by lovers. But when the evening was over it was Garvin who left with Jenny, and no regret could be discerned in her carefree farewells.

Jenny's resistance to Greg Dillon gradually became a campus legend, a source of pride and amusement to those who resented the ease with which he had taken over. To Garvin it meant much more; it was proof that her love for him was genuine, and for the first time he allowed himself to start planning a future that included Jenny.

At Christmas Jenny went to her parents in Greenwich and Garvin joined his family in the house they had rented in Florida. His older sister came down from Pennsylvania with her two small children, and because his brother-in-law was in Vietnam Garvin helped her out as much as he could, taking a new interest in the paternal role now that marriage was on his mind. His kindness took an ironic turn when his four-year-old nephew developed chicken pox and passed it on to Garvin.

The illness hit him hard. He ran a high fever for days, and had to be kept in bed and waited on until the risk of severe side effects was past. Classes were two weeks into the winter term before he could return to school after what had been his longest separation from Jenny.

He could remember everything about the way he had felt that first afternoon back: the dry-mouthed excitement with which he had hurried to Jenny's dormitory, then the let-down when he found her door closed and a message for him taped to it.

"Sorry, darling. Mr. B. adamant re. Physics Lab., so I'll see you at 6:00. WELCOME HOME!"

He had started to feel shaky while he read it over, and actually had to sit down for a minute on the steps before he started off to get some lunch. He was still recovering, of course, and hunger had intensified his weakness.

At five-thirty he had picked up the telephone to call Jenny, then, feeling an odd reluctance, had replaced the phone without dialing. He had taken his time getting back to her room, dawdling over his clothes, stopping to chat with the friends he met on the way. When he finally climbed the stairs again and saw that Jenny's door was still closed he did not feel surprised. Instead, he felt a sense of inevitability dragging him down like a heavy weight until his knees folded and he sank to the top step once more.

He sat there for two hours, his face growing so stiff and white as the minutes went by that any students who approached him were quickly warned away. At eight-fifteen he pulled himself to his feet and left the building, aware of the silence that fell as he stalked through the foyer and out past the couples who met there every night.

Very early the next morning when he was lying in bed sleeplessly watching the slow arrival of the gray dawn, he heard light footsteps outside his room, then the soft hiss of an envelope sliding beneath the door. He did not move, but waited grimly until he heard the footsteps depart; then he slowly stepped out of bed and picked up the letter, which he was not surprised to see was addressed to him in Jenny's hand.

In it she told him that she was engaged to Greg Dillon.

FIVE

FRANK LUNDY PULLED into Garvin Thorpe's parking area, turning so sharply that his wheels dug deep ruts in the gravel. He felt his heart thumping as he jumped out of the car and slammed the door behind him. Here he had been driving around for almost an hour waiting for nine o'clock and it looked like he was going to be late. What an incompetent fool he was—especially considering how much an hour of Thorpe's precious time was costing him.

In the reception room he stabbed at the buzzer to announce his arrival, then straightened his tie and tried to prepare himself to give a coherent description of his miserable weekend.

Thorpe opened his door too quickly, though, and Lundy was barely able to gasp, "Good morning." Just looking at the man's face set his mind in turmoil. The understanding he saw in the deep-set brown eyes set him trembling with eagerness to pour out his agitated thoughts. And yet the constraint was there, as always. Even now, on his fifth visit to Garvin Thorpe, he felt almost paralyzed with fear at the prospect of confiding his secret feelings to anyone, much less a person who until nine days ago was a total stranger to him.

The fear remained when, after they had sat down in their chairs and were regarding each other across the desk, Thorpe said, "How was your weekend, Frank?"

For a moment Lundy could not speak. His throat actually ached from his conflicting needs to unburden himself and to guard his privacy. "It was a disaster, thanks," he finally managed. He sat very erect with his knees locked together and his hands tightly clasped in his lap.

"Tell me what happened."

Lundy sighed heavily, but there was no relaxing of his stiff posture; clearly, he was exercising all the control he could muster.

"I was here on Friday, right?" Garvin Thorpe nodded, and Lundy went on, "Seems like longer. Anyway, Maria had a job that night, so I knew she'd be out late. What I wasn't ready for was four A.M."

He stopped and sat staring down at his clasped hands.

Thorpe prompted gently, "You must have been very worried about her."

"To put it mildly. I was ready to kill her when I finally heard her fumbling around at the door. I got there before she could open it, and I yanked it open and pulled her in, and I'm afraid I was pretty rough, but goddamn it, Thorpe, how much of this shit am I expected to take? Huh? Tell me, will you?"

Now his face was contorted with rage and pain, and his hands were no longer clasped but gripped the arms of his chair as if he were preparing to jump up and hurl it against the wall.

In a voice so soft that Frank Lundy had to strain forward to hear, Thorpe said, "Were you physically abusive to Maria, Frank?"

"Abusive? You mean did I hit her? No, but I pushed her around while I made her tell me what she'd been doing." He paused, glowering resentfully, then said, "What's abusive anyway, Thorpe? The way I see it, Maria's abusive to me in her own way, but if I lose control and pop her then I'm the sucker who gets nailed for being abusive."

"It is true that psychological cruelty often goes unpunished." Garvin leaned forward to pick up the glass frog from his desk. He turned it in his hand as he asked, "How did Maria explain her lateness?"

"Oh, it was the usual innocent fun with the customers, of course. All part of the job, which I would understand if I knew the first thing about show business." He spat the last words angrily. "I knew goddamn well she was lying, but I kept my mouth shut—like the spineless fink I'm turning into."

"Do you see your self-control as weakness, Frank?" Thorpe placed the small glass frog on his desk, frowning slightly as he shifted it to a spot where it caught the sunlight.

"Worse than that. You've got me so uptight I can't even function."

"Function in what way?"

"Well, after we got through fighting—this is Saturday by now—Maria pulled a switch, like she sometimes does. She started acting gentle, like she was sorry for me."

"And how did that make you feel?"

"Lousy. I sure as hell don't want that from her. And then, to make things worse, she gets sexy." Lundy stopped and brushed at his trousers concernedly; Thorpe saw that a faint pink color had risen to his cheeks.

"Why do you say 'to make things worse'?"

"Because it didn't work out—for the first time I can remember."

Lundy's face had turned a dark red; he was twisting uncomfortably as he relived his humiliation. Suddenly he struck the arm of his chair with one fist and shouted, "Goddamn it, Thorpe, I can't even act like a man anymore. What the hell is happening to me?"

Garvin said, "Many surprising feelings are coming to the surface, Frank. It is quite understandable that your sexual activity would be temporarily affected. You must not let that worry you, but keep working to resolve your inner conflicts."

"Conflicts? Are you implying I'm queer again? I don't have to take that, Thorpe, from you or anyone else." Lundy sprang to his feet and stood glaring down at Garvin with his fists clenched at his sides, his breath rasping in his throat.

Without moving, Garvin gazed up at him and said quietly, "Frank, did you take the opportunity this weekend to question Maria about Greg Dillon?"

Lundy's face did not change, but he stepped back to seize the arm of his chair for support as he said, "Hell, no. I told you I'm not planning to mention the guy to her."

"I know you did. I wondered whether during your 'confrontation,' shall we call it, you might have accused her after all."

"No. Give me credit for self-control, if nothing else."

"That must have been very difficult for you, Frank, especially in light of your sexual failure."

"Not to mention that bastard's sexual success, is that what you mean?" In an instant Lundy's face had become a crimson mask with white teeth gleaming in a manic grin. "Don't bother answering, I can read you like a book."

"Frank, I'm afraid you misinterpreted . . ."

"Just a minute, *Doctor,* I have one more thing to tell you." Lundy paused and the grin faded as he weighed the consequences of his words. "I did do something I wasn't planning this weekend. I bought a gun."

"A gun? What kind of gun?"

"A Beretta .25. It's small, easy to hide." He paused, defiantly waiting for an outburst, but Garvin said nothing.

"You said I should do what I could to relieve the pressure." There was the slightest quaver in his voice as Lundy went on. "Well, that helped; I felt real calmed down."

"You felt calm after you bought the gun? How do you feel now?"

"Okay." He looked determinedly into Thorpe's eyes and mustered a dry chuckle. "Well, sometimes it scares me to have it, but that's only natural. I even tried hiding it from myself." Again he bared his teeth in a grotesque attempt at a grin.

"What do you intend to do with the gun?"

"I'm not going to use it, of course; never meant to in the first place. I just thought it would make me feel less helpless, and for a while it did."

"I'm going to ask you to bring the gun in to me, Frank."

Lundy sighed heavily and said, "I thought you might say that."

"How does it make you feel to have me ask for the gun?"

"I don't know. Kind of angry. Yet kind of relieved, I guess."

Thorpe said, "Let's examine that. Giving it to me wouldn't be like returning it to the store, is that right? Would you feel that you still owned it in a way."

"Maybe. Could be. Even though I know you won't give it back if I ask for it. Or will you?"

"That will depend on many things, Frank." Thorpe spoke slowly, carefully choosing his words. "Right now I just have to ask you to bring me the gun, with no guarantee that you will or won't get it back."

Lundy stiffened. He started to speak, then stopped. He crossed his legs and began nervously jigging his foot as he said, "Well the problem is, I'm not all that willing to give up the gun. Then I'd look like a powerless wimp again."

"The gun represents power to you, does it? In what way?"

"I don't know, maybe because I'm sort of afraid of it, you know what I mean?" He bent forward and said earnestly, "I've never owned a gun before, so sometimes I get it out and study how it works. I aim it at something—maybe the mirror. But when I put my finger on the trigger it scares me stiff, makes me feel actually sick." He was squirming in his seat. "Look at me; I'm sweating now, just thinking about it."

Garvin Thorpe said, "Frank, I'm going to ask you to do two things. Today. Bring the gun here to my office, and ask Maria to come and talk to me. Will you do that?"

"If I don't will you have me locked up?"

Garvin stared at Frank Lundy in silence. He leaned back in his chair and watched as his face again turned red and his gray eyes darkened with anger.

Lundy's voice was trembling as he said, "You make me damn mad, Thorpe! You get me to unload with the idea everything I say in here is confidential, and then you threaten..."

"What did I threaten, Frank?"

"You're going to set the cops on me if I don't give you the gun, aren't you?"

"Is that what you think I should do?"

"Goddamn it, can't you give a straight answer for once?" Lundy had jumped to his feet; his body was quivering with rage.

"Please sit down, Frank, and I'll explain my position on this." Garvin waited while Lundy made up his mind to take his seat, then leaned forward and said slowly, "If at any time I feel a patient of mine is in danger of harming himself or another person I am legally bound to report it to the authorities. That is my responsibility—to society and to my patient. Can you see the logic of that?"

"You know what I see?" Lundy's face was still flushed, but his voice was cold and clipped as he said, "I see an over-educated fink who gets his kicks out of digging around in other people's dirt. You're perfect, right? Also perfectly gutless, that's what I say."

"You think I am weak, do you?"

"I think you're what I said: gutless." Lundy slowly rose to his feet and stood looking down at Thorpe. "So I'm not worried. You wouldn't want to call the police and have them find out what a lousy shrink you are."

"Frank, just a minute..."

"I'll think about bringing in the gun. I said *think* about it, got that? And I may or may not come back on Wednesday. How do you feel about that, Doc?"

He whirled, stalked to the door, wrenched it open, and, without a backward glance, stepped out, letting the door slam shut behind him.

That Evening

ALTHOUGH HIS DAY HAD BEEN especially long and trying, Garvin Thorpe quickly rejected Enid's suggestion that he postpone the meeting he and Jenny Dillon had set up for that evening to talk about the Mental Health Committee.

"Jenny sounded so enthusiastic and involved when she called yesterday," he said as he pushed his chair back from the dinner table. "I wouldn't want to discourage that by putting her off."

"You seem tense tonight, that's all, and tired. You have the look you get when a headache is coming on." Enid picked up their two plates and took them to the kitchen, observing that Garvin had not finished his meat loaf. That was almost the last of it too; she only hoped there was enough left for Thursday. Enid believed in conserving her time in the kitchen; therefore she cooked one major dish each week, then put dinners out of her mind. They went out to a restaurant almost every Wednesday, and were usually invited somewhere either Friday or Saturday night; Sunday was scrambled eggs in front of the TV, and that was that. Planning. If more women thought it out that way they would liberate themselves.

Garvin was right behind her with the salad plates, which he began rinsing under the water tap while Enid brought the empty meat loaf pan to the sink and scraped out the crumbs. He raised his voice to be heard over the running water.

"I was going to ask for your Mental Health file, but I decided I might make more of a contribution if I just started fresh with Jenny."

"I think you're right. Anyway, you and I don't always agree on these things. I do hope you'll emphasize the importance of preventive counseling though, Garvin, and I feel sure you will."

"Oh, don't worry. That's one area where we're in complete agreement."

Enid did not reply, and the word *agreement* seemed to hang suspended in the air until Garvin turned up the hot water and began forcefully scrubbing the pan. What he felt like doing was pitching the bent, crusted thing into the trash can. He tried to calculate how many times he must have washed it by now: every other week for four years, was it? He hoped not, considering his aversion to meat loaf. Yet he couldn't fault Enid for minimizing her cooking time; it was the only way she could work on her degree—especially since he wasn't interested in cooking, himself.

In ten minutes the kitchen was spotless, the dishwasher humming, the coffeemaker loaded for breakfast. It was exactly seven o'clock. Garvin was expected at Jenny's by seven-thirty; he had time to change his shirt.

Enid had settled herself in the study, as she did nearly every evening. He stood in the doorway, feeling faintly guilty as he watched her switch on the desk lamp. The sudden harsh light made her spectacles glitter with theatrical brilliance. Indeed, Enid might have been an actress portraying a part, so perfectly did her dress and manner and the setting in which she busied herself proclaim Professional Scholar.

Even though her work was, for the most part, solitary, Enid Thorpe was not to be found slouching about in jeans and baggy sweaters. She wore a neat khaki skirt and a crisp white cotton shirt. She had retouched her makeup after dinner and brushed her hair so that it shone, dark and glossy, in the nearly straight pageboy that suited her so well.

Garvin watched as she adjusted her desk chair, a sensible office model with wheels. Her lips formed a half-smile as she surveyed the folders and reference books on the desk with obvious anticipation. She sat down and reached for a pencil, then glanced up as if surprised to see Garvin standing there.

He said, "Isn't it time you took a night off?"

He spoke lightly. Any hint that she might be mishandling her life could make the eyes behind those shining lenses flash dangerously.

Enid smiled, pulling a folder of papers closer. "It's a little matter of persecution mania I'm dealing with this week—or maybe this year. If Freud couldn't get it straight it just may give me a bit of trouble too."

Mounting the stairs to his bedroom, Garvin chided himself for suspecting that Enid placed herself and her work on some exalted plane of scholarship that would remain forever beyond the reach of a money-grubbing ther-

apist like himself. He resented her attitude; he knew he
should face that without shame, for it was a normal human reaction. Still, he could not help enjoying the prospect of Enid's change in perspective once she started
treating patients. They would bring her down from her
ivory tower in a hurry.

Garvin sighed as he began unbuttoning his shirt. It
would take pushing to get Enid to leave her books and enter active practice; but for the sake of her emotional health
he must make the effort.

He showered quickly, put on a fresh shirt, then reached
for a pair of new gray flannel slacks he hadn't yet worn. He
stopped himself, however, and instead picked up the poplin trousers he had taken off. He wouldn't want Enid to
think he had dressed up to see Jenny as if he were going to
a party, or out on a date. He smiled to himself, remembering how eagerly he used to get ready for a date with
Jenny Cabot; even felt his heart give a long-forgotten lurch
of excitement.

He was in a youthful, buoyant mood as he hurried down
the stairs and gathered up a folder of papers from the hall
table. He turned on the front door light—it would be dark
when he got home, and Enid seldom thought about
lights—then stepped into the living room and switched on
a table lamp. The room had been nearly dark already; its
windows were narrow and hung with thick beige draperies
that kept it dim and cool on the sunniest days. The carpet
was beige; the sofa and upholstered chairs were covered in
the neutral beige and brown fabric they had worn in the
department store; the marble-topped coffee table was bare
except for a round copper ashtray and a stack of *Smith-
sonian* magazines.

On his way through the hall Garvin stopped once more
in the doorway to the study. "If a man comes by with a
package for me, don't be alarmed," he said.

Enid looked up, frowning with the effort of wrenching
her attention away from the pages before her.

"It will be a patient of mine, Frank Lundy," he went on.
"He may not show up, but I hope he does. Don't ask him

in, though, dear." He paused. "Not that he's dangerous, of course; I don't mean to alarm you."

Enid's expression switched from patient forbearance to grim comprehension. She nodded sharply. "I understand. Don't worry, I can take care of myself."

"You know the Dillons' number if you need me."

Again the quick, competent nod. "I'll be fine. Run along and enjoy your meeting."

THEY SAT OUTSIDE on the flagstone terrace until it was time to put Cabby to bed, the scent of lilacs and new-mown grass rising around them. The furniture was white, with trim white cushions, and the glass-topped table on which Garvin had spread his papers was centered with an enormous bowl of lilacs that Jenny pushed aside to make room.

"I suppose I should have asked you to come after Cabby's bedtime, but it seemed so late. Anyway, I wanted you to see him." Jenny smiled over at Garvin while she fondly ruffled the soft blond hair of the little boy who stood fidgeting impatiently, bored with being on display.

Garvin grinned at the child, trying to think of something to say. "Do you have a teddy bear?" It was the best he could do.

Cabby shook his head, looking across at Garvin appraisingly. "I'm into transformers," he said, and Garvin sat speechless for a long moment, facing the level gaze—Greg Dillon's exactly—while he tried to fathom the meaning of the child's words.

Jenny laughed softly as she got to her feet. "Oh, Garvin, if you could see your face!" She turned to her son and said, "Cabby, tell Mr. Thorpe—I mean, Dr. Thorpe—what transformers are. I don't think he's ever seen one."

"You change them into things, like R2D2 turns into an X-wing fighter. Mommy, come on."

Jenny shook her head apologetically. "You must think you've landed on Mars, Garvin, and in a way you have. I'll show you what they are l-a-t-e-r."

"Later? You mean after I'm in bed? I'll show him now, Mommy."

But Jenny took her son firmly by the hand and led him into the house. "I'll be down in fifteen minutes," she said as she stepped through the door. "Why don't we move inside and have a drink? You'll find everything in here in the bar."

Obediently, Garvin began gathering up his notes. He moved the heavy glass bowl of flowers back to the center of the table, then stayed bent above it for a moment, inhaling the fragrance. Lilacs had been his mother's favorite flower; he hadn't thought of it since her death, but now he vividly remembered how the house had been filled with them when he came home from school in the spring.

When he stepped into the living room he felt another wave of nostalgia. The room was decorated in the colors his mother—and Jenny's too, he recalled—had loved: pale lemon yellow with warm touches of coral and green. Mellow wood shone in the lamplight; crystal dishes sparkled, silver boxes and picture frames gleamed on tables and shelves. The room was immaculate, yet alive with color and light.

Garvin found himself smiling as he poured Scotch into a highball glass and added ice from the silver bucket. He looked around for stereo equipment and at that instant the soft strains of a Mozart sonata flowed into the room. He turned to see Jenny adjusting a switch near the entrance from the hall.

"That's uncanny," he said. "I was just thinking a little Mozart was the only thing lacking."

Jenny was smiling as she crossed the floor to join him. She wore a blue silk shirt and straight white pants that emphasized her long legs and slim waist. When she reached his side Garvin could not stop himself from briefly touching her cheek—the same ivory and apricot smoothness his fingers remembered from years ago.

"You haven't changed, Jenny," he said softly, "except to get prettier."

"Oh, Garvin, you're sweet to say that." She moved her face against his hand, savoring the caress, then straightened briskly and said, "Well, I see you have a drink. Vodka for me, please."

They carried their glasses to a low table that stood before the pale yellow sofa.

"We can spread things out here if you want to," Jenny said as she settled herself against the cushions. "But I think we've pretty much covered the preliminaries, don't you? Except for picking the committees."

Garvin said, "Frankly, I'd rather discuss Cabby. When did five-year-olds start to talk like that?"

Jenny laughed, her head thrown back against the cushion, her throat a lovely, arching line. Then she said, "Obviously you're not up on the trends. How can you treat your young patients if you don't know about *Star Wars?* I suppose you never play video games or go skateboarding either."

"But he can spell, Jenny. How do you and Greg keep any secrets around a child like that?"

Jenny had been about to take a sip of her drink. She stopped with the glass half an inch from her lips, then slowly and carefully lowered it to the table instead. In the same deliberate manner she turned to face Garvin, and he saw that all the smiling softness had left her face, leaving a stiff, impenetrable mask.

She said, "Secrets? There's no sharing of secrets in this house, Garvin."

"I didn't mean . . ." He was appalled at the effect of his words.

"Any secrets here are unilateral, you might say. Every man for himself." She reached again for her drink, and this time took a healthy swallow.

"Jenny, I'm sorry if I said something to upset you."

"But it can't be any secret that I have what is known as a philandering husband. You can't be the only person in town who hasn't heard about Greg's affairs."

"Look, Jenny . . ."

"Oh God, I'm sorry. Poor Garvin. I forgot for a moment that you're a therapist. You didn't come over to hear more of what you must listen to all day."

Her brown eyes were warm with remorse. She tried to smile, but her lips were trembling.

"We were friends, more than friends, long before I was a therapist. I had time for your troubles then, didn't I?" He smiled reflectively. "Not that you had many that I knew about."

"I can't remember having one single problem in my life until I married Greg." She looked at him wistfully. "Of course that can't be right, can it? I must have had some worries before."

"I seem to recall a little anxiety about getting your physics experiments done. I also remember the number of guys who wanted to help you out—including me."

"What a wonderful time that was, Garvin. I'll never forget the happiness of those days. If only I'd had sense enough to see how rare it was, how precious..." She paused, peering earnestly into his face, and he saw that her eyes were wet. "I threw away the greatest chance of my life, but I didn't know, I didn't know..."

She was weeping when he reached for her. He held her tight, cradling her head on his shoulder, feeling his shirt turn wet with her tears.

After only a moment she pulled herself away and sat shakily smiling at him while she brushed at her damp hair.

"Psychologists aren't supposed to hug their patients, are they?"

"Sometimes it's the treatment indicated." Now he was the one making an effort to smile. "And Jenny, you must know how glad I am that you've turned to me—finally— if only for what little comfort I can offer. It means more than I can tell you."

"Oh, Garvin, if you knew the number of times my hand has been on the phone to call you. I suppose it was pride that stopped me."

"Well, of course you wouldn't want me of all people to guess you'd made a mistake. That's perfectly understandable."

"But I don't think I can ever make you understand what Greg Dillon did to me; I don't think anyone could but another woman. He was so incredibly attractive—just the most appealing man in the world. Though I didn't let myself see it until you and I were separated for so long, and he was there, and I finally stopped trying to avoid what I knew would happen if I let it." She threw up her hands helplessly. "I was hooked, drugged! And the pathetic fact is, I still would be if he hadn't changed." She forced a bitter, trembling smile.

"I can't imagine a man wanting anything else if he had you." Garvin's voice was husky.

"I don't know what Greg Dillon wants; I only know that no one woman can give it to him. I wish I could warn the others somehow, as a public service." Her face was grim. "I'm serious, Garvin. God knows how many lives that man will wreck before he's finished. When I think of the families, the children.... He should be locked up. He should be exterminated, like any household pest."

She was on her feet, glaring down at him, her hands clenched at her sides. Her face shocked him. Stretched taut with anger, it came closer to ugliness than Garvin ever could have imagined. He felt his own anger surge as he got to his feet. Any man who did this to Jenny Cabot was indeed not fit to live among decent people.

He seized her hands, shaking them gently to bring her to her senses. He said, "Jenny, I would like to help you if I can. It must be terrible for you to feel such anger." He forced himself to add, "Maybe Greg would be willing to work with us."

But Jenny was slowly shaking her head, her eyes half-closed. "Greg is just waiting till the time is right—for him, that is—then he'll leave. Perhaps he'll say good-bye to Cabby and me and perhaps not. He told me, in so many words. All I can do is wait, just wait, for weeks, or months, or years." Her eyes flew open and she peered into his with manic intensity. "Won't it be amusing if it takes years? While I grow older and crazier, and Cabby catches on? What will life be like in this house, Garvin, tell me?''

He shook her hard, until she went limp. Holding her against him, he said, "You don't have to wait for that, Jenny. You can throw him out; you can leave him."

"But I can't." She looked up at him like a helpless child. "You see what he's turned me into? A spineless, will-less creature, the kind of person I always despised and still do." She drew herself away and stood facing him. "Isn't it ironic? He's not only made me hate him, he's made me hate myself. And for that I can never forgive him."

SIX

Tuesday, June 24 Morning

CARRIE PORTER PARKED her compact station wagon in the spot reserved for it in the lot next to the post office, then climbed out, dropping her car key into the pocket of her blazer. She pulled out her canvas tote bag, heavy with the weight of the manuscript it contained, and wondered as she crossed the street why she ever carried work home with her during the week, since it seldom got any farther than a chair in the front hall.

She stopped on the sidewalk to rummage in her handbag for the office keys, then started up the porch steps of the Victorian house that served as headquarters for the Porter Publishing Company. She paused to call a good morning to Pete Costello, who was carrying empty cartons out of his grocery store four doors up the street. Costello's occupied another of the pointy-roofed frame buildings that lined the main street of Rivervale, most of them former dwellings converted to shops and offices when the residents built new houses away from the center of town.

The porch floor creaked underfoot as Carrie approached the door, sifting her bunch of keys for the one she wanted. She inserted the key in the lock and immediately, before she had turned it, felt the old door slowly swing open. The well-worn lock had let her down again; she would call a locksmith that morning without fail.

The Porter Publishing Company had leased the four ground-floor rooms of the house, two on either side of a narrow center hall that ran through to the back door and was mostly taken up by a staircase leading to the second floor. The hall carpet looked even more disreputable than usual that morning, Carrie observed. Was it the cleaning man's day, or would she have to vacuum it quickly herself?

Musing on the inescapable nature of household chores, she opened the door on her right, and entered what was her working part of the office. Ben's office was across from hers, but since he did most of his editing at home, the room was seldom occupied, and he used it mainly to store files and the gear he needed for his early morning fishing expeditions.

Carrie dropped her bag on the leather-seated chair that faced her desk, then stood looking around the office with a frown. The air in the closed-up room seemed stuffier than usual that morning; in fact, she was aware of a faint, unpleasant odor. She sniffed, trying to identify the scent, then went to the front window and pushed it open. A squirrel or raccoon could have gotten trapped and died between the walls somewhere; it had happened before. A call to the exterminator moved into first place on her morning's agenda.

Carrie opened her second window, the one overlooking the narrow alleyway that ran along the side of the house to the river's edge. She took off her blazer and hung it in the small closet, then went to her desk and saw that, as on most mornings, the red light on her telephone answering machine was blinking to indicate waiting messages. She hesitated. One of them was likely to be from the Reynolds office requesting changes in the contract she had sent for the ethereal young author's first novel. Coffee would help.

She headed for the kitchen at the back of the house, passing through the office adjoining hers, which was used by their part-time secretary, Ted Marsh. Ted, like Ben, was an artist who liked to paint at home in his studio, but needed some steady income to live on.

Across from Ted's office was the bathroom, and beside it the small kitchen where Carrie made coffee every morning and frequently a sandwich for lunch. The one cupboard contained little but cans of coffee and tuna fish, with a few emergency chocolate bars tucked away out of temptation's sight.

She filled the coffee maker and turned it on; then, sniffing suspiciously for traces of the odor she had noticed, she went down the hall to Ben's office and opened the door. The stench was suddenly so strong that she recoiled and stepped back into the hallway. Her heart had begun knocking in her chest; the hand with which she still clung to the doorknob was slippery with perspiration.

Slowly and deliberately she pushed the door open once more, then forced her unwilling feet to move forward, into the suddenly ominous silence of Ben's empty office.

The inner wall of the room was taken up with filing cabinets; the outer had two windows overlooking the front porch and, between them, hooks that held the equipment Ben needed for his infrequent fishing trips on the river. His desk stood at the far end of the room, facing the door, with a window behind it and an armchair for visitors placed in front of it.

That morning something else had been placed on the floor in front of the desk, or more likely had fallen there. For a moment Carrie stared fixedly at the surface of Ben's desk while she postponed acknowledging that the shape at the edge of her vision was a man's body. Then she thought, But maybe it's a drunk who wandered in and passed out. Or maybe he's injured and needs help.

So she stepped forward and looked, really looked. And although she had never seen a dead body before, there was no question she was looking at one then.

It was the body of a man, casually dressed in blue jeans and a white shirt with rolled-up sleeves. His hair was light brown, his face swollen and puffy where faces are usually lean: around the forehead and the bones of cheek and jaw. His rigid mouth was twisted to one side and open in what might have been a smile, or a cry. His eyes were half-open, but she could not bear to look closely enough to see their color. The skin of his face and arms was a muddy blend of yellow and gray-blue, like moldy leather. He lay on his side with one arm bent under him, the hand protruding stiffly from beneath his body; the other arm was bent against his chest, the hand fixed in a half-open claw.

The poor drunken tramp had died there, that was her thought. The poor man must have been very sick to have turned that terrible color; he must have had some raging disease.

And as she thought it she knew it was not true, for from the crook of the arm that rested on his chest the handle of a knife protruded, and the dark patch beneath his elbow was not shadow, but blood.

Carrie grasped the back of the chair and stood swaying, rocking the chair on its feet. She could not stop looking, though the smell she had traced hung about her now in an invisible, choking cloud. Or was it her horrified recognition of the corpse that had closed her throat so she could not breathe?

For, deny it all she might, only one man had eyes with such long, dark lashes, only one a head of brown hair so youthfully streaked with blond; only one man besides Ben wore blue jeans streaked with paint. It was Greg Dillon who lay there stabbed to death on the floor of Ben's office.

Carrie's legs gave out, and she let go of the chair and sank to the floor, half kneeling beside Greg's body, feeling herself begin to tremble violently as she struggled for control. She pressed her hands against her cold lips to stop their trembling. She forbade herself to faint and lie there beside him. She would not do that.

Deliberately she erased every emotion but the stubborn determination to remain conscious. She refused to recall the way she had felt about Greg Dillon, refused to face the irony it would be to lie beside the dead body that so recently had teased and tempted her.

In a moment she felt able to get to her feet. She started shakily for the door, trying to decide whom to telephone first, Ben or the police. Ben would be easier; she wouldn't have to look up the number. But first there was something...

Carrie stood in the doorway, one hand clutching the frame, and made herself look slowly, methodically, around the walls of the room. She noted a cobweb in one corner, a crooked blind on one rear window, then the untidy tangle of fishing gear that in her opinion had no place in an office. A yellow oilskin hung next to a canvas bag of lines and reels, a long-handled net, and the leather scabbard in which Ben carried his fishing knife attached to his belt. The scabbard was empty.

She shifted her gaze from that black leather sheath to the knife handle that protruded from Greg Dillon's chest. It was wrapped with black leather like the one Ben had received by mail the previous week from Orvis. Exactly like it.

She looked back at the scabbard hanging on the wall, willing herself to see Ben's knife sticking out of it, but of course all her looking would not put it back where it belonged. That knife, Ben's new fishing knife, was now firmly planted in the middle of Greg Dillon's chest.

Wrenching her eyes from the incredible sight, Carrie turned and ran, stumbling, into her office to phone her husband.

"Now, THIS Porter Publishing Company is your own business, Mr. Porter? Is that right?"

The two policemen, Tom Finnegan and Vince Muzzio, were conducting their interrogation of Ben and Carrie in Carrie's office, since the comings and goings of coroner's men, photographers, fingerprint experts, and newspaper reporters had rendered the other three rooms uninhabitable. Carrie had courteously offered Lieutenant Finnegan the use of her desk for his note-taking, and she watched, entranced, as he settled his bulky form into her chair, busied his mitt-like hands with moving some of her papers and folders out of his way, then opened his blue spiral notebook to a clean page and held a stubby yellow pencil poised above it. Her desk and everything on it suddenly appeared to have shrunk.

"It's our business, Lieutenant, my wife's and mine."

Ben spoke from the small sofa where he and Carrie sat feeling a little like two children who had been summoned to the principal's office.

"Oh? I guess that's how Mrs. Porter happened to find the body this morning. You come in and help out sometimes, do you, Mrs. Porter?" A grin split Finnegan's face into rosy hemispheres. His pink neck folded neatly over the rim of his blue shirt collar as he nodded approvingly.

"Well, actually I come in and help out every day." Carrie swept her bright hair back from her face with a slender hand and darted a quick glance of amusement toward Ben, on her right. She continued, "My husband and I have a somewhat unusual working arrangement, Lieutenant. We both love book publishing, but Ben also likes to paint, so he mostly works at home and I come to the office."

"But you have children, I thought."

"Yes, a boy and a girl." Carrie smiled encouragingly. "We take turns ferrying them around, and of course Ben is there when they come home from school."

"I see."

Vince Muzzio crossed his legs, coughing to hide his amusement at Finnegan's baffled expression. If Mary Finnegan could hear this she wouldn't believe it.

"Okay. Well now, just how well were you two acquainted with the deceased and his wife?"

Carrie looked around at Ben and saw with some dismay that his color had returned and his eyes were sparkling happily. He too had found Lieutenant Finnegan's reaction entertaining.

She quickly spoke up. "Ben and I knew the Dillons casually, I would say. We've known them for about four years, ever since we came to Rivervale, but we've never been close friends."

Finnegan slowly recorded Carrie's reply in his notebook. He studied the words for a moment, then looked up and said sharply, "What does that mean, not close friends?"

"I guess it means that we saw each other mainly at parties, with other people around." Carrie was frowning with the effort of getting it exactly right. "It was never just the four of us, was it, Ben? I don't think so."

"Or just the two of you, the way Greg would have preferred." Ben smiled fondly at Carrie, ignoring her icy glare, then glanced innocently from one stunned policeman to the other.

It was Muzzio, the younger of the two, who found his voice first. "Are you suggesting, Mr. Porter, that Mr. Dillon was interested in your wife, um, romantically?" He readied his own spiral notebook for Ben's reply, but Carrie was first.

"Greg Dillon sometimes gave the wrong impression," she began, then stopped when she felt the pressure of Ben's fingers on her hand.

"I'm afraid I sounded flippant, Lieutenant. Probably because Greg Dillon's proclivities are pretty well known around town. Or so I thought." He raised his eyebrows questioningly, but received only a faint smile of acknowledgment from young Muzzio. Finnegan's broad face, though possibly a shade pinker, remained impassive.

Ben dropped Carrie's hand and bent forward earnestly. "I don't think I can be accused of maligning the dead if I say that Greg Dillon was 'romantically interested,' as you put it so well, in every woman who crossed his path. He was an incurable philanderer, in fact. Plenty of men must have felt like killing him at one time or another."

"The only one we're interested in is the one who felt like killing him last night. With your knife. In your office."

Finnegan's small blue eyes were glacial. He closed his lips firmly and studied Ben in silence, then he said, "I'd like you to come to headquarters with me, Mr. Porter. I have to get back, and there are a few more questions I'd like to ask you."

Carrie gasped. Her eyes opened wide with shock, and Ben took her hand once more.

"Lieutenant Finnegan isn't charging me with anything, Carrie. That's true, isn't it?" he went on. He twisted to face the police officer, who was pushing himself out of the desk chair. "Because of course I would want to call my lawyer if..."

"Don't worry, Mr. Porter." Vince Muzzio had risen as well. "For anything like that we have to warn you. It's the law."

"Excuse us a minute, will you?" Finnegan was ushering Muzzio toward the door. "Vince will have a few more questions for you, Mrs. Porter, and then you can get on with your work. Or whatever."

The door of the office closed behind the two policemen, and Carrie instantly turned on Ben.

"I can't believe what you said to them! Are you trying to get yourself arrested? My God, Ben..."

"I may have been rash, as it turns out, but there's something about that fat red face that challenges me. Have you ever seen emotions displayed so clearly?"

"But Ben, this is hardly the time to play around for your own amusement. That man seriously suspects you of murder. Are you aware of that?"

"Oh, come on, Carrie. In my own office, with my own knife? Do I look that dumb?"

"To Finnegan, yes. And, you force me to admit, sometimes to me."

"I was simply indicating what kind of a guy Greg Dillon was. That's damn useful information, as a matter of fact."

At that point the door swung open and Finnegan peered into the room. "We're set to go now," he said. "Vince is clearing everybody out, and then he'll want a few more minutes with you, Mrs. Porter."

Carrie looked at her watch. "I wonder if Officer Muzzio would come to my house? I have to pick up my daughter at nursery school and take her home for lunch. We can talk just as well there, I should think."

So the president and editor-in-chief of Porter Publishing emerged from their offices under police escort and, parting with no more than the coolest of nods, went their separate ways.

"YOUR HUSBAND PAINTS, and Greg Dillon was also a painter. Was there any rivalry between them, Mrs. Porter? On that score, I mean?"

Vince Muzzio felt his face grow warm and hoped that Carrie Porter would not notice that he was blushing. It was one thing, he was discovering, to discuss possible infidelity in the businesslike setting of an office, with Lieutenant Finnegan presiding behind the desk, and quite another alone in a comfortable living room with a knockout like Mrs. Porter.

Carrie's eyes widened at the novelty of the concept. "Why, I never thought of such a thing, Lieutenant. You see, my husband's work is totally different from Greg Dillon's. Totally. To compare them is like comparing Rubens—a far less talented Rubens, of course—with someone like Braque or Picasso. Do you see what I mean?"

Muzzio wondered how such a pretty woman could talk like that. Carrie had pulled off her glasses, which she held dangling in her hand, and was peering at him with the most intensely blue eyes he had ever faced. Discovering his mouth to be open, he closed it. He nodded automatically, trying to remember her question, then said, "No, to tell the truth, I have no idea what you're getting at."

Carrie smiled, setting off a sparkle in the blueness. "Well, like Rubens, Greg Dillon loved to paint women, and whatever they really looked like, they all appeared on his canvas as beautiful and sensuous, either lushly rosy and pink and cuddly, or tawny and sleek as a leopard. So, naturally, he was a huge success as a portrait painter, where Ben paints women as compositions of angles and planes— at the moment anyway." She chuckled. "Ben is in an experimental stage; probably always will be. Greg's style was set years ago."

"I guess I see," said Muzzio; but the pencil in his hand remained poised above his notebook.

"I never quite thought it out before," Carrie mused, "but Greg Dillon's total idea of women was expressed in his paintings. No wonder..."

"Did he do your portrait?" Muzzio asked softly.

"No, indeed. He was the last artist Ben would have wanted to paint me."

Muzzio detected a hint of wistfulness in Carrie's voice. She must have heard it herself, for she straightened in her corner of the sofa and shook her head in dismay.

"I don't know why it seems to be impossible for either my husband or me to speak of Greg Dillon without giving you the impression that there was some torrid love affair going on."

She put on her glasses and gazed at Muzzio thoughtfully. He was young, with straight features and healthy, rose-tinged olive skin.

Carrie said slowly, "I think I can be perfectly honest with you, Lieutenant Muzzio, because I have an idea that occasionally you may feel about someone the way I felt about Greg Dillon. He was a very attractive man, and when he turned his charm on me it was impossible not to feel slightly—tempted, shall we say?"

She smiled at him, and Muzzio thought that if he had never before understood her meaning, at that moment he most emphatically did.

"Are you married?" she asked, and when Muzzio nodded she went on, "Then I'm sure you know that you can be happily married and still sense an attraction like that without ever intending, or even wanting, to do anything about it. Isn't that true?"

Muzzio nodded again. "Yes, I see." He cleared his throat. "Then you're telling me there was really nothing between you and Greg Dillon that would have made your husband angry enough to..."

"To kill him. No, definitely not. And anyway, I have to tell you that when they put Ben Porter together the killer instinct was completely left out." She paused. "Otherwise, can you imagine him leaving it to me to run the company? No, Ben is different; that's what's so wonderful about being married to him. He's the most gifted editor I know, and he likes to cook, and paint, and be with his children. He makes other men seem one-dimensional."

"Then would you say that you are pretty much the breadwinner in this family? Is that the way it works?"

"No, no. Ben is just as responsible for the business as I am. He selects manuscripts, edits them, and works with other editors to improve the books. He has a great instinct for what will sell, and thinks of brilliant promotional ideas. What I do is make it all happen: supervise the daily workings of the place, try to get people to meet their deadlines, work with agents on the contracts."

She stopped and looked around the room, then back at Muzzio. "And when Ben's sick of cooking I cook, and if I need a day off he runs the office. We're interchangeable, or close to it."

"Sounds like a great arrangement..." Muzzio glanced through his notes, then got to his feet. "I don't see any reason to keep you any longer, Mrs. Porter. Thanks for your help."

Carrie stood up and straightened her beige linen skirt. "I'm glad to give you any help I can, Lieutenant. It is upsetting to have a friend murdered in my office. I can't help wondering why there. Do you think the spot was picked deliberately?"

"We may not know that until we find the killer, but for your sake I sure hope not. Good-bye, Mrs. Porter."

Vince Muzzio took his time on the ten-mile drive to police headquarters in Springfield, and when he pulled into the parking lot he did not get out of the car immediately, but sat staring blankly through his windshield, trying to pin down an elusive, nagging thought. Giving it up, he reached for the door handle just as Ben Porter emerged from the building and walked down the short flight of stone steps.

Muzzio froze. That was it. Carrie Porter had done a good job of convincing him, Vince Muzzio, that she had not had an affair with Greg Dillon, but how about her husband? Had she ever taken the same pains with him? Muzzio hoped so, for he suddenly saw that the crux of this case could be not what actually had happened between

Carrie Porter and Greg Dillon, but what Ben Porter *thought* had happened. That was the question that must be pursued.

SEVEN

Tuesday, June 24 Early Afternoon

"WAIT A MINUTE, Enid, please. How did he act when he handed you the package? Did he seem nervous?"

Enid Thorpe had started for the study, carrying her lunch: a plate of lettuce and bean sprouts and a carton of vanilla yogurt. She stopped in the kitchen doorway and turned to frown over at Garvin. He was making a bologna sandwich at the kitchen counter near where a brown paper parcel rested that had been lying there when he came in from his office.

"I don't know whether I would use the word *nervous*. He did seem tense, and he was pale. But of course I'd never seen him before; maybe that's his normal coloring."

"It is nowadays, though I've been trying to make him get some exercise." Garvin smiled at his wife. "That's as much of a losing battle with Frank Lundy as it is with you."

Enid's tight little grimace might have been meant for a smile. Nothing irritated her more than a lecture—as it always sounded to her—on physical fitness.

"Well, anyway, he asked if I was your wife, then he hesitated until I said you had told me to expect him. Then he handed over the package and said, 'Tell him I kept part of the bargain at least.'"

She turned away and would have left the room if Garvin had not stopped her once more.

"How about eating in here with me for a change?" He put his sandwich and cup of coffee on the small, round kitchen table and drew out a chair, peering at Enid invitingly.

She stood undecided, looking at her husband almost suspiciously until he added, "I'm interested in how you happened to ask him what was in the package."

At that, she approached the table and slowly set down her plate and the yogurt carton. She kept her eyes on them, as if she might snatch them up again as she replied, "I guess it sounds silly, but you told me not to invite him in, and he did look rather strange. I thought of a bomb. It's all the terrorist stories we read, I guess."

A faint pink had risen to her cheeks, and Garvin felt a stab of tenderness. He knew how she detested, even feared, ever appearing fanciful or illogical.

He said softly, "Seems to me an intelligent precaution."

Enid flashed him a quick glance of appreciation, then, relaxing a little, sat down and pulled her chair close to the table. "I was relieved, actually, when he said it was a gun. He looked a little alarmed then, as if he was sorry he had told me, so I smiled, reassuringly, I think, and said only that I would be sure to give it to you the minute you came home."

"And then went to sleep instead."

Enid's mouth dropped open and she looked so chagrined that Garvin patted her hand where it lay beside her plate. "I don't blame you, Enid; it's all right. I was late getting in; I'm just glad I didn't disturb you."

"I thought if I took the thing to our room it would be all right. I was very tired. And you may laugh, but I hid it in my closet under a stack of sweaters so it would be out of sight. I've heard of women shooting their husbands when they took them for intruders. I didn't want to do that."

"Too bad having a gun around doesn't make everyone that uncomfortable. It might lower the crime rate."

Enid picked up her fork. "Some day I'd like to hear about Frank Lundy's case," she said. Garvin started to speak, and she held up her hand to silence him. "I know it would be unethical to talk about it now, in the midst of treatment. I can wait."

The telephone rang and Garvin rose to get it from the bookcase beside the table, glancing at his watch. "It'll be for me, I think. My one o'clock appointment..."

Enid reached for the morning paper, and began to eat her lunch. She paid no attention to Garvin's conversation until she heard him say, "You're certain he was stabbed, are you?"

She lowered her fork then, and sat staring at the geometric design of the beige and white wallpaper.

On the phone Garvin was saying, "I think you should come and see me, Frank. I'll cancel my next appointment." A pause. "Later, then. Stop by around five. I think it's important for you to talk about it." Another pause. "One more thing, Frank. What time do they think it happened? Do you know?"

Garvin listened for a moment, then said good-bye and rang off. He did not return to the table, but stood very still with the telephone in his hand.

"Enid," he said. "What time was it when Frank Lundy brought the gun last night?"

Her glasses had slipped forward on her nose, and she pushed them up and peered through the shining lenses at her husband.

"Why? What's happened, Garvin? I heard the word *stabbed.*"

"Greg Dillon has been murdered. Carrie Porter found his body this morning in her office. Or in Ben's office, actually. He was stabbed, apparently, and the police think it was shortly after nine o'clock."

He stood very still, holding the telephone, and Enid saw that the color had left his face. I've never seen him so pale, she thought. She felt clinically detached, an onlooker watching from a distance.

"I don't know exactly when Lundy arrived, but it wasn't more than an hour after you went out."

"I left the house about seven-fifteen. Do you think, then, that Frank came to the door before eight-thirty?"

"Yes, I would say so. But why, Garvin? What difference does it make?"

"Well, it's too much to go into right now, but Frank Lundy was carrying a load of hostility against Greg Dillon, and he was getting close to the breaking point. Though God knows I tried my best."

"I'm sure you handled it perfectly. You must have, obviously, or he wouldn't have turned in his gun to you."

Garvin nodded slowly, but his lean face remained a tense, white mask. "Anyway, Greg was stabbed, not shot. That makes a difference."

Enid pushed her chair back from the table. "That makes all the difference, it seems to me. A man who is obsessed with the idea of shooting someone doesn't suddenly give the gun away and stab the person instead. Anyway, stabbing is another kind of violence, isn't it? Would he make a switch like that?"

"He might, he might. Who can say for sure?" Garvin replaced the telephone on the bookshelf and moved abstractedly to the table. He stood staring down at his coffee cup with distaste.

Enid said, "There's more hot coffee, Garvin. Would you like some?"

"What? Oh, no thanks." He sat down, picked up his cup, and drained the contents, peering over the rim at his wife while he swallowed. Still keeping his eyes fixed on Enid, he set down the cup and said, "If Frank Lundy doesn't come to see me this evening, as he very well may not, I think I've got to tell the police about his case."

"Why don't you call them right now? You're obviously very concerned."

Garvin shook his head. "If Greg had been shot and if Frank hadn't turned in his gun to me I would, of course, call them immediately. But as it stands my first responsibility is to my patient. I have to see how he feels now that his enemy has been removed; apparently quite by coincidence. At least I hope that's what it is."

"What are you suggesting? That perhaps Frank Lundy got someone else to kill Greg?"

Garvin looked startled. "I hadn't thought of that."

Enid had pulled off her glasses while she stared thoughtfully into the distance beyond Garvin's shoulder. "I think you'll be able to tell when you talk to him, don't you? He'll reveal his guilt somehow, don't you think? Or his innocence?" She turned to him and Garvin saw that two spots of pink had appeared on her cheeks. "Oh, Garvin, I'd give anything to sit in on that interview this afternoon." He started to speak, but she interrupted. "I know I can't, of course; but will you tell me everything he says? Let me see your notes? It's a fascinating case."

She was peering at him with shining eyes, and he remembered how her enthusiasm had attracted him years ago when they took a course together. Psychopathology, was it? Or Behavioral Science; something they had studied in senior year.

Finally he said, "This may turn out to be a complicated situation, Enid. Much as I would enjoy sharing all the details with you, I think I must stick to the rule of confidentiality for your protection, as well as my patient's."

She had picked up a pencil and was frowning at it as she turned it in her fingers. "Don't be angry," Garvin added. "When it's all over you can read every word of my notes, I promise."

She glanced up in surprise. "I'm not angry. You said just what I expected you to. No, I was just wondering: Did Frank Lundy tell you anything about the murder weapon, the knife or whatever it was? Do you think he knows?"

"I never thought to ask him, and no, he didn't say what weapon was used to kill Greg. He just said he had been stabbed. What difference does it make?"

There was a faint suggestion of superiority in the smile that flickered across Enid's face before she bent and began drawing with her pencil in the margin of the newspaper.

"I just wondered if it was something a killer might bring for the purpose, as he would bring a gun, or if it was a makeshift weapon of some sort. In other words..." She kept her eyes fixed on her doodling. "Was the killer planning to kill Greg? Did he meet him there for that purpose? Or was it a sudden, overpowering impulse?'' Enid's intent gaze was once more focused on Garvin's face. ''It could matter, don't you think?''

Garvin regarded his wife in silence. He was suddenly aware of a pulse throbbing almost painfully in his throat.

He said, ''Enid, will you do me a favor and cancel my next two patients? I think I should get over to Jenny Dillon's right away.''

Without waiting for a reply, he headed for his office wing to get his engagement pad.

Mid-Afternoon

''I DON'T REALLY THINK you're dumb, darling. You know that, don't you?''

''Don't get carried away and say a lot of things you don't mean just because you're so glad to see me walk in here a free man.''

''Oh, I am glad; I certainly am.'' Carrie pulled Ben's head down to hers and kissed him again.

He grinned, holding her tight against him. ''I'll have to get arrested more often.''

Carrie pushed herself away. ''Oh, please. If you had any idea how scared I was...'' She sighed, remembering, then took her husband's hand and drew him to the sofa where a few hours earlier they had sat together answering Lieutenant Finnegan's questions. ''Tell me everything that happened. Don't leave out one single question.''

Ben sat down beside her and slumped into his usual relaxed position with his long legs stretched out before him, his head on a level with Carrie's shoulder.

''They took my name, address, Social Security number—why that, do you suppose?'' Carrie shrugged impatiently, and he went on. ''They asked me all that stuff again about how long we'd known Greg, and how well, and then Finnegan really zeroed in on you and Greg: Had I ever caught you together? In fact, had I ever caught you with anyone?''

" 'Caught me,' I like that. Sounds as if you spent most of your time hiding in closets and skulking in corners to spy on me.''

"Maybe I should. I might have more colorful tales to tell the fellows down at headquarters.''

"Well, what in the world did you tell them?''

"I couldn't have been more honest with them. I went all the way back to the office Christmas parties at Foote and Marshall—how enthusiastically you'd kissed your boss, now that I thought of it; and that New Year's Eve when Chuck Gibbons cornered you in the hall. Oh, their questions made me think, Carrie; I can tell you they opened my eyes.''

"They didn't break your spirit, obviously.'' Carrie shook her head wonderingly. "Do you get yourself suspected of murder every week or so, but forget to tell me? I don't understand how you can be so flip about it.''

Ben patted his wife's knee. "To tell you the truth, I don't quite understand it myself. Unless it's because Greg Dillon never seemed real to me, so murdering him almost isn't a real crime. Do you know what I mean?''

Ben twisted his head to peer up at Carrie. "He never acted like an adult; he thought there were special rules for a glamorous guy like him. He wasn't in the world, was he? Not the same one we live in.''

"He was in it enough to cause some very real pain, Ben, to more than one woman. You'd agree with that, wouldn't you?''

"I guess so, I guess so.'' Ben struggled to his feet and walked over to the desk. He turned, leaning back against it, and said, "Could you ever take a guy like that seriously? I always thought any smart, grownup woman could see right through that type. But I must have been wrong, hmm? If someone got serious enough to kill him.''

"Perceptive as you are about most things, you are dead wrong if you think Greg Dillon was a figure of fun to any woman. I felt his attraction myself; there's no point in denying it.''

"Not any more.''

"Don't be so callous; it's disgusting."

There was a silence while Ben and Carrie Porter regarded one another from opposite sides of a chasm that had suddenly opened between them.

After a moment Ben said slowly, "I guess this thing has shaken us more than I realized. We've never been this close to violence, have we? Especially you—coming in and finding Greg's body on the floor like that."

"And it's horrible that a murder took place in your office. You're still reacting, I guess. Nonetheless . . ."

"Nonetheless, murder is not a thing to be taken lightly. Even when it's Greg Dillon."

"Damn you, Ben Porter—"

At that point the telephone rang. Ben picked it up from the desk, listened a moment, then said, "I'll ask my wife; she may have it here somewhere." He looked at Carrie and said, "Do you happen to have Maria Lundy's phone number or address? Apparently there's more than one Frank Lundy in Springfield."

"I'll see. Who wants it?" Carrie went around to the other side of the desk as she spoke. Once there she began flipping the revolving card file to the letter *L*.

Covering the phone's mouthpiece with his hand, Ben replied, "The police. I'll tell you why in a minute."

Carrie looked up, shaking her head. "Did you tell them her husband has an office? Isn't he an accountant or something?"

"Right. I'd forgotten." Ben informed the caller of Frank Lundy's profession, then hung up.

"I suppose they want to question Maria because she posed for Greg." Carrie sat down in her desk chair. "Did you tell them that?"

"I'm afraid I did when they were asking about my painting versus Greg's; what kind of subjects we painted, etcetera. Her name came to mind because she was the only model we both used, as far as I know."

"But Ben, surely you didn't suggest—"

Settling himself in the chair that faced her desk, Ben replied, "I didn't suggest anything. I merely said our only possible professional link was that we both used the same model occasionally. Finnegan snickered at that. I guess the word *model* has a salacious connotation to a cop. I said all serious painters employ models, both male and female, and he gave me a look with those piggy little eyes that was like, 'Sure, fella, I catch on.' It's illuminating to come up against the brutish police mentality.''

''I don't think Vince Muzzio is brutish. In fact, he strikes me as a pretty sensitive man.''

''*Vince* Muzzio is it? Well, well.''

Carrie ignored him. ''We had a really good talk at home after I'd put Brooke down for her nap. I'm pretty sure I convinced him that there was nothing going on between Greg and me; nothing more than a slight attraction, at least. I thought I did it rather well, in fact. I wish I could have taped the conversation for you.'' She smiled reflectively. ''I think honestly confessing to my own human frailty was a brilliant stroke. An adulterous person wouldn't do that, do you think?''

''I don't know how adulterers reason, if they do. Right now I'm more concerned about the thought processes of the police.'' Ben ran his fingers through his already disordered brown hair. ''God, Carrie, it's frightening to see how quickly they build a case in their own minds. Finnegan had it all settled this morning, didn't he? I'm jealous of Greg on two counts: His paintings sell, mine don't; and my beautiful, blond wife is in love with him, not me. So I get him to come to my office, where I stab him with my fishing knife, brazenly leaving the body on the scene. Let's see, how would Finnegan figure that?''

''As a macho gesture of defiance. A sinned-against husband, justified in defending his territorial rights.''

Carrie stopped abruptly and stared wide-eyed at her husband. She gave a little shiver and folded her arms tightly across her chest. ''It's entirely too possible, Ben. Will you call Howard Keating right now and tell him what's happened?''

''I don't know as we need to bother Howard with this just yet.''

Carrie reached for the phone. "Will you call him right now or shall I?"

"Okay, go ahead. You're probably right. But I think he goes to Hartford on Tuesdays."

Carrie consulted the card file, then dialed their lawyer, and was informed by his secretary that Mr. Keating was out of the office for the day, but would be able to call the Porters that evening.

"Please ask him to, without fail," said Carrie. "Tell him it's very important." Then, politely declining the opportunity to speak to Howard's partner, she hung up.

"I wonder . . ." Ben was thinking out loud, frowning in the direction of the hall. He slowly rose to his feet saying, "I wonder if Greg was stabbed in my office where you found him, or if someone dragged him in from outside. Let's have a look."

Carrie rose to join him. "I remember noticing that the hall carpet looked terrible when I came in. In fact, I was planning to vacuum it as soon as I had my coffee."

In Ben's office they studied the area in front of the desk where Greg's body had lain. Carrie frowned at the plum-colored broadloom she had long been wanting to replace. "Now can we get new office carpeting?" she said, and Ben looked at her reprovingly.

"Now who's being callous? But you're right, it's time." He knelt and pressed his hand against the surface of the rug. "Doesn't feel damp, exactly, but it's kind of matted."

Carrie walked slowly in the direction of the front door, stopping every foot or so to study the rug's texture.

"It looks as if something had been dragged across from the door. Or am I imagining that?" She stooped to peer more closely. "Now I know why Sherlock Holmes carries a magnifying glass."

"I see it too. Except here and there where the nap seems to go in circles. As if someone had scrubbed . . ." Ben sat back on his heels and looked around. "Then what did they do with the scrubber, the cloth or brush or whatever?"

"Took it with them?" Carrie straightened, pondering; then she started for the kitchen at the far end of the hall. "A brush wouldn't do it; you'd need a cloth or something absorbent."

She stepped into the tiny kitchen and Ben heard her exclaim, "Aha!" She emerged brandishing a depleted roll of paper toweling; only two or three squares remained on its cardboard core.

"This was brand-new yesterday morning," she said. "I put it up myself. In fact…" Carrie disappeared again into the kitchen and came out carrying a plastic wastebasket.

"Look! Here's the wrapper, right here, and only about two used towels. Somebody used up that whole roll, Ben, mopping up blood, I'll bet."

Ben ran his hand across the carpet, then dusted his fingers. A faint showering of lint floated to the floor, and he said, "That looks like paper towel to me. But then what? After the mop-up he'd have this bundle of bloody paper…"

"And he'd take it out and throw it in the river."

Carrie put down the wastebasket and hurried to the door that led outside from the rear of the hallway. "Paper towels wouldn't float, would they? Especially blood-soaked ones."

Together Ben and Carrie stepped out into the sunny square of grass that led to the riverbank. A small wooden dock floated on the water, and they walked out on it and gazed around, shielding their eyes from the dazzling reflection that sparkled up from the wind-ruffled surface of the river.

Ben said, "We could hardly expect to find any evidence still floating around, but this looks like the logical place to toss it. Couldn't have taken more than a minute."

"But what would it prove anyway if we found Greg was stabbed outside and then dragged into the office?"

Ben stepped back onto the riverbank and turned to extend a steadying hand to Carrie. "I suppose the location might reveal something about the killer—his strength, his motive, I don't know."

"Greg was not a huge man, but nobody could drag a dead body very far—especially without being seen. He had to be killed on our property, inside or out, and with your knife; there's no way around it."

"None that I can see. Oops, there's the phone!" They had left the back door open, and Ben sprinted across the lawn and into the house.

Reluctant to exchange the bright river for rooms now burdened with tragedy, Carrie dawdled to search along the bank for rocks and branches that might have snagged a shred of toweling. A bullfrog squawked at her approach and cannoned into the water with a flash of white legs. Close to shore Carrie saw a swirling brew of tadpoles and paused to watch them. There must be a jar in the kitchen, she thought; she would scoop up some tadpoles and take them home to the children.

Starting for the house, Carrie felt lighthearted for the first time that day. Her mind could not accommodate tadpoles and children and murder simultaneously, and thank heaven for that.

Late Afternoon

GARVIN THORPE WAS ENGAGED with another patient when the buzzer indicated that Frank Lundy had arrived. He could hear Lundy moving restlessly about the reception room, and half expected him to stalk out without waiting; but when he finally ushered his patient out, Lundy was standing beside the sofa, apparently absorbed in a magazine.

He tossed it onto the table and greeted Garvin with his customary unsmiling nod. In the office the two men settled in their chairs, then sat regarding each other in silence, each waiting for the other to begin.

Thorpe's expression was faintly questioning, his heavy brows slightly lifted over the probing, intelligent eyes. On Lundy's face, however, he saw only the expression of exaggerated calm he wore at the start of every interview. His face revealed no sign of the relief or amazement a man might be expected to feel after the fortuitous demise of his wife's lover.

Lundy said, "If you're wondering how I feel about Dillon being killed, I can tell you in a nutshell: good riddance."

Thorpe nodded slowly. "I suppose for you that is an understandable reaction, even to such a violent murder. You are glad the man is gone."

"You're damn right I am."

"What other feelings did you have when you first heard the news?"

A fleeting spark shone in Lundy's gray eyes, perhaps ignited by the rays of the afternoon sun that slanted into the room across Garvin's shoulder.

He said in a perfectly level tone, "I was surprised, of course."

"Do you feel relieved?"

"Not exactly." Lundy paused to reflect. "In a way I guess I do, and yet..."

"Yes?" Garvin prompted.

"Well, it's funny, but I don't feel as good as I'd have expected." Lundy looked up quickly, as if startled by his words. "I mean, I don't feel as good as I always thought I would if something happened to the guy. In a way it doesn't solve anything."

"Do you mean it doesn't solve anything between you and Maria?"

"Yes. It isn't as if she gave him up, is it? On her own? I'll never know what would have happened if he had lived. I'll always have to wonder, won't I?" Lundy spoke the final words with a querulous tremor.

Garvin said, "You won't *have* to, Frank; and I hope you won't choose to. It will be up to you."

"Up to me. Sure, I guess that's right."

"What about Maria? How did she take the news?"

"I haven't seen her, so I can't say for sure, but she sounded okay on the phone." He paused, then added hopefully, "She didn't cancel her job for tonight. That's a good sign, isn't it?"

"She is supposed to sing at her cousin's nightclub tonight?"

"Yes. After I talked to her I called Joe DeLucca and he said she's still going on."

"Then you didn't ask her that question?"

Lundy shook his head, scowling. "I'm not supposed to know about her and Dillon, remember? So I can't make a big thing of this, just act like she knows the guy because she poses for him, and so forth. Phony as hell."

Lundy fell morosely silent while Thorpe slowly turned the pages of his notes. After a moment he closed the folder on the desk before him, looked across at Lundy, and said, "Frank, Greg Dillon's murder compels me to take a step that may disturb you. I am going to have to tell the police something about your state of mind over the last two weeks."

Frank Lundy looked up sharply. "Why the hell...? I did what you wanted. I brought my gun over here. And Dillon wasn't shot anyway. I don't see where there's any connection."

"Perhaps there isn't. Still, I have an obligation to report anything that might have a bearing on the case. Surely you can see that."

"You're just going to stir up a hornet's nest about nothing. You know damn well I didn't kill Greg Dillon."

"I don't know that, Frank. You're the only one who knows with certainty what you did. And if you are innocent it won't matter if I tell the police that you were angry at Greg and had threatened—"

"I never threatened him! I said I was mad, and with good reason. You'll agree to that, won't you?"

"I agree that you were in a situation that would anger most people, yes. But not everyone buys a gun."

"And then turns it in to a shrink, like some kid giving teacher his water pistol."

"Were you glad after you gave the gun to my wife? Did you feel relieved to be rid of it, or deprived?"

"God, I don't know. To tell you the truth I'm getting sick of thinking about how I feel all the time. I think I've had enough of this, Garvin. I guess you mean well, but let's call it a day. Okay?''

"I would want you to think about that decision, then see me once more, if you will. But whether you continue therapy or not, I hope you understand that I will be speaking to the police.''

"Well, look, can you put that off for a couple of days? I need some time here. For one thing, I'd better tell Maria about you if you're going to the police. That's what you've been wanting me to do, right?''

"Yes, I agree that Maria should be told.''

Garvin sat silently weighing the risk of delay. Perhaps he had happened on the lever that would force Lundy to bring his wife into therapy, an essential step if the treatment were to be effective. Meanwhile, he might inadvertently be providing the opportunity for further violence.

He said slowly, "Well, let's say this. I will consent to wait for a short time—no more than a couple of days—if you will try to persuade Maria to see me, and if you will come in here to the office every day yourself.''

"Every day? I don't know, Doc.''

"That's the deal, Frank. This is a crucial time for you, and for Maria, too. I must insist on your cooperation or I will go to the police immediately.''

"Well, I can't promise about Maria. I might have to give her some time to get over the shock.''

"Two days, Frank; that's all I can promise.'' Garvin rose as he spoke and after a moment's hesitation Frank Lundy also got to his feet. Without expression the two men reached across the desk to shake hands; then Lundy strode to the door in silence, pulled it open, and departed.

EIGHT

Wednesday, June 25 Morning

MARIA AND FRANK LUNDY lived in a four-room apartment in a red brick building that had been erected in a rundown section of Springfield when it had looked as though the neighborhood was about to make a turnaround. Indeed, in the three years since Frank had carried Maria over the threshold many of the old frame houses on their street had been bought by upwardly mobile young couples and "restored," as they liked to say, although the term implied an architectural or historical importance few of the houses could claim.

What all the refurbishing had done was to make Maria hate her square, characterless apartment even more than she had when she moved in.

"It'll do for a year, while we look around for something great," Frank had persuaded her; but then he had decided to get his CPA certification, and then to open his own office, and there was no money to spare. A house was a postponable luxury; so was a baby, which seemed ironic to Maria. Certainly her mother had never thought of babies as luxuries and didn't now. When the touchy subject came up at all she would look from Frank to Maria in bafflement, wondering about the reason for their barrenness, but too shy to press the matter.

A baby would put an end to Maria's nightclub singing; for Mrs. DeLucca that alone would make it worthwhile, for as things stood, Maria had nowhere near enough to do and could hardly be blamed for having crazy ideas about a show-business career.

At least it was her cousin's nightclub—that was some small comfort—and since it was the only spot in town that offered live entertainment, Maria was not offered other jobs. Just the modeling, and a baby would take care of that very nicely too. Mrs. DeLucca would nod grimly when she pictured her daughter's shapely body bulging in pregnancy. Motherhood would settle that girl's hash, as it had many a one before her, and to that end Maria's mother had made a novena every month for a year at St. John's R.C. Church.

A baby figured in Maria's dreams that morning, a plump little creature that studied her from the depths of its lace-trimmed cradle with a strangely wise and sad expression. It made no sound, but when she bent to pick up the infant it began to dissolve, and soon she was gazing in horror at a small heap of empty baby garments.

She woke sobbing. Tears, real ones, were sliding down her face, and her terrible sense of loss was even greater than it had been in the dream. Propping herself on one elbow, Maria reached for a tissue. She sank back, mopping her eyes, still sobbing uncontrollably, and in an instant recollection struck. Greg was dead. He was gone forever, and all temptation with him. All joy, all adventure, all color had been drained away, and her life, recently so electric with the excitement of guilty love, had become a drab gray wasteland.

Realization stopped her tears, but she felt spent, as exhausted as if she had come to the end of a long, arduous journey. She glanced at her husband, and felt dully grateful that her sobs had not wakened him. He was always a sound sleeper, a convenience over the last few months, she thought bitterly. It wouldn't matter anymore, however, when he woke up, or if he woke up.

She stared at his still form. Perhaps he was dead too; it wouldn't be any particular shock, not today. But she saw a slight movement; he was breathing, and she was glad, really. She couldn't blame Frank for her sorrow. He loved her, she knew he did, or he wouldn't have been suffering so terribly: suspecting the worst, but afraid to accuse her because he could not bear to hear her confession.

Maria slid out of bed, careful to leave the covers in place. It was only six-thirty; she had time to bathe and make up her face, maybe fix Frank something nice for breakfast before getting him up to prepare for their appointment at police headquarters.

In the shower she shampooed her hair and thought about what to wear. For once she should play down her figure, so a dress might be preferable to pants—her blue silk shirtwaist, perhaps, and pumps, not sandals. Her idea was to look conventional, well-bred, with no suggestion of being in mourning.

The thought of mourning, of the way she would have to conceal her grief over Greg's death, brought the prickle of tears again, but she clenched her teeth and forced herself to stare resolutely into the mirror until her eyes were clear and her lips had stopped trembling.

She brushed her thick black hair into shape, using the dryer just to get the wetness out, knowing it would dry naturally in soft, shining waves; then she applied mascara and eyeliner with a light touch. Today the natural look was her goal; she wanted to appear sincere and forthright—not only to the police, she admitted to herself, but in her husband's eyes as well.

She heard the bedroom window close. Frank was out of bed. Tightening the sash of her white terry cloth robe, she opened the bathroom door and stepped out to say good morning.

"THE REASON WE'RE talking to you separately, Mrs. Lundy, is that we want you to feel perfectly free to tell us the truth, with no worries about your husband's reaction. Okay?" Tom Finnegan spoke softly, bending over the heaped papers on his desk to bring his face closer to Maria's.

"I understand, Lieutenant." Maria's voice was even softer, and she did not draw away from the beefy expanse of perspiring flesh, but actually inclined her lovely head in Finnegan's direction, Muzzio observed, like a flower seeking the warmth of the sun.

Freeing himself with an effort from the pull of Maria's velvety eyes, Finnegan sat back, cleared his throat, and picked up one of the crumpled papers before him. He said in a firm, businesslike manner, "We asked you to come in because we have looked over the paintings in Greg Dillon's studio and found that you figure prominently in many of them. In other words, you obviously spent a good deal of time posing for the deceased. That is true, is it not?"

Maria nodded. "Yes, I often posed for Mr. Dillon, and for other artists as well, of course."

"Including Ben Porter?"

"Yes, now and then; but Mr. Porter's style is different. He uses all sorts of models—old people, local characters, and so forth—where Mr. Dillon was mainly interested in, well, younger, more feminine types."

Maria listened to herself saying the words as if she were observing from a corner of the room this poised, detached person who clearly had no personal stake in the fate of Greg Dillon.

"Beautiful women, you're saying." Although it did not disturb her protective shell, she heard Finnegan's voice and, as if on cue, felt herself blushing.

"I didn't mean to sound . . ." The velvet gaze was focused on her clasped hands now; Finnegan saw only the rich sweep of curling black lashes against the curve of Maria's rose-tinged cheek.

"No use beating around the bush, Mrs. Lundy; you're a gorge—that is, you're a very good-looking woman. You don't need anyone to tell you that."

The darkly glowing eyes once again engaged Finnegan's tiny blue ones and even Muzzio found himself listening breathlessly as Maria replied, "You're awfully nice to say that, Lieutenant."

Enough. This could go on all morning.

Muzzio said, "What we're curious about, Mrs. Lundy, for reasons you can well imagine, is your relationship with the murder victim. Just how long have you been posing for him?"

She twisted in the straight-backed wooden chair to face the young officer, who sat at one end of the desk holding a pencil and a spiral notebook. In contrast to his bemused superior, Muzzio appeared to be taking her presence in stride. Maria felt, in fact, a pulse beat of recognition flash between them, and with it the first faint stab of fear.

"I believe my first modeling job for Mr. Dillon was about two years ago. I would have checked my engagement book if I had known you—"

"And how many times a week did you sit for him, on average?" Muzzio interrupted, and saw Finnegan frown reproachfully.

"Why, maybe three times a week, I would say, when he was working hard. Sometimes he traveled, of course."

"With his family? His wife and son?"

"Oh, certainly. They went to Cape Cod in the summer, for a few weeks anyway, and usually to the Caribbean in February or March."

"Were the Dillons happily married, as far as you know?"

"Now just a minute, Vince," Finnegan spoke up. "It's not up to Mrs. Lundy to make a judgment on that."

"You're right, of course. I apologize, Mrs. Lundy." But Muzzio had seen Maria's body tense, and observed that she remained unnaturally still, a polite smile fixed on her lips, as she waited for him to continue.

However, it was Finnegan who said, as gently as a parish priest, "What about your own marriage, Mrs. Lundy? Are you and . . ." He glanced at a form on the desk before him. "Are you and Frank happy together? It's a routine question, you understand, in cases like this."

Cases like this? Muzzio marveled. Finnegan had probably handled two murders in his entire career in Springfield.

"Frank and I are very happy, Lieutenant." Maria's smile softened as she shifted her attention to Finnegan, and he smiled paternally in response. She glanced shyly at her folded hands once more and said, "Of course, we would like to have children. That is the only flaw, I would say. It's been a disappointment."

"But you're very young; you have plenty of time."

He might as well have added, "and plenty of fun trying." Muzzio had to glance away, afraid he might catch Finnegan literally drooling.

"We have talked to Mrs. Dillon, briefly of course, in view of her bereavement, and I have to tell you that she described her marriage as a disaster." Never afterwards was Muzzio able to explain, to himself or Finnegan, the impulse that triggered his next harsh words. "She claims her husband was unfaithful repeatedly, and she implied that you were one of his frequent partners. That was how she put it: one of them."

Maria gasped. While he was speaking she had swiveled around to face him, and now he saw that her eyes were huge and black with shock, her skin drained of color.

"That's a lie!" She stopped to gulp for breath. "Just because he didn't love her she thought he couldn't love anybody. But he loved me—tell her that!" She was bent nearly double, shouting the words in Muzzio's face, panting like a cornered animal.

There was no sound in the room but Maria's labored breathing. Then the telephone rang shrilly, and as if she had been struck Maria went limp. She dropped her head to her hands and slumped in the hard chair, sobbing in great, painful spasms while Finnegan and Muzzio looked on, speechless with shock.

"I WOULD LIKE YOU to wait here while your testimony is being typed up and then read it over and sign it if it is accurate. Any problem with that?"

Maria shook her head. The mug of coffee she clutched in her hands had lost nearly all its warmth; still it was a comfort, a link with normality, so she took tiny, infrequent sips, wanting it to last.

Finnegan had put on his wire-rimmed spectacles to read the notes he had taken, and Maria saw that the earpieces stretched out to the sides of his fat, pink face before bending back to hook onto his ears. He should get some new glasses, properly fitted; but she supposed it wasn't up to her to tell him that.

He was saying something, peering at her over the gold wire rims. She felt as if she had been sitting on the bare wooden chair for days. She could imagine how she looked after her outburst, but for the first time she could recall in her entire life she didn't care.

"I want to be absolutely clear on one point, Mrs. Lundy. You say that you visited the deceased several days before the murder in order to break off your affair. Is that correct?"

"Yes, it is."

"*You* were breaking it off, on your own initiative, not Mr. Dillon; do I have that right?"

"Yes. Actually Greg wanted to go on as we were. He saw no reason to end it."

"But you were under a strain because of your husband, your fear that he would find out."

"And my knowledge that I was hurting him. I just couldn't keep it up any longer."

"But it wasn't until the night of the murder that you went back to the studio, around eight o'clock, to get some clothing and cosmetics you had kept there. You talked briefly with the deceased."

"I had asked him to be out, you understand, but he was there, which didn't surprise me."

"Yet you remained firm in your resolve, and packed your belongings into your car and left. Around eight-thirty, is that right?"

"As near as I can tell. I was upset, of course, and not paying much attention to the time. All I wanted was to get it over with."

"Of course. Well, I think that does it." Finnegan pulled off the glasses that had looked so tiny on his hamlike face and shuffled his notes into a neat pile. "Give these to Gladys," he said to Muzzio, "and ask her to send Mr. Lundy in."

Maria bent forward anxiously, still clutching her coffee cup. "I want to ask you, Lieutenant. Is it necessary to...I mean, do you have to tell my husband everything I've said in here?" Her mouth was shaking so that she had to stop. She felt tears rising once again and she angrily blinked them back.

Muzzio looked hard at his boss, but it was all right.

Finnegan said, "Everything you have said in here is confidential, Mrs. Lundy. Unless, of course, it has to come out in court at some point. You can understand the necessity of that, I'm sure?" Maria nodded, and he went on, "We're gathering information, not dispensing it. It's up to you to tell your husband whatever you think best."

She'll have to tell him something, Muzzio thought, watching her slowly get to her feet. The face he had compared to a flower was as bloodless as parchment, the once-velvet eyes were like dull black stones.

Gently he took the coffee cup from her stiff fingers and opened the office door. He led her into the large room that opened onto the street and was occupied by the desk sergeant; the secretary, Gladys; a group of officers drinking coffee and reading newspapers while they waited to come on duty; and Frank Lundy, who sat at one end of a wooden bench staring at the floor beside him while his fingers drummed restlessly on his thighs.

He jumped up as they entered, and Muzzio found himself stepping in front of Maria as if to shield her. He murmured, "There's a rest room over there if you want to freshen up," and caught her quick glance of gratitude.

Before she could move, however, Lundy was at her side, seizing her arm and turning her around to confront her. Muzzio saw his anxiety switch to horror as he stared at her ravaged face.

He breathed, "My God, Maria..." and at once her eyes filled with tears.

"Frank, don't. I...it's all right." She was pulling away from her husband, and Muzzio, once again motivated by some obscure protective impulse, grasped Frank Lundy's arm, forcing him to loosen his grip of Maria's.

He said firmly, "Lieutenant Finnegan is waiting for you, Mr. Lundy. Would you go right in, please?"

Then, as Maria began walking uncertainly toward the door marked "Women," Muzzio tugged her husband into Finnegan's office.

NINE

BEN PORTER FELT a pleasant sense of anticipation as he pulled his car into the drive leading to Greg Dillon's studio. He had never visited the place while Greg was alive and had never had the slightest interest in Greg's working arrangements, probably because he held a low opinion of the results. Now, however, it seemed that Greg's murder on Ben's own premises had established a kind of morbid kinship between them, and Ben felt the sort of curiosity about the studio that he would have about that of a relative or schoolmate who had become famous.

In any case, he loved all artists' studios, with their generous space and clear light and clean, intriguing smells. He enjoyed seeing and touching the paraphernalia—the many kinds of brushes, the pots and tubes of pigment, the stacks of thick, textured paper and ranks of stretched canvases. Sometimes he thought he had taken up painting not out of a real need to create, but simply because he liked the materials involved.

Two blue and white police cars stood before the entrance to the shingled cottage, and Ben parked behind them, wondering who Lieutenant Finnegan had brought with him in addition to the indispensable Muzzio. He also wondered, as he approached the screen door, why Finnegan wanted to see him there, specifically. In hopes, possibly, that a look at Greg's work would evoke a revealing snarl of envy? Ben smiled grimly at the thought of such childishness. He knocked on the rim of the door, at the same time glancing at his watch. It was 2:25; with Finnegan's permission he had asked Howard Keating to join him there at 2:30.

Vince Muzzio appeared in the dimness inside the door, and at the same instant Ben heard tires crunch on the gravel and looked around to see Howard's black Mercedes pull up beside his own Mustang convertible.

He said to Muzzio, "Hello, Lieutenant. I believe this is my lawyer arriving," and they waited, Muzzio holding the screen door ajar while Howard stepped out of his car and buttoned the jacket of his dark suit before walking over, in his deliberate, unhurried manner, to join them.

Ben grinned, reflecting, as he watched him approach, on the entertainment value of Howard: the fun of knowing what an acerbic wit and unpredictable spirit of mischief were masked by that stolid, bankerish facade.

He started to introduce the two men, but Howard said, "Lieutenant Muzzio and I have met, Ben."

Muzzio smiled and said, "Many times. How are you, Mr. Keating?" He pushed the door wide and they all shook hands as they entered the small hallway.

Peering ahead at the bright, high-ceilinged studio, Ben saw that Finnegan was directing two policemen as they lined up a number of large, brightly colored canvases to lean against the wall.

"Come in, Mr. Porter," Finnegan called to him, then nodded to Howard Keating. "You're his lawyer, are you, Keating? We want Mr. Porter to take a look at these paintings. Tell us what he thinks."

"What he thinks of them as works of art?" Howard smiled his greeting to the young officers, then turned back to Finnegan. "You want his professional opinion of them, Tom?"

"Sure. Anything he has to say."

Ben was already walking slowly along the rows of canvases, pausing to study the ones that interested him. These were apt to be portraits, in various stages of completion, of women he recognized. Greg had posed most of them in the traditional manner, seated in a small Louis XV chair or leaning against a piano; all wore evening dresses with low-cut necklines, usually filled in with a string of pearls.

"It's very traditional, rather ordinary work, I'd say."
Ben had stopped in front of a half-figure of Madge Dexter, wife of the president of the Bank of Springfield. "But he gives them something; he glamorizes these women."
Madge, he knew, thought of herself as the First Lady of Springfield. At social gatherings she usually planted herself in a key spot, as if to receive homage, while appraising with her sharp, flickering glance the heft of the other women's jewels and the provenance of their dresses.

In Greg's rendering, however, Madge's hard, bright eyes were soft and glowing and her normally firm, no-nonsense mouth curved appealingly. Not bad, Ben thought, feeling an unexpected twinge of respect; if he could do that to a harpy like Madge it was no wonder the guy had been popular.

Greg had been industrious, that was evident; the row of unfinished portraits stretched almost the length of one studio wall. At the end there was a change. Quite literally, Maria entered the picture.

Ben's initial reaction, following a pleasant shock of recognition, was amusement at the contrast between Maria's lovely, piquant features and the plainer and in most cases, older, faces in the other paintings.

The first "Maria painting" was a large close-up with her face almost completely filling the canvas, and Ben fell into a reverie as he studied the limpid, dark eyes, the slightly parted lips, the superbly balanced curves of the bone structure. The artist's pleasure could be seen in the caressing brush strokes, and Ben recalled his own enjoyment when he painted Maria, although so very differently.

"What do you think?"
Ben started. He had not been aware that Finnegan had joined him and now stood at his shoulder, evidently impatient for his opinion.

"I think he could be damned good when he felt like it."
Ben glanced over the three remaining portraits of Maria, then crossed to the paintings lining the opposite wall of the studio. Finnegan followed, and Ben quickly realized why.

Greg's work had been arranged, not haphazardly, but in a calculated progression from the conventional portraits of local matrons through the facial studies of Maria, then several full-length paintings in which her body was fully or partly draped with fabric, followed by a series of nudes that were large, exuberant, glowing with life.

Ben walked slowly along the row of canvases, then turned and went back, here and there bending to examine a work more closely.

He stopped abruptly and was nearly knocked down by Finnegan, who had been dogging his heels.

Ben threw out his hands. "What can I say? These nudes are first-rate. I had no idea Greg Dillon could paint like this."

"I suppose you recognize the model?" Finnegan's tiny eyes were shining as he brought his wide pink face close to Ben's.

Ben caught the scent of tobacco mingled with perspiration, and stepped back a pace. "Yes, I recognize the model, of course. I've told you that Maria Lundy sometimes poses for me."

"Like that?" The expanse of pink face was moist, Ben observed with distaste. "She poses for you, uh, nude like that too?"

"Sometimes, not always. She is an excellent model. You can see that." Ben felt his own face growing warm with anger. There was nastiness in Finnegan's tone; the oaf was practically leering.

"Mrs. Porter know about this?" Finnegan jerked his head toward the canvas. He was grinning broadly; the blue eyes had become slits.

Now it was Ben who thrust his face at Finnegan. His whole body twitched with fury as he shouted, "What the hell are you suggesting, Finnegan? Of course my wife knows I use nude models; I told you that the other day. All artists do. You think it's obscene or something, Finnegan? What's your problem?"

He felt a hand grip his arm and heard Howard Keating say, "Take it easy, Ben. I don't think Lieutenant Finnegan is implying..."

"Lieutenant Finnegan is implying one thing and one thing only." Finnegan's voice rasped angrily. "That Mr. Porter here may have had more than one reason to want to get Greg Dillon out of the way. First, Dillon is sniffing around his wife—and she's the breadwinner, as I see it. Second, Dillon's beating his time with this gorgeous dish, Maria Lundy, and that's the final straw."

Ben was aware of Howard's fingers biting into his arm, and heard Howard's voice, fuzzy and far away as in a poor telephone connection, saying, "Let's get out of here, Ben; that's it, come on," and then they were once more standing in the drive before Greg's cottage.

He tried to speak, but something had gone wrong with his breathing. His legs wobbled; he might have just staggered in after a long, hard race. Howard pushed him into the front seat of the Mercedes and stood watching him through the open door.

"We could get coffee, except I don't want to give any impression of retreat, if you know what I mean." Howard's square face was impassive; but Ben sensed the wariness in his stance. He was ready to spring if his client should decide to burst back into the studio to follow up on Finnegan.

Ben managed a shaky grin. He dug out his handkerchief and mopped his face. He said, "Tell me something, Howard. Just how abusive is Finnegan allowed to get, within the law?"

Howard shrugged. "He's trying to solve a murder, so he can make wild accusations in hopes of scaring out a confession. As long as he doesn't get physical or print anything in the paper.... Hell, you're perfectly able to take care of yourself. All you have to do is deny it—which, in a way, you just did."

Ben stared through the windshield. "I never thought of that one: Greg and I competing for Maria. I could see professional envy, and anger because he lusted after Carrie, but an affair with Maria never entered my mind."

"Cross your heart and hope to die?"

Ben laughed, but meeting Howard's quizzical gaze, he saw a concentration in it that belied the flippancy.

He said slowly, "No normal man could even meet Maria Lundy, much less see her in the nude, without thinking of sex. I'm sure you're well aware of that. But when I start painting I'm concerned with something else; there's a detachment, Howard, and I never had any great urge to break it with Maria, the way Greg did, apparently. You can see it in the work. He painted her as if he were making love; every stroke is sensuous, lingering, while my pictures are like geometric theorems—or so Carrie tells me."

Howard smiled. "That's what I thought, but I had to hear you say it. Now I'm going back in there." He nodded in the direction of the cottage. "You can come along, or wait for me. I don't think you should leave."

"I'll come along." Ben emerged from the car, unfolding his long body with the caution of a tall man. "I can be civilized even if Finnegan can't. Anyway, I want to stay in touch, get in on any information the police get. I may have to solve this case myself to save my own neck."

Late Afternoon

"ALL RIGHT, I'M SORRY. I'm not bullying you. I'm just trying to get it straight once and for all."

Frank Lundy was enduring the most painful moments of his life, as far as he could remember. He was finally getting the truth out of Maria, and whatever horror he had anticipated in such a scene was agonizingly exceeded by the reality.

Hearing her actually utter the words confessing her infidelity had made him ill. He had felt a lurch of nausea, then, as the details emerged at the slow pace of some exquisitely refined torture, a dull pain began to twist about in his stomach.

"If you had been in any state to listen I would have explained everything last night."

"What do you mean by that?"

"You were drunk and you know it. Just the way you usually are when I come home, only worse."

Maria had turned sullen. She slumped in a corner of the sofa and stared resentfully at her husband—her inquisitor, as he seemed to her—and as merciless as the one she had faced that morning.

At first, when she had begun to recover from her interview with the police, she had felt an overwhelming tenderness for Frank, coupled with an almost religious need to confess. Compared to the gross Lieutenant Finnegan, Frank had appeared strong and fine; he deserved to know the truth, and when all was straight between them they could make a fresh start, their marriage would be purified, renewed. But Maria had overestimated her emotional capacity.

Since early morning her feelings had ricocheted between heartbreak, fear, anger, and remorse. Now, although she could see that her sharp words had wounded her husband, she could not seem to care.

She saw that there were tears in his eyes, and she looked away. His voice trembled as he said, "I think I can stand it if I can only believe that you were really breaking up with him. If you can make me believe that..."

"I don't know what more I can say to convince you. I told him I was coming to get my things because we were finished. I asked him to be out when I got there and I told him exactly what time that would be." She did not add: I knew what might happen if I saw him again.

"But he was there, is that right?" She nodded, and Frank jumped to his feet and stood glaring down at her. "He threw you out—that's what really happened, isn't it? You're trying to save your skin by saying you left him. Well, Greg Dillon wasn't the type to let any woman walk out on him. I know that much!"

For an instant she gazed up at his distorted face, waiting for him to strike her. Then, unexpectedly, she found herself on her feet, shouting, "Well, I'm not the type to be two-timed by Greg Dillon or anyone else. You might as well know that if you know so much!"

"What do you mean? Greg had a new girl?"

"It was just a question of time, I could see that. Finally. It took long enough, but I finally caught on that if he wouldn't leave his wife for me it was because he intended to go right on doing what he always had." She had begun shaking again, and she reached for the back of a chair to steady herself. "Women were always calling him..."

"You mean while you were there, in his studio?"

"Oh, yes, we never had a sitting that wasn't interrupted. Usually he would cut them short, but lately there was somebody..."

Tears were filling her eyes; she paused to draw a long, shuddering breath. "She made him laugh; he would talk longer to her, and he didn't want to stop. I could tell. I'd be sitting there, waiting, and I could tell..."

She was sobbing helplessly, and Frank felt his own eyes fill as he watched her. He drew her down onto the sofa and pulled out his handkerchief to dry her eyes.

"Come on, honey," he murmured. "Don't cry over that bastard. He's not worth it. Any guy who would treat you like that..."

"Oh, Frank, I've been so mixed up. So selfish, so cruel to you; and it didn't even make me happy, that's the crazy thing. I could never believe him, never trust him, and all the time you were going through hell."

"It's over, that's the main thing. You finally saw the light."

Maria sat up and pushed her damp hair back from her eyes. She had cried off all her makeup; her face was as pale and forlorn as a punished child's.

Frank gently dabbed away a final tear, and she managed a small, grateful smile. He did not return it, but glanced away and began folding his soaked handkerchief as carefully as if it had just arrived fresh from the laundry.

He said, "Did you tell Lieutenant Finnegan about your...affair with Greg?" His hands were still; he sat frowning down at them, waiting for her answer.

"I guess I did."

"What do you mean, you *guess* you did?"

"He sort of got it out of me, Frank. Or the other one did, Lieutenant Muzzio."

"And you told them you were splitting up, right? Do they know you went to the studio Monday night—before Greg was killed?" Still he did not look at her, but continued frowning at his hands.

"Yes, I thought I'd better tell them before they found out some other way."

"Did you tell them why you were leaving Greg? Because of his other women?"

"I think I probably did. I can't remember too well, Frank. I was awfully upset." She placed a tentative hand on his arm, but he did not turn to face her.

"So they know you had a good reason to be angry at Greg that night."

"What? Well, I suppose they could look at it that way."

Now he slowly swung around, and she saw that his face was impassive. She could not gauge his mood.

"What did you tell them about me? Do they think I knew?"

"I couldn't have said that because you didn't. Oh, I know you were unhappy, you wondered, but..." Her dark eyes widened. "You couldn't have known, Frank, could you? And not said anything to me? No one could do that."

He was silent. He gazed at her without expression. His eyes were opaque, unfathomable, and staring into them, Maria felt a sudden thrill of fear.

She said quietly, "Please stop looking at me like that, Frank. I can't stand any more. I've been honest with you; maybe it was a mistake. Anyway, I can't handle any more of this, not now."

Her face began working again and, as Frank watched her fight for control, his stern expression slowly relaxed. Gently he put his arms around her, pressing her head against his shoulder, crooning to her as if indeed she were a child who had transgressed.

"It's all right, honey. I'll take care of you. I don't care what happens. We'll get through this somehow, don't you worry."

It was not until later, when Maria had at last fallen asleep in the darkened bedroom, that Frank Lundy allowed himself to face the question that had been hovering at the edge of his mind: Had Maria really seen the light? Had she left Greg to save her marriage, or because she thought he was about to dump her for another woman?

He could never be sure of her until he knew the answer.

TEN

THE PORTERS' KITCHEN was a square, open room, divided by a working counter into two areas: one for the cooking and cleanup, the rest used at various times for dining, painting, proofreading, and whatever activities might seize the imaginations of Brooke and Terry.

It was a most inviting room, flooded with sun by day, and at night often warmed by a fire in the big stone fireplace, as well as by the heartening sounds and smells of dinner being prepared—usually by Ben.

It was he whose cooking habits dictated the arrangement of the space, for Ben was a sociable cook, who liked to have company while he chopped, peeled, and stirred. If he sometimes became distracted by the conversation and glanced at the wrong recipe; if, for example a breeze flipped the page from *Oiseaux sans Ailes* to *Côtes de Veau à la Languedocienne,* the resulting dish was sometimes, not always, hailed as a discovery. However startling the combination, the food was never wasted, as the entire Porter family, including four-year-old Brooke, looked upon eating as an adventure and every one of them felt impelled from time to time to make his own contribution. With a chair to stand on the children could flour chicken pieces for frying, or beat up pancake batter, and Carrie sometimes devoted most of a Saturday to making her mother's vegetable soup. "The only way to get plain home cooking around here is to do it yourself," she had observed.

It was close to seven-thirty when Howard Keating arrived. Carrie was upstairs getting the children ready for bed, and Ben had blanched the vegetables for his pasta

primavera and set out the cream and cheese and herbs that
would go into the sauce.

"Good timing," he said as he slid open the wide glass
door to the deck to admit Howard. "I'm about to make a
drink."

"I don't know how you waited this long." Howard
shook his head wearily, and stepped into the room. "That
was quite an afternoon we put in."

Ben's smile was grim. "It's a good thing you were
along."

"I know. Or right now I'd be raising bail for you." He
followed Ben to the pine cupboard that served as a bar.
"You've got to learn to be tactful with guys like Finnegan, Ben. He may look like a side of beef, but he's very
sensitive, very easily upset."

"I noticed." Ben poured Scotch into two glasses and
added ice and a splash of water. He gave Howard his
drink, then raised his own glass in a toast. "To a speedy
resolution of this mess."

"I'll drink to that. I'm supposed to join Mary at the
Cape next week."

Seating himself in one of the low, upholstered chairs that
flanked the hearth, Howard saw that two pads of yellow
paper lay on the table between them, along with two
freshly sharpened pencils.

"What is this, a directors' meeting?" he asked.

Ben set a plate of cheese and crackers on the table and
sat down. "I thought we should put everything on paper:
what happened, as far as we know, what we found out
from Finnegan, and what it all seems to point to."

"You mean you're seriously going to work on this case?
Ben, I strongly advise you not to do that. You don't know
how to go about it; you've already antagonized Finnegan—"

"Look, Howard, a friend, sort of, was found stabbed in
my office, with my fishing knife, and if I hadn't convinced Finnegan that I was home with Carrie when it happened I'd be in jail right now. He's still suspicious anyway,
it's obvious. So how can I help getting caught up in the

case? I've got a big stake in the outcome, you must admit.''

"True enough, and I have to confess that when he told us about Greg's activities last night—his visit to the drugstore—I felt like questioning George Chapman myself.''

"Drugstore? Greg went to the drugstore last night? When? What for?'' Carrie had come into the room and Howard stood up to give her a kiss.

"Did Ben tell you about our interesting session with Lieutenant Finnegan?'' he asked.

"Only sketchily. It hasn't been very peaceful around here until now.'' She sat down on a hassock, smiling expectantly at her husband, and he rose and started for the bar.

"Did he get as far as Finnegan suggesting that Ben might have had something going with Maria Lundy?''

"Yes. I found it a fascinating theory.''

"Well, when we went back in after Ben had recovered himself Finnegan seemed a little chastened. I think Vince Muzzio may have put in a word. In any case, I pointed out that Ben obviously found any imputations of guilt extremely upsetting, and that his reaction attested to his innocence as well as to his fervent desire to see the case solved and his name completely cleared.''

"Because I was a leading citizen of Rivervale, a responsible and devoted family man whose integrity had never been in doubt.'' Ben handed Carrie her glass, then turned to Howard admiringly. "I hope you're around to write my obituary, Keating.''

Carrie said, "So then Finnegan told you all his secrets?''

"The police don't know much more than we do,'' Howard replied. "The only clue so far is the drugstore visit, which George said took place around eight-thirty or eight-forty-five and was very brief. Greg had walked over to get a pack of cigarettes. He didn't hang around, but left immediately.''

"And George thinks he heard him speak to somebody outside his door. He isn't certain because the phone rang just as Greg left and George was taking down a prescription number; but he got the impression Greg had run into someone he knew." Ben picked up his pencil and pad and made a notation.

"Was it a man or a woman?"

"George couldn't say. He was too distracted to pay attention, and of course he had no idea it was going to matter." Ben frowned thoughtfully. "Suppose that was the murderer accosting Greg. Why would he take him down the block to our building to do him in?"

"And even if he had picked Porter Publishing as the ideal site for a killing," Howard put in, "how would he get Greg to go there with him? Especially at such an unlikely hour?"

Ben grinned at Carrie. "Told him we had come up with an irresistible offer for Greg's memoirs? Not a bad idea, actually."

Carrie said slowly. "Could a woman have killed Greg? An average, not especially athletic woman?"

Howard said, "I think so, but we won't know for sure until after the autopsy."

"Ben's fishing knife is very sharp." Carrie shuddered, then took a sip of her drink. "I was thinking of Maria Lundy and her hot Latin blood. She's a DeLucca, you know. Her cousin owns the Crazy Cat."

"But Maria was probably crazy about Greg. That's what I'd say after looking at those paintings. What do you think, Howard? Would Greg paint her like that if they didn't have a very special relationship?"

"I don't see everything you do in pictures, of course; but the number of them alone implies an awful lot of time spent together in what was at least a potentially intimate situation." Howard smiled reflectively. "And since Greg Dillon was apparently free of moral constraints—unlike you, Ben, with your position in the community..."

"And idyllic family life."

Ben glanced sharply at his wife, who sat primly on the hassock with her hands folded in her lap. "Your tone leaves something to be desired," he said, then turned back to Howard. "As I think I explained to you, Howard, it was the passion I saw in Greg's paintings that convinced me they were having an affair. Maria was obviously much more than a beautiful body to him, and it seems likely that she returned the feeling—if Greg was as irresistible as my own wife says he was."

Howard cleared his throat. "Assuming you're right, both of you, I can't think of any reason why Maria would kill Greg." Carrie started to speak, but Howard said, "Excuse me, but if they were having an affair wouldn't either Frank Lundy or Jenny Dillon be much more strongly motivated?"

"Jenny Dillon could never, never be driven to such lengths, I'd stake my life on it." Carrie was vehement. "Jenny Dillon has never so much as raised her voice in anger, and she's taken on some of the most maddening jobs in town. Plus the fact that she utterly adored Greg. She had to. Any woman who wasn't totally addled over him would have gotten out long ago."

Howard scribbled quickly on his yellow pad, then looked up. "I wonder how she's taking this. Have you seen her?"

"Not yet, but we're going over Friday for the memorial service."

Ben got to his feet with his empty glass, and held out his hand for Howard's. He said, "Frank Lundy is an unknown quantity; at least to me. I've never met him."

"We know he's an accountant," Carrie pointed out. "I gather he has his own business."

"Accountants are generally steady, controlled types, at least in my experience, but there must be exceptions. Why doesn't one of you give Frank Lundy a call? Couldn't Porter Publishing consider a new accounting firm?"

Ben grinned down at his friend as he handed him his drink. "I thought you wanted us to stay out of this, Howard, but never mind. That's a good idea."

Instead of sitting down again, Ben glanced at his watch, then walked over to the kitchen area. Carrie pushed herself up from the soft hassock and followed.

She said, "Getting back to Maria, I think it's quite possible, sadly enough, that she had plenty of motive." She pulled two bar stools close to the wide counter and, looking over at Howard, patted one of them invitingly.

Ben was filling a pot with water, and when he had finished he said, "You mean jealousy, I presume?"

Carrie nodded. "A man like Greg wouldn't stick to one woman for long; it wasn't in his nature. He might be obsessed for a while with a girl as lovely as Maria Lundy, but I'm sure he was always, maybe unconsciously, on the prowl. He was programmed that way."

Ben peered at her quizzically over a clove of garlic he was about to peel. "You seem to have known Greg Dillon a lot better than I realized."

Howard joined them, bringing Carrie a freshly filled glass. He said, "I think you're probably right about Greg's loyalty factor. It seems highly likely that he was cheating on Maria, or planning to. Still, there's little question he was cheating on Jenny, and Maria on Frank Lundy. So I think they're the ones to be considered."

Ben crunched the garlic clove into a heavy skillet and stirred it around in a puddle of olive oil. Over his shoulder he said, "We seem to be assuming that Greg's murder was a crime of passion. Couldn't there be some other motive?"

"How about blackmail?" Carrie suggested. "Somebody threatens to tell Jenny about Greg's affairs, then when Greg gets angry the blackmailer kills him in self-defense?" She stopped and shook her head. "No, that doesn't make sense, does it?"

"Not really. Jenny must know more about Greg's naughtiness than anyone else." Howard climbed awkwardly onto his bar stool.

"Have you considered robbery? That Greg might have been attacked like any other victim, simply because he was alone and looked prosperous?"

Ben squinted down at the mound of onion he was mincing with a large chef's knife. "Has that ever happened in Rivervale? In front of a brightly lighted drug-store?''

Carrie said, ''Rivervale is changing, you know that, with so many big companies moving out to the country. I've seen some distinctly unsavory types around recently. And anyway...'' She paused to count the knives and forks she had taken out of the drawer beneath the counter. ''Greg wasn't killed in front of the drugstore. For some reason he didn't turn around and go right back to his studio after buying his cigarettes; he wandered up the street to our building.''

''Where it was darker.''

''And somebody could have been skulking around, needing money for a fix.''

''You make our peaceful village sound like Times Square.'' Ben added chopped tomatoes and a handful of basil to the skillet, then turned down the heat and covered the pan. Drying his fingers on a dish towel, he moved over to where he had placed his drink on the counter. He frowned across at Howard. ''Your idea is best, I think. I'm going to tackle Frank Lundy. Maybe I can get him to come over here tomorrow and have a look at our books.''

''And we'll both see Jenny Dillon Friday afternoon.'' Carrie was arranging place mats and silver on the round marble-topped table. She said, ''Maybe I should try to see Maria Lundy tomorrow morning.''

''That's awfully obvious, don't you think? Both of you moving in on both Lundys on the same day?'' Howard was cut short by the ringing of the telephone placed near him on the cluttered counter. ''Shall I get that?'' he asked, and Ben nodded and turned his attention once more to the pot now steaming on the stove.

Howard picked up the phone, and at the same instant Carrie heard a wail from the direction of Brooke's bed-room. She hurried upstairs to quell any uprising that might disrupt dinner, and when she returned a few minutes later, after soothing Brooke back to sleep, found Howard just hanging up.

He said, "I have a news bulletin for you, folks," and Ben swung around from his cooking pots while Carrie paused in the doorway.

Howard said, "That was Lieutenant Muzzio, the good guy. He wanted you to know, in confidence, that the autopsy shows that Greg was not killed with your fishing knife. He was shot first. That's what killed him. The knife was planted afterwards, apparently to throw suspicion on Ben—or anyway to confuse the issue." Howard slowly shifted his gaze from Carrie's bewildered face to Ben's. "Now, how does that revelation affect us?"

"It's done wonders for my appetite." Ben grinned hugely, his teeth gleaming white in his heat-reddened face. "Plates, Carrie!" he said briskly. "Howard, please pour the wine. We have some celebrating to do."

ELEVEN

Thursday, June 26 Morning

GARVIN THORPE HAD LAIN awake half the night, tortured by his decision to allow Frank Lundy a grace period before reporting his emotional state to the police. During the two days since Greg Dillon's murder, every ring of the phone had filled him with dread, even though he had replayed his tape recordings of the sessions with Lundy and felt convinced that his handling of the case had been ethical as well as compassionate. In spite of that he was sweating with impatience as he prepared for Lundy's appointment that morning. If Lundy did not appear, in fact, if he did not bring Maria with him, he, Thorpe, would feel free to go to the police immediately and get the matter off his conscience.

So it was almost with relief that he opened the door to Lundy alone. He looked about the reception room, then said, "I gather your wife is not with you."

"Right." With his customary brisk nod of greeting, Lundy stepped into the office. "I couldn't force the issue, Doc, not after the day we had yesterday. I'm going to need more time."

Stifling a quick rebuttal, Thorpe moved to his seat behind the desk and said, "Do you want to tell me what happened?"

"Boy, it was some workout." Lundy was shaking his head as he pulled out his chair and sat down. "First the cops quizzed her all morning, and then they tackled me."

"You were apprehensive about that when you came in yesterday. Was it as bad as you feared?"

"Not for me." Lundy lifted his chin defiantly. "They soon found they couldn't push me around; but they had a field day with Maria. I've never seen her so wrecked. When she came out of Finnegan's office she could hardly walk. It's scary to see your wife like that, I'm telling you."

"It must have been very hard for you."

"Well, there was worse to come. Worse for me, that is." Lundy folded his arms on his chest and stared out the window at the sunlit garden with the same grim expression he might have worn viewing a disaster site.

Garvin said in a mild conversational tone, "How long did the police keep you?"

"It seemed like all day." Frank Lundy's face cleared while he considered the mundane question of time. "Let's see, I dropped Maria off around ten-thirty while I checked my office, and it must have been after noon before they finished with her. Then she had to wait while I talked to them—one of the sergeants brought her a sandwich, but she couldn't eat it—and we didn't get out of there much before three. They had a nerve making her wait around in her condition."

"I wonder why they kept her so long."

"Oh, they had to type it all up and get her to sign her version and me to sign mine. Finally they let us leave, but Maria was like an invalid—all white and shaky—so I took her home and let her rest while I went to the office for a while."

"You didn't discuss your separate experiences with the police?"

"Not until later. We needed a breather. But, boy, it all came out then." He paused and his face sagged unhappily; he sank back in his chair as if defeated by the painful memory. "I bought pizza on my way home so she wouldn't have to cook, which was a good thing because when I got to the apartment she was just sitting in the dark in her bathrobe, doing nothing. She didn't fix up her hair or her makeup, even when I came in, and that's a bad sign with Maria. I was worried, so I made her a drink, and then we talked, and she told me... she told me it was true."

Lundy's voice had faded to a whisper. He seemed unable to say any more.

"She confessed to an affair with Greg Dillon?" Garvin spoke briskly, and saw Lundy look up in annoyance.

"Well, what do you think we've been talking about? Yes, sure, it all came out, the whole damn story—or as much as I could stand to listen to."

"Do you want to tell me . . . ?"

"I want to forget about it, Thorpe, and telling you won't help with that. Except her version of how they split. She claims it was her idea; he was getting ready to cheat on her, but she wasn't having it." He shook his head slowly. "If I could believe that . . ."

Garvin said gently, "I'm hoping you will be able to give less and less importance to that question as time passes and your relationship improves. How did you end the evening?"

"We were more together than we have been for a long time, I'd say. I felt sorry for her. That surprised me. And she . . . well, I got the impression that she wants to stick with me, have a normal life and all. But first I've got to be convinced."

"Frank, Maria must have had love affairs before you met. How do you feel when you think of those attachments? Is it painful to think of her loving someone in the past?"

"Not really, because they're just that—in the past. She could have had any of those guys, but she didn't take them."

"She wanted you instead."

"I guess so. But this thing. . . . This is like she might have picked that bastard over me. If she could have had him."

"She can never have him now. Doesn't that put him in the past with the others?"

"No, because I'll never know. God, I didn't expect this! I wish I could wake him up. I wish I could see them together; then I'd know. That's the only way."

"Frank, I would like you to think about what is going on here. You are still feeling angry about a situation that no longer exists, do you see that?"

"You think it's left over, the feeling? And when I get used to the idea that he's gone I'll be normal again? I sure hope you're right."

"You need time to get over this. You need to regain your trust in your wife, to reestablish the comfortable, loving relationship you must have had once. It will happen if you both want it and work for it. Did you tell Maria about coming here, as you said you would?"

"I don't know why I can't seem to find the right time to bring that up. I meant to, but when I got home and saw how weak and tired she was I didn't want to upset her."

"I'm sorry to hear that, Frank, because I have given you as much time as I can."

Lundy started to interrupt, but Thorpe held up his pencil, gesturing silence.

"I think I understand why that is so difficult for you, but for me it is a matter of the law. Whether or not you can bring yourself to tell Maria about your therapy, I am obliged to make my report to the police. I hope you are able to accept that."

"Accept, that's all anybody thinks I'm good for anymore." Lundy pushed back his chair, gripping the arms in exasperation. "Accept being two-timed by my wife—she's only human, poor thing, right? And the cops—accept getting pushed around by them. Accept it like a little man when they bully my wife!"

He sprang up and the chair teetered on its legs. "And now my own shrink wants to expose my private, confidential thoughts to the same goddamn bullies, and I'm supposed to accept that!" He paused, panting angrily as he watched Garvin slowly rise to his feet. "You do what you want, Thorpe. I don't give a damn. You've seen the last of me."

Garvin said, "Frank, it is very important that you try to understand..."

"Do you understand what I'm saying, Thorpe? I'm saying screw you and your whole phony profession. I hope for once I've made my feelings clear."

BEN PORTER HAD LEFT his office door ajar so that he would hear Frank Lundy arriving and be able to deflect him from Carrie's office, where she was negotiating a complicated book contract. At 9:25 he heard the street door open, and he got up and went over to peer into the hallway.

The man he saw hesitating outside Carrie's closed door was of medium height and slender, and he swung around instantly upon sensing Ben's presence with the quick, nervous alertness of a good tennis player.

He strode across the hall, extending his hand, saying, "You're Ben Porter. Sorry to be late. I was delayed by a client." He did not smile as he spoke, but looked intently into Ben's eyes, then swept a quick, evaluating glance around his surroundings, as if he had been given two minutes to memorize the layout.

"That's okay," Ben replied. "Gave me a chance to get some figures together for you." The two men shook hands, then Ben gestured for Lundy to precede him into the office.

They sat down, Ben behind his desk, Frank Lundy in a leather-seated armchair facing it. Once again he looked about appraisingly, then, apparently satisfied with the plain, utilitarian style of Ben's office, turned and said crisply, "Do you have someone handling your accounts at the moment, Mr. Porter?"

Ben smiled. "My wife and I—Carrie is my partner, you see—have pretty much taken care of the books ourselves. Except for taxes, that is, when we've had to have help. But the business is growing, getting more complex in some ways, and we feel we need an accountant who would take a real interest."

Frank nodded. He reached into the breast pocket of his gray suit and brought out a pair of spectacles, then he suddenly stiffened in his chair and Ben saw an expression of shock appear on his lean face.

Lundy said, "Good Lord, I've forgotten my brief-case." He stared at Ben, his gray eyes so round with alarm that Ben felt he was about to leap up and run out of the room.

"Well, we can manage," he began soothingly, but at that moment the telephone rang and Ben, with a gesture of apology to his visitor, picked it up and said, "Hello. Porter Publishing."

"Hello, Ben, this is Garvin Thorpe," was the response. "I believe a...friend of mine, Frank Lundy, has an appointment with you this morning."

"Yes, Mr. Lundy is here now. Would you like to speak to him?"

"That won't be necessary. Just tell him his briefcase is here, will you, Ben? I imagine he's wondering where he left it."

"He just realized he didn't have it. Thanks very much, Garvin. I suppose we'll see you at Jenny Dillon's, won't we? How is she doing?"

"She's been remarkable so far. But the service will be an ordeal, of course. She'll appreciate the support of her friends."

While the conversation went on Ben watched Frank Lundy's expression change from apprehension to intense embarrassment. By the time he hung up the phone Frank was actually squirming in his chair, and his face had turned quite pink.

He forced a chuckle as he said, "That was Garvin Thorpe, right? About my briefcase?"

Ben nodded, but before he could speak Frank had gotten to his feet and was striding toward the door. "I'd better get over to the Thorpes' right away," he said. "Sorry. We can pick this up another time, okay?"

Ben said, "I have a pretty full calendar, Frank. I'd really like to continue our talk if you don't mind. We can get to the paperwork next time."

Lundy turned with the same athletic lightness Ben had observed in the hall. Again he gave a nervous chuckle, then he shrugged and slowly returned to the desk, where he stood facing Ben for a moment before he sat down.

"Thorpe and I are old friends," he said. He grinned, prying his lips apart. His eyes had taken on a feverish glimmer. "We get together a lot."

"Oh, do you live near each other?" Ben spoke softly. He might have been gentling a mettlesome horse.

"Yes. That is, no we don't. He's here in Rivervale, of course. I live in Springfield. My wife Maria, and I."

"Yes. I know Maria. She's posed for me a few times. But of course you know that." Ben smiled. "She's an excellent model—very professional."

Frank opened his mouth to speak, then closed it again. He looked suddenly wary.

Ben went on, keeping his voice low and gentle. "Modeling is not easy, you know. There's a good deal of skill required. Intelligence too. A model should have some grasp of the artist's aims, but so few do." He shook his head. "Maria is especially understanding," he said.

"You mean she understands what you're trying to do when you paint a particular picture?"

Ben nodded. "Exactly. And she doesn't waste a lot of time, you know, talking, fussing with her hair. As I said, she's very professional, very good at her job."

Frank Lundy said, "She'll be glad to hear that you think so. She could use some cheering up right now."

Ben raised his eyebrows questioningly. He said, "No problems, I hope?"

"Well, no real problems. She just... you know Maria, how softhearted she is. She used to pose for Greg Dillon, did you know that?"

Frank was once again moving restlessly in his chair, crossing his legs, brushing at his trousers. He did not look at Ben as he spoke, but busied himself placing his glasses carefully into their case.

"Oh, of course." Ben nodded understandingly. "I hadn't put that together, but Maria must have been very upset by Greg's death."

"Not that they were that close or anything." Again Frank forced a chuckle. His eyes engaged Ben's, man to man, then flicked away. "It's more the way it happened, the violence..." He shuddered dramatically. "The thought of someone you know being stabbed... It's just about made Maria sick."

"Greg wasn't stabbed to death, it turns out. He was shot first."

"What? What are you saying, shot first? How crazy, how weird. I don't understand." All color had left Frank's face; the gray eyes were once more glassy with alarm.

Ben said, "I know it sounds crazy, but that's what the autopsy turned up. It was the shot that killed him. No one knows why he was stabbed afterwards—with my fishing knife, by the way. You can imagine how I've been feeling about that."

"Yes, yes, I certainly can." Frank sprang to his feet and began moving restlessly about the office. "Shot, then stabbed. That makes it worse. I don't know how to tell Maria. You see, she's so unbelievably sensitive." He swung around and Ben saw that his pale face shone with perspiration, giving his skin the look of waxed paper. "Just reading in the paper about violence—attacks on total strangers—will have her in tears. Sometimes she'll cry for hours. This, knowing the man, I don't know how she'll take it."

"Maybe you'd better not tell her. Wait a while, you know, until she's recovered from the initial shock."

Frank Lundy stared unseeingly at the wall behind Ben's head. "I think she would be angry if I did that. We try to be completely honest with each other. About everything. We're very close, you see." Now he focused on Ben and once more managed a stiff grin.

Ben said carefully, "Last time I talked to Maria I got the impression—tell me if I'm wrong—that she and Greg had had some kind of disagreement." He smiled companionably. "Of course it's none of my business."

"You mean that she was angry at him? At Greg? Oh, no, no, no." Frank was shaking his head emphatically. "No, Maria and Greg had an excellent working relationship. Very businesslike. As you said, she had a completely professional approach to her modeling." He drew a deep, shuddering breath. "Anyway, she hadn't seen much of Greg recently. She hadn't posed for him in several months, so they couldn't possibly have had any arguments."

Ben shrugged. "Well, it's beside the point, isn't it? Now Frank, let me tell you a little about our company."

He glanced from Lundy, still on his feet, to the chair he had vacated, but clearly the man was far too distracted to embark on a business discussion.

He said, "I'm afraid I really must get my briefcase, Mr. Porter, before I can settle down to work. I'll call you later to set up another appointment."

Without waiting for Ben's response he strode to the door, wrenched it open, and disappeared down the hall.

TWENTY MINUTES LATER Ben read over the notes he had made following Frank Lundy's departure. When he had finished he tiptoed to the door leading to Carrie's office and listened, hoping to find that her visitors too had left. He was disappointed to hear the discussion still going on, however; he would have to wait until after lunch to share his impressions of Frank Lundy, and in that case, he decided, he might as well go home and release the baby-sitter.

He left a message on the answering machine telling Carrie what he was doing, then locked his desk and left the office, taking his notes with him. Approaching the street door he heard the loud braying of the fire alarm, and he stepped out onto the porch in time to see the shiny red fire engine pull out of the fire station a block away and head north along Main Street. He watched as it rumbled past with siren shrieking, and when he reached the sidewalk found himself irresistibly drawn to follow its progress as long as he could keep it in sight.

This was longer than he expected, as it turned out, for the fire truck's destination was less than a mile away, where the riverside studio of the late Greg Dillon had suddenly and inexplicably burst into flames.

TWELVE

Friday, June 27 Afternoon

IN THE THREE DAYS following Greg's death Jenny Dillon lived in an emotional kaleidoscope. At times grief held the upper hand, and she felt a bottomless desolation over her loss. Then memory would intrude, bright shards of anger would nudge aside the grief, and she would curse her dead husband for tormenting her as cruelly after his death as before.

She could not let her confusion show, of course. Her parents had come to stay with her, and to them and Cabby and the friends who called she maintained the appearance of a normally grieving widow. Her pride would not allow her to destroy the facade she had built over the years; she would lower that protective shield for only one person: Garvin Thorpe.

Garvin's presence had become essential to her. He spent hours with her each day, listening while she poured out her feelings of grief and rage, providing the tranquilizers that allowed her some rest, and answering Cabby's questions with patience and understanding.

He had also helped her plan a memorial service that would be a suitable tribute to Greg while avoiding the hypocrisy of a formal religious rite. It was held in the garden, where a small group of relatives and close friends listened to the minister's reading from the prayer book, then shared their own recollections of Greg.

It was exactly right, Jenny thought, as she accepted a glass of wine from her cousin, George Cabot. The sparkling summer afternoon, the soft breeze that stirred the skirts of the women's light dresses, Jim, who waxed everyone's floors, wearing a white jacket to pass the silver tray of sandwiches—the scene was perfectly attuned to the side of Greg they all knew best and that even she could remember with fondness. As for the other, the faithlessness, the deliberate cruelty, she would try to forget for Cabby's sake, but it would take time; her wounds were deep.

"I gather they saved most of Greg's paintings," George said. He drank from his glass, and Jenny saw a drop of wine land squarely on the face of the small orange tiger embroidered on his black tie.

She looked up at George and saw by his expectant look that he was waiting for some kind of answer. Greg's paintings—oh yes, the fire.

"I don't know what they saved, to tell you the truth," she said. "And they're not letting anyone in to look around until they make sure it's safe."

"Not even you? Well, I guess that's sensible."

"I'm not awfully anxious to see it, George." She felt her eyes filling with tears and quickly looked down and concentrated on taking a sip of her wine.

"I suppose not, but you're the only one who can assess the damage accurately." George's face was stern, and Jenny remembered that he was in the insurance business. "You may have a substantial claim."

"Oh, I do. There's no question about that." She turned to greet a couple who were hesitating nearby, waiting to speak to her. Substantial claim. The term was more apt than George Cabot could have guessed.

"Such a shame about the fire," the woman was murmuring while her husband solemnly nodded in agreement, and it occurred to Jenny that the burning of Greg's studio was perhaps a subject people could discuss more easily than the emotionally loaded one of his violent death.

The notion provided a welcome distraction for her as she moved through the afternoon. In her mind she kept a rough score of condolences received on the fire against those for the loss of her husband. They came out almost even, she decided during one of her escapes to tend to her hair and makeup. Gazing into the mirror at a face that

appeared remarkably normal, she reflected that whoever
had set the fire had performed a service in a way by making the occasion more comfortable for her and her guests.
She was frowning as she turned away, wondering why she
felt so certain the fire had been set. That had been only one
possibility suggested by Bill McCarthy, the volunteer fire
chief, but in her mind there was no doubt.

On her way back she found Garvin Thorpe standing just
inside the French doors to the terrace with a tentative smile
hovering on his lips. It seemed to Jenny that for three days
his face had been excessively mobile, as if it were on loan
to her and primed to adapt itself instantly to her changes
of mood.

He said, "There you are. I've been looking for you."

"Are people leaving?" She smiled, and saw his uncer-
tainty vanish.

"There are some hopeful signs," he said cheerfully,
"but no one will go without saying good-bye to you, so
you'd better come back out."

He opened the screen door for her, and as she stepped
through it Jenny saw Enid walking toward the terrace. She
looked very smart in her black linen suit and massive silver jewelry, and she moved past the clusters of chatting
people with the air of one who would allow nothing to deflect her from her goal.

In a moment she would be upon them, and Jenny
touched Garvin's hand and said, "Enid's coming to say
good-bye, I think, and I want you to go with her tonight,
Garvin. You have been so wonderful to me, but it's time
to get back to normal." He opened his mouth to protest,
and she added, "I really mean it; I'll be just fine."

"Jenny, I've got to go." Enid was beside them, her clear
gaze fixed on Jenny assessingly. "You're all right, I see. If
I thought I could be useful I'd stay, you know that."

Jenny took Enid's hand in both of hers. "I do know
that, Enid, and thank you. I'm sending Garvin with you.
It's time I stopped monopolizing him."

Enid turned her attention to her husband, and a look passed between them that Jenny could not read, but she sensed a sudden wariness in the air.

"You might as well stay until the others leave," Enid said to him with complete neutrality. "Jenny's bound to feel let down then." She paused, then added with the same absence of feeling, "I'm going to be working most of the evening."

Garvin said slowly, "We could go to the club for dinner if you'd like to."

"The way the food has been lately? No, thanks! Call me soon, won't you, Jenny?" then, turning to Garvin, "I'll check your messages and call you if there's anything urgent."

She gave them each a brisk, friendly nod, pulled open the screen door, and stepped into the house. In a moment they heard the firm click of her heels on the marble floor of the front hall, and Garvin smiled helplessly.

"Let's do it Enid's way, shall we?" he said, and for the first time that week Jenny actually laughed.

"You know something? I didn't really want you to leave. But Enid knew it and I didn't." Jenny linked her arm in his and looked up into his face. "Thank her for me when you get home."

The laughter was gone from his eyes as he said, gazing down at her, "I will thank her, Jenny; you may be certain of that."

Without haste they moved apart and started across the wide terrace to join Jenny's guests.

That Night

JENNY'S LONG DAY finally ended at ten. It wasn't until then that she was able to persuade her mother, dizzy with fatigue, to leave the kitchen and the hopeless task of cleaning up after what had seemed a seventeen-course supper. Most of the guests had left soon after Enid, but Jenny's close friends had hovered, uncertain whether their moral support outweighed the trouble of feeding them, and a good dozen deciding that it did. The house was full of food, in any case, both refrigerators loaded with casseroles, cakes, cookies, and platters of ham and turkey.

"It's the automatic reaction to bereavement," Jenny's mother had said at one point, "the women's, that is. And not only because the mourners need to be fed, but because providing good food is a gesture of defiance—an assertion that life matters more than death."

"I'm not so sure of that," Garvin had said, hurrying through to the bathroom with Cabby, who had suddenly gone white-faced and glassy-eyed as the result of unsupervised cookie consumption.

Jenny had been impressed by her own and the other adults' consumption, not of food but of liquor. She had lost count of the number of times her wineglass had been refilled; nonetheless, when her father suggested a nightcap after the last guest had gone she instantly complied. Even the stiff drink of vodka he poured for her seemed to have little effect, possibly because it was one of the rare occasions in her life when she would have welcomed a feeling of intoxication.

Instead, her mind seemed to function with unusual clarity, as if the hours of intense emotion had scrubbed it clean. When her father began to slur his words she briskly packed him off to bed. She poured his unfinished highball down the sink, then added a splash of vodka to her own glass, which she carried with her while she went slowly through the downstairs rooms closing windows and turning off lights.

She relished the silence, the freedom of being alone after days of constant companionship. As she walked slowly around her house she looked at the furnishings appraisingly, observing the faded condition of the chintz draperies in the den and the spots on the hall rug, deciding to replace an easy chair she had never liked as soon as she could get to Bloomingdale's Springfield store. She would start replying to her letters of condolence first thing in the morning, she decided, and as soon as possible she would have to clean out Greg's studio. But she could get a decorator in by the first of the following week, and after they had decided on colors and fabrics she might take Cabby on a little trip. It would be good for them both to go away together—something they had never done while Greg was alive.

When she had placed her glass in the dishwasher and turned on the machine Jenny stood looking around the still-disordered kitchen. Her mother had efficiently stacked the platters and casseroles that needed returning on the breakfast table, but had she labeled them with their owners' names? Jenny was about to check them over when a wave of fatigue struck. Her knees went wobbly, and she seized the back of a chair for support.

SHE WAS GLAD to feel tired at last. Now she could sleep; she felt certain of it as she switched off the kitchen light and started for the hallway. "Sufficient unto the day," she said to herself. What was the rest of that, the part that didn't make sense to her? "Sufficient unto the day is the evil thereof." Could that be right? She would have to look it up.

In the upstairs hall, where a small night-light cast a dim glow, she saw that Cabby's door stood ajar the way he liked it, and she tiptoed into his room to check on him, just as she did every night. Standing beside his bed, she felt comforted by the sight of the sleeping child sprawled on top of his covers in the oversized T-shirt he insisted on wearing instead of pajamas. His rounded cheeks were flushed, his lips slightly parted, and his blond hair lay damply molded against his well-shaped head.

He's beautiful, Jenny thought, as beautiful as his father. If he suddenly woke and looked up at her it would be with Greg's fine brown eyes, she knew. How wonderful that something of Greg lived on; she prayed that Cabby would not inherit his father's destructive vanity as well as his handsome features. Silently she vowed to guard against that with all the vigilance at her command.

She slipped out of the room and went down the hall to her own. Passing the guest room she heard her father's snoring through the closed door and wondered how her mother managed to sleep through it. Greg had never snored. Perhaps only older men did. It occurred to her that Greg had been spared something he would have found extremely damaging to his self-image.

On the threshold of her bedroom Jenny paused. The room was dark, reminding her that all week, until exhaustion made her forget, her mother had been turning down her bed each night and lighting a lamp to ease her loneliness. Well, she would have to get used to this blackness, though it seemed especially dense that night; it felt as if the room had been packed with some substance to keep her out.

She drew a deep breath and started forward, but at the same instant a puff of cool air struck her cheek and from the corner of her eye she saw a sudden flicker of white. She gasped, shrinking against the door frame; but almost immediately she saw that it was only a corner of the curtain that had lifted when a vagrant current stirred the quiet night air.

Later the recollection would amuse her, she supposed; but at the moment Jenny had to muster all her courage to step into her own bedroom and switch on the bedside light—the white Wedgwood lamp her aunt had sent from Tiffany's as a wedding present. The room was suddenly comfortingly familiar, the blackness replaced by the soft colors she had chosen so carefully when they moved into the house: the pale ivory of the thick rug, the watercolor tints or rose and green on draperies and bedspread, the blurry green checked linen on the two small armchairs. Between the chairs stood a low table where she had imagined she and Greg would have their breakfast, but they never had, not once.

Feeling her throat thicken and her eyes mist with tears, she glanced away. There was time enough ahead for grieving over unfulfilled dreams of happiness; right now she must deal with the realities of exhaustion and loneliness. She must make herself strong enough to build a new life and to be both mother and father to her son. Thank God for Cabby, she thought; out of the wreckage of a marriage, of a life actually, there remained that fine, beautiful child.

She unzipped her dress and stepped out of it. Heading for her closet she paused to take off her rings and place them on the dresser, and, as always, her eyes sought the photographs of Greg and Cabby that stood there. There were several of each of them, some of the two together, some that included her, one excessively flattering studio portrait of Greg she had kept only because he liked it. Now she could throw it away, yet somehow that would seem disloyal.

She must have removed some of the pictures, however, for the dresser top looked less crowded than usual. Pulling on her nightgown, she tried to remember when she had last rearranged them, but of course the events of the last few days had erased any such mundane recollections. Then, in the midst of brushing her teeth, she recalled the picture of Cabby his kindergarten teacher had sent when school closed for the summer. She had put it in a silver frame; she knew she had. It must be there with the others; she had simply missed it.

Jenny dropped her toothbrush and clutched the rim of the basin while she stared into the mirror in horrified comprehension. Her legs began to shake as she turned and walked slowly back to the bedroom and up to the dresser, where she stood and methodically scanned its surface from one end to the next. She knelt and searched the floor beneath, then peered behind it as best she could, to see if the photograph might have gotten caught somehow as it slipped off the back.

But it was gone. Her most recent picture of Cabby, the one that showed him exactly as he was at this moment, had disappeared. Without a word to her someone had taken it.

Again she gazed at the reflection of her own face petrified with shock, this time in the wide mirror above her dresser. What had she been doing, thinking about decorating, planning a trip?

There were no such normal activities in store for her, Jenny Dillon. For she was not just a newly bereaved wife, but a woman whose husband had been murdered with savage violence.

And now she knew that violent murder was possibly only a prelude to the most unthinkable tragedy of all. If someone had stolen Cabby's photograph it was not for the value of the silver frame; other larger and heavier ones had been left behind. Identification must have been the purpose; identification for the purpose of doing him harm. And who in the world would want to harm a five-year-old boy?

The only logical answer—if any logic existed in her new nightmare world—was Greg Dillon's killer. Whatever bizarre motivation had dictated the murder of the father might now be directed at the son. Since Jenny's mind could not tolerate such a concept it blessedly shut itself off, and she sank, unconscious, to the floor.

THIRTEEN

Saturday, June 28 Morning

"THIS IS GARVIN THORPE, Frank. Please call me back as soon as you can. If I've left my office you can reach me at my home number."

Frank Lundy pressed the stop button on his answering machine. He had no desire to hear his other messages a second time, only that one. His hand hovered over "rewind," but he did not press the button that would erase the tape.

Instead he got to his feet and slowly walked over to his office window. He stood staring through the dusty pane, which provided a view of the parking lot four stories below. Gazing along the rows of parked cars, he picked out the roof of his red compact station wagon. I think I know what he's calling about, he thought, but he doesn't know I've heard. I wonder what he'll do if I don't call back— have me arrested?

He glanced down at the dried-up azalea plant on the window, a remnant of the congratulatory gifts he had received when he opened the office in the spring. He carried the plant to the wastebasket beside his desk and dropped it in, listening to the heavy thud it made when it hit the metal bottom. Then he pushed the playback button and listened to Garvin Thorpe's message for the third time.

Funny how it makes me feel, hearing his voice, he thought. I think I'll go and see him tonight, if he has any time. But if he's calling to tell me Dillon was shot and now he's going to the police for sure, isn't it better if he doesn't get me? Or has he already told them whatever he's going to?

He hasn't much to report anyway. It won't be news to the cops that I was upset about Maria; I told them that myself. The only thing would be the gun, but how would Garvin find out Dillon was shot?

Frank picked up the telephone. I've got to give the guy a chance. I know he was threatening the other day; he wouldn't turn me in. He's probably calling because he wants me to come in again, and I'd really like to. I need him to help me sort this out. He might come up with an answer.

Slowly Frank pressed the first four digits of Garvin Thorpe's office number; then he paused and stood holding the instrument in both hands while he stared at the tiny message tape, trying to remember Garvin's exact words. Had he sounded normal or were the police forcing him to lure Frank to his office?

Perhaps the call was a warning.

He replaced the telephone, then pushed the playback button on the answering machine. Once again the familiar voice filled the room: "This is Garvin Thorpe, Frank. Please call me back..."

BEN PORTER WAS SITTING on the deck with his breakfast coffee and a partially read manuscript when he heard a car enter the driveway, then the solid thunk of a Mercedes door closing. In a moment Howard Keating appeared on the side lawn, making for the stairway to the deck.

"I tried to call, but your line was busy," he said as he mounted the steps, "and I wanted to catch you before you went out somewhere."

He sank into a chair, breathing hard from the climb, and Ben frowned at him in mock dismay.

"I hate to see my lawyer so out of shape."

"Well, if you would stop complicating my life I could get to the Cape and play some tennis. Meanwhile..." With a nod of thanks Howard accepted the coffee cup Ben handed him. "Meanwhile you'll be wanting to hear what the police found in Greg Dillon's studio."

"You mean they saved some paintings? The way that fire was burning I'm amazed."

"You might say they saved some paintings. Where's Carrie, by the way? I'd like her to hear this."

"She's taking the children to the club pool with a sitter. She ought to be... in fact, here she is."

Carrie had pulled her car in next to Howard's, and the two men rose to watch as she crossed the lawn wearing a short white tennis dress that set off her slim, graceful figure and tawny legs. She paused to wave to them, the sun glinting bright on her tousled blond hair, and Howard drew a sigh of appreciation.

"Best-looking legs in Connecticut," he said when she arrived at the top of the stairs. "Possibly on the Eastern Seaboard."

Carrie laughed and presented her cheek to be kissed. She tossed her handbag into a chair and poured herself a cup of coffee. "What have I missed?" she asked as she pulled a chair over and sat down.

"I was about to tell Ben that they found some pretty sensational paintings in Greg's studio."

"More nudes of Maria?"

"No, but nudes, *total* nudes, I gather, of some of the best-known women in town. They were locked in a closet apparently, away from prying eyes."

"And that's why the fire was set."

Howard frowned at Ben. "What? Oh, I see. You're assuming that the fire was set in order to destroy the paintings. Hmm, I suppose that is a possibility. But it would be terribly risky, Ben. Arson is a criminal offense, after all, and often easy to detect."

Carrie said, "Come on, Howard, more about the naked ladies. We've simply got to find out who they are, don't you see that? Because one of them may very well be Greg's killer."

"Muzzio was adamant. He was furious at Bill McCarthy for telling me about the paintings; but Bill was still pop-eyed when I caught him leaving. He couldn't keep quiet about the sensational find."

"All his hours of volunteering finally paid off." Ben smiled reflectively. "What exactly did he say about the paintings?"

"He said there were ten or twelve of them stacked in a closet at the back of the cottage where he figures the fire got started. That's why they are badly damaged, some unrecognizable. But he could see that they were all nudes, and most in extremely—how did he put it?—suggestive poses. But what shook him were the faces. He was bursting to tell me who they were, but he said Finnegan would kill him. Said the police carried them off under wraps."

"Am I going to have to make a play for Vince Muzzio? Are we that anxious to solve this case?" Carrie peered at her husband. "Careful how you answer that, Ben Porter."

"I have no doubt that you could drive the lieutenant mad with your wiles, but you're already so busy with your work and the children..."

Howard said thoughtfully, "Even if we can't learn the identity of the subjects the fact that the paintings exist tells us something, doesn't it?"

"That Greg Dillon was naughty in ways we never imagined." Carrie wrinkled her nose. "I liked him better before."

Ben said, "The guy must have had a prodigious appetite. It's awesome to contemplate."

"I suppose the paintings were done as a turn on."

"You mean a lady would go to have her portrait done, with her pearls and velvet dress, and then..." Carrie pulled off her sunglasses and turned from Ben to Howard with an incredulous grin. "Oh my, it's too funny to be sexy!"

"You told me Greg could never be a figure of fun to any woman, and this seems to bear you out. What do you think, Howard? And did he keep the paintings for purposes of blackmail, do you suppose?"

"Blackmail for what? He didn't need money, and apparently had no problem with seduction."

Carrie said, "I imagine he kept them for the same reason authors save every word they write: Artists just can't stand to throw away their work, no matter how bad it is. Or, as in this case, how compromising.''

"Howard, did Bill happen to tell you whether the salacious paintings were all of different women? Were there any repeats?''

"He wouldn't get into specifics, but I gather there was quite a variety. Certainly they weren't all the same person.''

"Too bad. Then we'd have something to work with.''

"We do anyway.'' Both men turned their attention to Carrie, who lay back in her deck chair squinting up at the sky. "We know now that whatever Greg had going with Maria Lundy wasn't keeping him totally occupied.''

"We already knew that. Remember Cousin Barbara at the Boat Club Dance?''

"Right. Now the question is, does that make Maria more suspect or less?''

"More.''

"Less.''

"I know what her husband thinks," Ben said. "At least I'm pretty sure after talking to him Thursday.''

Howard sat up straighter in his chair. "That's right, you did see Frank Lundy. What came of it?''

"Two interesting points, I'd say. Lundy was so anxious to impress me with Maria's kindness, her horror of violence, and her fondness for Greg that I feel certain he thinks she killed him.''

Ben paused to watch Howard's reaction. Satisfied by his expression of shock, he continued. "And I'm pretty sure Lundy has been seeing Garvin Thorpe for counseling of some sort. He got purple in the face when Thorpe called to say he had left his briefcase in his office, then put on a big act about what good friends they were. I didn't press it.''

"We thought I could drop in on Garvin today, Howard. What do you think? Better I than Ben because of the Mental Health Committee. I always have some excuse to talk to Garvin, or Enid, for that matter.''

Poised on the edge of her chair, Carrie waited for Howard to voice his approval, but instead he reached for the pad and pencil he had placed on the table and said, "First let's go over your interview with Frank Lundy, Ben. Start at the beginning."

Carrie jumped up. "Sorry, Howard, but Ben and I have spent a lot of time on that interview, and what I'm dying to do now is get over to the Thorpes' without any more deliberations. I want it to seem impulsive, do you know what I mean? I'll report back, with any luck, in an hour or so."

Glancing at her watch, she hurried into the house to change her clothes.

When Carrie pulled into Garvin Thorpe's tastefully concealed parking area she was surprised to find it empty. She had come prepared to wait for an opening between Garvin's many Saturday patients; now it appeared that his office might be closed. She walked up the neat brick path to the office door anyway and pressed the button beside the brass nameplate. She was not surprised when there was no response to her ring.

Carrie hesitated on the doorstep for a moment, then walked across the lawn to the front door of the house. Garvin might have been called away on some emergency, or he might be relaxing at home between appointments. If she found him having a lazy Saturday with Enid, so much the better; her visit would seem a spontaneous, friendly call.

She stepped onto the flagstone stoop and knocked with the antique brass knocker the Thorpes had brought back after their year in England. In a moment the door was opened by Enid, whose look of polite inquiry changed to a welcoming smile when she saw Carrie.

"I was just going to call you!" she exclaimed, pulling the door wider. "Come in. Garvin was wondering about the agenda for the meeting next Tuesday."

Carrie stepped into the hallway, and the two women stood peering at each other in the dimness until Enid, after an appraising glance toward the living room, invited Carrie to follow her down the hall to her study.

She was wearing neatly tailored poplin pants, a crisp white shirt, and, as usual, the heavy silver earrings that so dramatically complemented her sweep of smooth, black hair.

"Were you going out, Enid?" Carrie asked. "Don't let me keep you from anything."

"No, Saturday is just another workday for me." Enid flashed a brilliant smile over her shoulder, "as you'll see by the mess in my office."

The room they entered was indeed a shock to Carrie, accustomed as she was to Enid's fastidious grooming and neatly organized thought processes. A green-shaded lamp cast a glow across a litter of papers and books. One volume lay spread open on the desk for reference, others were piled on the floor nearby or tumbled into the seats of two wide leather chairs. Hundreds more filled the bookshelves that lined the walls from floor to ceiling.

Enid removed the books from one of the big armchairs, stacking them on the floor beside it. When she had finished she looked around the room with a smile that was at once helpless and proud.

"Scholars are untidy, let's face it, Carrie. A good housewife couldn't stand this for a minute." Again she managed the smile that fell so short of apology. "Sit there," she said, indicating the emptied chair, then picked her way to her own seat behind the desk.

Settling herself, Carrie was glad she had changed into a denim skirt; her brief tennis dress would have been quite out of place in the lamp-lit, book-strewn office.

She smiled at Enid. "This is where you spend your time, I can see that. Are you still working on your thesis?"

Enid nodded, slipping on the glasses she had located beneath a pile of notes she apparently had been working on when Carrie interrupted her. "The work goes on and on. Garvin thinks I'm unwilling to finish up." Behind the shining lenses her dark eyes narrowed thoughtfully. "I have an idea why he likes that theory."

Carrie said, "Maybe you just want to be sure it's good. That seems worth doing."

"Worth doing. Who's to say?" Enid's lips twisted quizzically. She sat staring so fixedly at the papers on the desk before her that Carrie began to regret her words.

She said, "You know what I mean, Enid. You're a perfectionist, or so I've always thought. You don't give up on any project until you're satisfied with it. That's why we're going to miss you so much on the Mental Health Committee."

At that Enid looked up with such a clear, knowing gaze that Carrie felt she had gone too far. Instead of challenging her, however, Enid merely said, "You'll have Jenny Dillon now. She has more time to give and she'll be excited about the work because it's new to her. And she needs to keep busy right now." The dark eyes softened. "Poor Jenny. She'll be a long time recovering from the shock of Greg's death. Months, I would think, maybe years."

"You and Jenny are good friends, aren't you? I didn't realize that until I saw you at the house yesterday."

"We were in college together, she and Greg, and Garvin and I, but I never knew her well. We had differing interests." Enid smiled tolerantly. "Socially, Jenny was the most sought-after girl on campus. I was there to learn—a very old-fashioned idea, I know."

"But Jenny was a good student, wasn't she? Somebody told me she was Phi Beta—"

"Oh, yes, yes, of course she was, but for Jenny good marks came easily, like everything else." A quick, wry smile. "She never wanted to invest the intellectual energy that real scholarship demands." Enid's flat tone told Carrie all she needed to know about those shared college years.

She said gently, "Isn't it a coincidence that all four of you ended up in the same small town?"

"Well, yes and no. It was Jenny who suggested Rivervale when we saw her at reunion three years ago. Dr. Schmidt was leaving, Garvin was ready to set up his own practice, and I—well, I think you know I'd had a spell of depression."

"That was the year you went to England, wasn't it? The climate was probably responsible."

Something changed in the wide dark eyes behind the lenses, a minute shift, perhaps an instant's inward glance. Enid pursed her lips reflectively.

"I think not," she said quietly. "Whatever the cause, it seemed like a good idea to try a new environment, and Jenny raved about the advantages of Rivervale: a small town that wasn't suburban, yet not provincial, because of being near the university in Springfield. Of course Garvin would follow Jenny to the ends of the earth."

Carrie twisted in her chair. "Oh? Were they...?"

Enid nodded. "For a while. Nobody lasted very long with Jenny. Until Greg Dillon."

There was a moment's silence, then Enid spoke so softly that Carrie had to lean forward to hear her. "And now Greg is gone, while Garvin..." With an impatient movement she pulled off her glasses. "It seems funny, doesn't it? Jenny getting everything she wanted all those years, and now she's alone." She stopped and swallowed hard. "Except for her friends, of course. Garvin is over there with her right now. I don't know how she would have gotten through this without him."

"You have both been wonderful to her, I know that." Carrie sat back in the chair and folded her arms. The room felt chilly all at once.

Enid was gently shaking her head. "Garvin is the one who will help Jenny recover. He is not only wonderfully qualified, you know, Carrie; Garvin is a truly talented psychiatrist. He has such humanity, such intuition." She paused, then added, "I shouldn't say it about my own husband, I suppose, but it's true. Garvin is outstanding in his field."

"I don't see anything wrong with appreciating our husbands. I think mine is very talented too. It's too bad..." Carrie stopped with a regretful smile. "I guess I'd better not say it."

"What were you going to say, Carrie? It's all right."

"I was thinking it's too bad more marriages aren't like yours and mine. Ben and I have been worrying about a couple we know professionally who are having such problems that, actually, we've been trying to get them to see Garvin for counseling. And then yesterday Ben found out that Frank, the husband, has been coming to Garvin for some time, so now we feel hopeful." Carrie wondered if her smile looked as stiff as it felt.

Enid said, "I'm sure Garvin is helping him, or them. Did you say the husband is seeing him? In marriage counseling it's necessary to have the husband and wife work together."

"Why, yes, I imagine it is. But Ben got the impression that Frank was coming in on his own. If you think it's important perhaps I could speak to his wife; she might listen to me."

"She might be more willing to take advice from you than from her husband at this point. Look, I shouldn't do this, but if you want me to I'll check and see if they're both on Garvin's books. What is the last name?"

"Oh, Enid, I don't want to put you on the spot, but maybe it would do some real good. They're the Lundys, Frank and Maria. He is an accountant we work with sometimes, and Maria is a model. She poses for Ben."

"Just a minute. I'll be right back."

Enid got to her feet and made her way to the door, picking her way among the piled-up books with the agility of a goat on a rock-strewn path.

While she was gone Carrie reviewed their conversation, congratulating herself on her luck in finding Enid at home instead of Garvin. She had never before caught her in such a communicative mood, perhaps because she was on her home ground. Without being quite certain what she was learning, Carrie felt sure that Enid was revealing more than she intended, and it gave her a heady sense of power, as if she were the psychiatrist and Enid the trusting patient.

In five minutes Enid was back. "I found Frank Lundy's file," she said as she sat down behind the desk, "and you were right. Lundy is coming in by himself—and apparently not for marriage counseling."

"But we got the impression . . ." Carrie paused. "Don't tell me anything you shouldn't, but in general terms what else would bring him to Garvin?"

"Psychotherapy, of course." Enid sounded uncharacteristically brusque. She did not meet Carrie's eyes as she spoke, but shuffled the papers on her desk as if she were looking for something.

"I'm sorry to be stupid," Carrie said, "but most of us are unfamiliar with what goes on in a psychiatrist's office."

"A lot goes on, some of it beneficial, some destructive. Unintentionally, you realize." Enid sighed. "We walk a fine line in this profession, Carrie. The wrong choice of words, even an unfortunate intonation, can increase a patient's anxiety when, naturally, our goal is to relieve it."

"Is that the most common problem? Anxiety?"

"One of them, along with depression and various phobias. I can't tell you Frank Lundy's problem, of course; that would not be ethical. But I can tell you that Garvin has talked to me about the case." Enid allowed herself the faintest smile of satisfaction. "He sometimes calls me in to consult. All therapists do that when a case is particularly baffling. And I have wondered whether Garvin is on the right track. I think this is the first time we have disagreed."

"Frank Lundy seems so well balanced I find it difficult to think of him as having a baffling neurosis." Carrie shrugged. "But I suppose we all have our hidden selves."

"The shadow side, yes. Like the dark side of the moon. A primary goal of psychotherapy is to discover what that darkness conceals."

"But you feel that in Frank Lundy's case—"

"Oh, Carrie, I shouldn't have said one word to you about that. Please put it out of your mind if you can." Enid's handsome face was taut with concern as she bent forward across the desk. "You and I have worked together so closely on Mental Health that I almost think of you as a professional. You are extraordinarily perceptive, I've always thought. You would have made a good therapist.''

"Why thank you, Enid. But I had no intention of winkling secrets out of you. I hope you understand that.''

Enid straightened in her chair and reached for a manila folder on the desk. "Now let's put Frank Lundy's case aside and get on with the agenda.'' But the folder remained unopened while Enid reflected, biting at her lower lip. Finally she said, "I want to clarify one point first and then I hope we can drop the subject. No matter how gifted the therapist—I'm thinking, of course, of a genius like Garvin—his effect on his patient is unpredictable. Intense feelings are brought to the surface in the course of treatment, and while many patients find wholesome means of channeling these emotions, others are not so fortunate. Do you understand what I am saying?''

Carrie nodded slowly. "I think I do. I think you're saying that a therapist should not be held accountable for his patient's actions.''

Enid said solemnly, "It's a good deal more complex than that, but your interpretation will do.'' She smiled apologetically. "Forgive me. I don't mean to sound didactic. We can explore the subject further if we ever need to, but I can't think why we would. Now, about the Tuesday night meeting . . .''

FOURTEEN

Saturday, June 28 Late Morning

UNDER THE BRIGHT BLUE SKY of a perfect June day the
blackened remains of Greg Dillon's studio looked particularly forlorn. At least half of the once-charming cottage
now existed only as a heap of ashes and charred timbers.
What was left of the shingled roof sagged dejectedly into
the ruins, a subject of discussion for Bill McCarthy and the
other volunteer firemen who had assembled to secure the
building.

"We'd better knock it down before somebody gets
hurt," Bill said finally. "But first you guys have to get the
furniture out of the other part. The whole roof may come
down when we start on it."

As Bill started over to his truck Howard Keating said,
"What do you think, Bill? Does it look like arson?"

McCarthy shrugged. "Hard to say. A painter's studio is
a fire trap, with all that turpentine and kerosene. Oil paints
are highly flammable, not to mention the canvas and paper and all the rags just asking for spontaneous combus-
tion."

"The insurance must be astronomical." Ben Porter had
joined the two men and he and Bill exchanged a nod. "I'm
impressed with the job you did, Bill. You must have saved
a good third of the place."

"Yeah, that's why I want it cleared out before we pull
the roof down. Greg's desk is intact and so is a lot of other
stuff Jenny will want to go over." He began walking slowly
to the open door of the cottage and Ben and Howard followed.

"How about paintings? Aside from the ones you told
me about?" McCarthy frowned, and Howard added, "It's

okay. Ben is a consultant on the case. Unofficially, you understand.''

"Oh?" Bill looked at Ben appraisingly. "That's right, you're a painter too, aren't you? You'd better come in and look around. We saved most of what was in this end of the building."

The three men stepped across the threshold and passed through the tiny hallway to the studio beyond. There they stopped, struck by the serenity of the undamaged area, where Greg's desk stood before the window on the east wall, a chair pushed back from it as if he had just gotten up to go to his easel at the far end of the room. The wicker chair and sofa from Jenny's parents' house were grouped a few feet away, and Ben decided that the pots of African violets on the low table between them had been Jenny's contribution—or possibly Maria Lundy's.

He was seized with a desire to record the scene, to attempt to capture the poignant contrast between the untouched space, which looked so cosily habitable, and, at the opposite end, the blackened ruin gaping open to the summer sky. He looked about for a sketch pad and, seeing what might be a supply cabinet standing at the edge of the burned-out area, asked Bill McCarthy if he could help himself.

"I guess so," Bill said, "but I don't want anything else touched until Jenny gets here. I thought she'd be here by now."

While Ben located a pad and drawing pencil Howard paced slowly around the room. At Greg's desk he paused to study the four or five family photographs grouped there: a close-up of Jenny's smiling face, a charming shot of her with Cabby at the beach, and several of the little boy alone. A Polaroid camera lay on the desk top, and Howard saw that an open metal file box beside it seemed to contain preliminary shots of Greg's subjects. His fingers itched to rifle the box, but Bill McCarthy had joined him, apparently to see for himself whether the telephone was working.

Bill picked up the instrument, listened, then replaced it, saying, "The phone's out, of course. Too bad. I'd like to give Jenny a call so we can get on with this job."

Howard said, "The police ought to see this bunch of Polaroids, Bill. Might tell them something about the ladies in those, shall we say 'special,' paintings you found."

"I looked them over last night," Bill replied. "Didn't see any of the same faces. Can't be sure about the bodies though, can I?" he leered. "They kept their clothes on for the Polaroids—unfortunately."

"Careful. Here comes Jenny."

Standing in the doorway to the studio, Jenny Dillon presented a classic image of grief. Her dark blue dress blended into the dimness of the hallway behind her so that her white face with its shocked brown eyes stood out like a tragic mask. She stared silently at the scene before her, ignoring the three men while she took in the details; then she sighed deeply, turning to the man who had come up behind her, and Howard saw Garvin Thorpe place a comforting hand on her shoulder.

They entered the room together, and Jenny went immediately to Bill McCarthy and shook his hand, saying, "I'm very grateful to you and all the others, Bill, for saving so much of the studio. You can imagine what it means to me." She stopped. Her lips were shaking and her eyes had misted with tears, but she quickly collected herself and greeted Howard and Ben.

"Why, you're sketching the room, aren't you?" she said to Ben. "What a good idea." She managed a tremulous smile. "I didn't think to bring a camera, and I don't have a single picture of the interior of the studio."

Ben lightly kissed her cheek. "I'm glad I had the impulse," he said, "but I'd better work fast. Bill wants to pull down the roof before it does any damage."

"If you'll tell me what you want done with the furniture I'll get it taken out first," McCarthy said to Jenny. "The desk is probably full of things you will want."

Jenny walked to the desk and after a moment's hesitation pulled the center drawer open. She stood staring at the contents, then looked over at Garvin, her face once more filled with unbearable sadness. He quickly stepped to her side and pushed the drawer shut.

He said gently, "You don't have to go through it now. Let's just decide where to have these things put until you're able to deal with them. How about your basement or the garage?"

"Yes, fine. That's a good idea." Jenny sounded distracted, and Ben saw that she had fixed her attention on the photographs standing on the desk top and that her already pale face had turned ashen.

"I'm taking these." Jenny's voice was harsh as she seized the pictures of Cabby, then looked around at the men defiantly, as if daring them to prevent her. She clutched the photographs with shaking hands and began trying to stuff them into her handbag.

"Here, Jenny. I'll put them in the car." Garvin Thorpe spoke gently, but Jenny swung away from him, shaking her head emphatically.

"No, Garvin. This is my job. I'm going to lock them up in a safe place." She stared at him, concentrating. "Mother and Dad have lots of pictures of him; I'll have to get those too. And the school. They must have copies of that new one. Come on, Garvin, I've got to hurry."

She darted toward the door, and Garvin followed as the other men looked on in astonishment. In a moment they heard the screen door slam, and Howard said, "What was that about?"

"I don't know, but I want her to get back here and make some decisions."

Bill McCarthy strode out of the room in pursuit of Jenny, and Howard and Ben exchanged a look of bafflement.

"She seems to have flipped," said Howard.

"Strange. She was very composed yesterday at the service. Seeing the studio must have upset her. Her associations here can't be happy ones." Ben looked at the sketch in his hand with distaste. "I don't think I'll finish this."

"I'd go ahead with it, Ben. Five minutes ago Jenny thought it was a great idea." Howard started toward the door. "I'm going to try to catch her and see if she'll let me borrow these Polaroids for a few hours."

Left alone, Ben went back to work on his drawing, giving particular attention to details that might be meaningful to Jenny. The gleaming mahogany desk, for instance, which seemed too handsome a piece to have been relegated to the studio. Perhaps it had been Jenny's wedding present to Greg, a symbol of her hopes for his career. Ben felt an ache of compassion as he thought of the bitter disillusionment that gradually must have replaced those hopes.

In a few minutes he heard the others returning, and he quickly went over his drawing to note the colors: the intense blue of the sky glimpsed beyond the charred timbers, the paler blue of the cushions on the wicker chairs, the rich wood tones of the sunlit desk.

The screen door opened, and Jenny and Garvin entered the cottage. They came into the studio and Ben saw that Jenny had recovered her composure.

She said, "I had a terrible shock last night, Ben, although Garvin thinks I'm probably making too much of it. My most recent picture of Cabby is missing. Someone must have taken it, and I can only think..." She stopped to draw a deep breath, reaching blindly for Garvin's steadying hand, then she went on. "I can't even say it, Ben."

"Don't try, Jenny. But I think there must be some explanation. Why would anyone threaten Cabby? Why would they persecute you that way?"

"Why would anyone murder Greg? That doesn't make sense either, but it happened."

There was no reply to that. Ben looked at Garvin for help, but could read nothing in his expression except the gentle concern that had been there all week.

Feeling a faint stab of annoyance, Ben said, "What's your opinion, Thorpe? As a professional? What motivation do you see here?"

Instantly the gentleness was gone from Garvin's dark eyes, which now bored into Ben's with a clear message of caution.

"I mean, do you think there's a pattern, any connection..." Ben was stumbling in confusion. Was Garvin warning him against pursuing the subject to spare Jenny, or did he feel Ben had put him on the spot?

"Jenny has taken steps to protect Cabby; she has employed a man to stay with him..."

"I've hired a bodyguard, Ben."

"And I hope the picture will turn up soon, or that she'll remember taking it to be repaired or something..."

"I did not take it anywhere. The last time I looked it was there on my dresser."

"In any case, until the police discover who killed Greg and why, I don't see how we can make a connection."

"Unless..." Ben stopped.

It would hardly be tactful to speculate in Jenny's presence that Greg's killer might want to wipe out his whole family. Or that he might be threatening her child in order to punish Jenny. But for what? Ben was so distracted by his new avenue of thought that he could not think what Howard meant when he heard him say, "Ben, I explained to Jenny that it might be useful if we could look through the box of photographs on Greg's desk."

Frowning, Jenny walked over and picked up the small file box. She picked out several of the photos and studied them, then slipped them back in place.

"They're shots of Greg's subjects," she said. "He always photographed them in several poses to see which would work best for a portrait."

She offered the box to Garvin, who took it and examined several of the photos, as Jenny had done. He pushed them back into the tightly packed file, then flicked his finger along the top.

"Very impressive," he said. "Greg must have been a busy fellow." He smiled at Jenny. "Remember when I had the idea that he should paint Enid? How she resisted?"

Jenny said. "I've always thought that Enid disapproved of Greg's style." She paused and glanced around at the others. "Don't misunderstand; I love my husband's work, but I think Enid would want a more uncompromising artist to do her portrait—someone like you, Ben."

There was a snort from Howard, and Ben raised his eyebrows inquiringly. "Yes, Howard? Do you have something to add to Jenny's evaluation?"

"Only that I have heard many comments on your approach to portraiture, but never in my presence has the word *uncompromising* been used. Very apt, I would say."

Ben studied his friend coolly for a moment, then glanced at his watch and said, "Time for me to report for duty. What do you say, Jenny? May we have the Polaroids for a day or two?"

First eliciting Garvin's faint nod of approval, Jenny handed the box to Howard, saying, "You can take them, as far as I'm concerned."

"Thanks, Jenny; we'll be careful."

When Howard and Ben stepped outside they found that Bill McCarthy had lowered the tailgate of his truck and was waiting with undisguised impatience for the signal to begin removing Greg's furniture from the studio.

"Any minute now," Ben said as he passed, and Bill sighed heavily and tapped his watch.

"Two hours I've wasted, on the best fishing day we've had yet."

"You're a fine person, Bill."

Ben and Howard continued walking down the drive toward the entrance, where Howard had left his car parked in the street. Not until they had passed through the stubby stone pillars that marked Greg's property did Howard say, "Pretty cosy, wouldn't you say? I mean Jenny and Garvin Thorpe."

"I think they are old friends, Howard, and being a psychiatrist besides, Thorpe is probably a big help to her right now."

"I suppose you're right. Still, comforting a wealthy young widow is not bad duty. I wonder how Enid feels about that."

"She probably hasn't noticed. Has her mind on higher matters."

Ben opened the door of Howard's Mercedes, which was parked at the curb close to Greg Dillon's metal mailbox. Unprepared for the weight of the door, he swore as it swung heavily against the wooden post that supported the mailbox, causing the flap to spring open and release a cascade of advertising circulars.

"Looks like the glamorous Greg Dillon got just as much junk mail as the rest of us." Ben gathered the leaflets into a bundle that he clutched while he carefully climbed into Howard's front seat. "If you can wait a second I'll see if any of this stuff is worth taking back to Jenny," he said.

As he began going over the stack of mail Howard said, "The police are going to want those Polaroids, you know."

"Yes. I'm surprised that Garvin let us take them."

"Maybe he didn't think of that. What we'd better do is make a list of the subjects in the snapshots. Then we can take our time checking them against the paintings of Greg's that we've seen."

"Right, and that will give us a possible clue to the paintings they won't let us see—the nudes."

"It won't be definitive though, Howard, because a lot of Greg's portraits must be hanging in their owners' houses."

"And every artist has some commissions fall through after the preliminaries, I should think."

"Too true." Ben sighed. "Let's go. I'll pitch this out at home. Somebody ought to notify the post office to stop the flow."

"I imagine that has to come from Jenny." Howard started the car. "Home or office?" he asked.

"Office, please," Ben replied. "Carrie might be there, since obviously she didn't get to talk to Garvin Thorpe."

As they pulled up before Ben's building Howard said, "Talking to Thorpe is apt to be counterproductive, in my opinion. No reliable psychiatrist is going to hand out information about his patients.''

"I don't know about that. Carrie has her ways." Ben was smiling as he stepped out of the car clutching his armful of pamphlets. He bent to speak through the car window. "I'll call you if she has anything to report. Meantime I sure wish you could think of a way to get a look at those secret paintings of Greg's."

"It's hopeless, I'm afraid, but I'll have a chat with Finnegan."

Howard drew away, and Ben ran up the porch steps and pushed open the door to the Porter Publishing offices.

"Is that you?" Carrie poked her head out of her office door, and Ben saw that her cheeks were flushed with excitement. "I've had the most fascinating talk with..." She stopped, glancing around the deserted hallway. "Come on in; I can't wait to tell you."

Ben followed her into her office and allowed the stack of circulars to slither onto the nearest tabletop. Then he kissed his wife keeping one eye on the clock on her desk.

"It's one o'clock," he said. "What do you say I get a couple of sandwiches before we report on the morning's activities?"

Carrie said, "All right. Rare roast beef for me, please. I'll make coffee."

Ben started for the door. "You might take a look at that stuff from Greg's mailbox. It looks like straight junk to me."

When he had gone, Carrie went back to the small kitchen and filled the coffee maker. Returning to the office, she began looking over Greg Dillon's mail, tossing the catalogues and premium offers into the wastebasket one by one. A bright yellow card slipped from between the pages of a loosely folded pamphlet and fluttered to the floor. Retrieving it, Carrie saw that it was not an ad, but a repair notice from an appliance company.

"Sullivan's Electronics," it read, "Appliances Large and Small, Retail Sales, Repairs. 51 Hinkley Ave., Springfield, Conn." A telephone number followed. A form message was printed beneath: "The appliance you left for repair is ready. Please pick it up at your convenience."

Carrie placed the card on her desk, feeling pleased that it gave her an excuse to call on Jenny Dillon and possibly find out more about her friendship with Enid and Garvin Thorpe. She would invite her to dinner as well; Jenny would need extra attention from friends during the first weeks of her bereavement.

"All right, let's hear all about it." Ben pushed the office door shut with his foot and carried his bag of sandwiches over to Carrie's desk. Taking the neatly wrapped packages out of the bag, he placed hers on the blotter and his own on a paper napkin on the opposite side of the desk. He carefully unwrapped his sandwich and took a bite, then, as Carrie handed him a cup of coffee, he moved the yellow postcard aside to make room.

"I salvaged that from Greg's mail," Carrie said, slipping into her chair on the other side of the desk. "I ought to take it to Jenny, don't you think?"

"What is it?"

"A notice that some appliance has been repaired. Doesn't say what it is." While Carrie started on her sandwich Ben picked up the yellow card and studied it.

"It was sent to Greg's studio, so it must be something he used there, not at home." Ben turned the card in his hand while he sipped his coffee. "A lamp maybe?"

"Whatever it is, it gives me a good reason to see Jenny."

"I shouldn't think you'd need one."

"Well, oddly enough, I sort of feel that I do; because of what we're up to, I suppose, and then what Enid told me." Carrie paused for a gulp of coffee, her blue eyes shining at Ben over the rim of the white cup. She lowered it and said, "Enid Thorpe is so envious of Jenny you can practically see it oozing out of her pores. And has been for years, what's more."

"For years?"

"They were in college together—Enid, Garvin, Jenny, and Greg—and apparently Jenny and Garvin were an item for a while and he's still somewhat under her spell, or anyway Enid thinks he is. Jenny was a campus queen, of course; you can see how she would be.''

''And Enid a grind, probably shy and lonely in those days.''

''But attractive to Garvin because she was bright, and different . . .''

''And impressed by him.''

''Very. In fact, the awe is still there when she speaks of him: Garvin is brilliant, intuitive; I believe I heard the word *genius* as well. That was when we got to the other intriguing part of our conversation, the bit that has me slightly baffled.''

The phone rang, and frowning with impatience, Carrie reached over to switch on the answering machine. She took another bite of her sandwich and a sip of coffee, then sat back to compose her thoughts.

''I'm going to write down our interview before I forget how it went because I had the feeling that the discussion was following a scenario that had been devised very deliberately by Enid.''

''To what end, Carrie? What was her point?''

''That's where I'm confused. She was surprisingly forthcoming about Frank Lundy. I had barely mentioned his name before she ran off to get his file. And then, while emphasizing Garvin's almost magical capabilities as a therapist, she said she had disagreed with his treatment of Lundy.'' Carrie paused. ''Does that make sense to you?''

''Not yet, but you've got me hooked. What next?''

''Well, it all seemed to lead to one point that she was strangely anxious to make: that a therapist has no real control over the actions of his patient.''

''And should not be held responsible?''

''That wasn't spelled out, but yes, she seemed to be making a disclaimer. She made me think of an overprotective mother leaping in to squash any possible hint of fallibility on the part of her darling. As if no blame could attach to Garvin even if Frank Lundy committed a crime.''

''Such as murder.''

"Yes. Or that's what I inferred."

Ben said nothing, but got to his feet and walked slowly around the room. He gathered up the sandwich wrappings and threw them into the wastebasket. He picked up the yellow postcard and read its message once again, then tossed it back onto the desk. He swallowed the last of his coffee and stared into the empty cup trying to decide whether to have more.

Finally he said, "I hope you will record everything you remember about that interview while it's still fresh in your mind."

Carrie looked up from a legal pad on which she had been rapidly scribbling. "That's what I'm doing, darling. Almost finished."

Ben clicked the telephone to its operative mode, then, peering down at the yellow postcard, dialed the number of Sullivan's Electronics. Carrie heard the tinny sound of a recorded message and watched as Ben listened, then slowly replaced the instrument.

"Closed for vacation until Monday, June 30th." He reached for the appointment calendar that stood on the desk, flipped to June 30, and jotted a note on the page. He was about to tuck the yellow card into the calendar when he changed his mind and instead slipped it into Carrie's top desk drawer.

He said, "Let's follow up on this ourselves, okay? It's one little chore we can do for Jenny."

"But Ben, I wanted to go and see her."

"You don't need a pass to call on Jenny Dillon." He stood looking down into Carrie's face, absently stroking her blond hair back from her forehead. "I want to find out what appliance Greg was having repaired before Jenny does. I don't even want her to know that Sullivan's Electronics has something of his. Not at this point anyway."

Carrie slowly pulled off her horn-rimmed glasses to study her husband's face. "You think it might be something Jenny would conceal from the police, don't you? But that can only mean . . ."

"I'm not sure what it means, maybe nothing. But for now Sullivan's Electronics is our little secret and I say let's keep it that way."

FIFTEEN

BEN PORTER LEFT for the club around two o'clock and, watching him go out into the bright afternoon, Carrie had felt a rare surge of resentment. While he played three or four sets of tennis and then joined Terry and Brooke at the pool she would be closeted in the office making amendments to Sam Blake's contract. She glared at the folder of papers on her desk. This was the fourth book Sam had done with Porter Publishing; his new agent might have trusted them to do right by him, but no, the man had revised almost every clause of the contract. Now Carrie must study his changes and hope that in her impatience to be finished she did not allow any terms disadvantageous to the company.

But it was such a gorgeous day! She pushed back her chair and strode out to her office and down the hall to the back door. She stepped out onto the small porch and could not stop there, but compelled like a sleepwalker walked slowly across the thick, green grass to stand at the edge of the river. There a soft breeze caressed the water, carving its surface into brilliant scallops of silver that lapped against the grassy bank.

Carrie sighed, lifting her face to catch the sun's warmth. She pictured the scene at the club pool, the gaggle of small, tanned children with shining, sun-bleached hair, the teenage sitters with their smooth, perfect bodies stretched out to catch the last iota of sun, the young mothers gossiping together a few feet away, out of hearing.

It would be nice to be there with them, Carrie thought wistfully—for about ten minutes. She found herself grinning, back in touch with reality. Sunday afternoons at the pool were all she could tolerate; if she took the day off, she would be fidgety with boredom by this time tomorrow.

She walked back to the house, her thoughts once again on Sam Blake's new contract. She would ask Howard Keating to go over it when she was finished; then with any luck she could get it in the mail by Friday. Except that Thursday was Brooke's fifth birthday, and Carrie would of course take the afternoon off for the party. She hoped Ben had remembered to arrange for the pony ride...

"Hello, Mrs. Porter."

Carrie gasped. As she stepped into the hallway, half-blinded by sunlight, a lean figure emerged from the shadows. It was a man, she saw as her eyes adjusted to the dimness, one whose tense, white face was strange to her. She moved back toward the door, her eyes instinctively scanning him for a gun or a club; but his hands hung empty at his sides, and he appeared genuinely sorry to have alarmed her.

"I didn't mean to startle you," he said, "but the door was open so I knew someone was here. I thought I'd find your husband. We talked last Thursday; maybe he told you." He paused expectantly, then went on, "But of course we haven't met. I'm Frank Lundy."

"Well, how do you do?" Carrie advanced to shake Lundy's hand, adjusting her mental image of the man to the reality. "I thought you would be...older." She had actually pictured Frank Lundy as large and dark and probably somewhat unkempt. This slim, tidy person dressed in a neat gray suit seemed too organized, too collected; until, as he followed her into her office and stood waiting to be invited to sit down, she saw the tension in his rigid body, the alertness. He was like a wary bird poised for flight at the first sign of danger.

Carrie felt her own nerves tighten in response, but she sank into her desk chair and said as cordially as she could, "Please sit down, Mr. Lundy. I understand your conference with my husband was cut short Thursday. I'm sorry he isn't here now. Was he expecting you to come in?"

"No, I just dropped by on the off chance..." He pulled the visitor's chair a few inches back from the desk, then seated himself and crossed his legs with what appeared a calculated economy of motion. "I hoped to find one of you in so I could make another appointment." His smile flickered briefly. "I would very much like to do some work for your company."

Carrie smiled. "We need a good accountant, one who would take a real interest in our situation at the moment and our plans for the future. But Ben told me he explained that to you. The next thing..."

"Your husband described our conversation to you? He quoted..." Lundy twisted in his chair as he darted a quick, searching glance around the room. "He didn't tape it, did he? Our interview, if you could call it that?" He stared at Carrie as if challenging her to tell the truth.

She shook her head, but before she could speak he chuckled softly and sank back as if amused by his own behavior. "I guess I sound kind of paranoid, don't I? As if Ben Porter would have any reason to tape our discussion. Why, there wasn't a word of it worth recording. He probably told you that, didn't he? How I had to break it off before we even got to the point? Dumb." He shook his head, marveling. "I'm not usually so disorganized, I hope you understand that. I came by hoping to set up another appointment when I'd be better prepared to show you what I think I can do for your company."

Carrie pulled her desk calendar closer and flipped to the following week. "How about Monday afternoon? Two o'clock?" She looked up inquiringly and Lundy nodded. "If I find Ben has other plans I'll call you."

Again Frank nodded, and Carrie penciled in the time, then pushed back her chair and said, smiling up at him, "I'm so glad to have met you, Mr. Lundy."

But she saw at once that there had been another change of mood.

"I'd like to ask you a question, Mrs. Porter, if you won't think I'm too fresh." The easygoing facade had vanished as quickly as it had appeared. Lundy's gray eyes were fixed sternly on her face, and Carrie felt her irritation rise.

"I came to the office because I have work to do, Mr. Lundy. I'm afraid I can't talk any longer." As she spoke she rose to her feet.

"So I guess you know what I was going to ask you, right? Yes, I can see why you want to get rid of me. You're afraid you'll fall apart just like..." He stopped, swallowed, then went on. "You fell for him too, just like the rest of them, didn't you? Sure, you're good-looking and young, you're here on your own a lot. Plenty of chance for..."

"Will you leave, please? Right now? Before you say what you apparently came to say?"

Carrie slipped from behind her desk and strode to the door but, moving as swiftly as a cat, Lundy reached it before her. He stood leaning against the door, one hand firmly gripping the knob, and his expression was like that of a little boy tormenting his sister—except for his waxy pallor and glassily shining eyes.

Later Carrie was amazed at her coolness, but truly she did not feel afraid or insulted, only immensely baffled by this strange young man's behavior. What could be his motivation? Why was he suggesting that she must have been one of Greg Dillon's lovers? It was like a deadly guessing game. If she got the answer right she would be safe. If not? Well, she would soon find out.

"What's on your mind, Frank? You seem a little upset." Her tone was friendly, sympathetic; she managed a confiding smile.

"Upset! God, everyone thinks I'm upset these days, when they're the ones..." He shook his head in wonder and his lips parted in a stiff attempt at a smile. He let go of the doorknob and, crossing his arms, leaned back against it and studied her with narrowed eyes.

"I suppose you're going to claim you had nothing going on with Greg Dillon, right? When he was killed right here in your husband's office. I mean, it had to be you or your husband; any idiot could see that, but not the stalwart members of our local police force." Again he shook his head wonderingly. "Those so-called detectives."

"Would you like to see where Greg's body was found?" Some instinct was guiding her, Carrie decided, as she watched Frank Lundy's eyes widen in surprise. There was no guile involved; she was fighting craziness with craziness and it seemed to be working.

"Why, sure. Did you find him yourself?" Lundy stepped away from the door and courteously opened it for her. She preceded him into Ben's office, feeling dazed by his abrupt change of manner.

"Did I . . . ? Oh, yes, I found him lying right there when I came in that morning." She stopped beside the spot in front of the desk, which after three days looked no different from the rest of the well-worn, raisin-colored carpet. Still, something kept her from stepping where she knew Greg's body had lain, and she saw that Frank Lundy skirted the area just as she did, as if in some mystic way her knowledge had been communicated to him.

He stared at the spot for a moment, then looked up at her and said, "That bastard deserved to die." There was a steely glint in the gray eyes that bored into hers. "He had it coming if anyone ever did. Whoever shot him ought to get a medal."

Carrie could feel anger emanating from the man like heat from a radiator. She also felt the anger reflected in herself. In a short space of time he had insulted her, as much as accused her of murder, and now, though no threat had been voiced, he held her prisoner. Yet she could not respond in kind and oddly enough did not want to. Her immediate need was to get him out of the building. She recalled his swift change of mood only minutes earlier. He was intelligent, and like most intelligent people, inquisitive; that was the lead she must follow.

"You know what I've been wondering?" she said in a light, conversational tone. "I've been trying to figure out not only why Greg was killed here on our premises but how the killer got in. And you know? I've just thought of something."

She turned and walked briskly out of the office and down the short stretch of hall to the front door, not daring to look behind her, expecting at any moment to feel him roughly grasp her arm. But when she reached the door and seized the handle he merely stood close beside her, frowning thoughtfully as he watched her turn the knob.

She pulled the door inward, carefully avoiding any appearance of haste, though she could not help drawing a grateful breath of the fresh, warm air that met her face.

Looking around at Lundy with a conspiratorial smile, Carrie said, "Come with me; I want to try something." Then she stepped out onto the porch, and he followed like a docile child.

She pulled the door shut, giving the knob a sharp tug to make sure the latch had caught. Again she smiled at Frank Lundy, and said, "Now, give it a push. Go ahead."

First darting her a quick glance of puzzlement, he pushed against the door with one hand, then lifted his eyebrows in surprise as the feeble latch gave and the door swung gently inward.

"I don't know why I didn't think of it sooner," Carrie said. "We just get used to things not working right, don't we?"

"I'd get a locksmith over here right away if I were you." Lundy tugged the door to, then pushed it open again. He frowned at Carrie, disapproving of her carelessness. "I could fix it myself if I had the tools. I'm surprised that your husband . . ."

"Oh, you know artists." Carrie chuckled indulgently as she strolled across the porch and down the four wooden steps to the sidewalk. There she stopped to say good-bye to Lundy, who had accompanied her.

Standing there in his neat gray suit, he looked every inch the accountant. His pale face was fixed in a grimace as he squinted into the sun; still his manner was one of friendly deference as he said, "Please tell Mr. Porter I'll see him on Monday."

With perfect, businesslike courtesy on both sides, they shook hands and parted. Frank Lundy turned and started walking up the street to his car, while Carrie crossed to her parking lot, hoping she wore the air of a sane, collected lady who had her car keys in her pocket—which she did not, and which she had no intention of retrieving from her office until she saw Frank Lundy drive off in the red compact station wagon he was approaching.

Until then she thought she would just climb into the front seat of her car and sit there and shake.

SIXTEEN

Sunday, June 29 Morning

AFTER HE HAD PULLED into a space at police headquarters, Ben Porter switched off the ignition, and then sat holding the key in his hand while he prepared himself for his forthcoming confrontation with Lieutenant Finnegan. If a brief telephone conversation had resulted in Ben's slamming down the phone with a clearly uttered obscenity a personal interview might be expected to place an intolerable strain on his self-control.

Carrie had urged him to wait, but obviously Carrie did not fully realize the danger or she could not have handled Frank Lundy so skillfully. Even so, the strain had been terrible for her. Picturing her tense, white face as she described the encounter, Ben closed his eyes and shuddered. At breakfast that morning she had still been shaky, and had dropped a plate on the kitchen floor. Ben felt his own hand trembling and, opening his eyes, saw that he was clutching the ignition key in a tight, white fist.

He drew a deep breath, dropped the key into his pocket, and stepped out of the car. Finnegan is a conscientious cop, he lectured himself as he crossed the drive and mounted the stone steps. He's a limited guy, but a good guy; don't let him get to you.

Ten minutes later Ben was watching the deliberate progress of Finnegan's stubby yellow pencil across one of the lined pages of his spiral notebook. The hand was musclebound, Ben decided; that must be Finnegan's problem. How did he manage his buttons with those fat sausage fingers? Possibly his wife helped him out—or one of their children. Ben had seen five-year-olds form letters on a page faster than Finnegan was doing it.

The lieutenant looked up suddenly, fixing his small blue eyes on Ben so sternly he might have been reading his thoughts.

"I don't see anything here about Lundy actually threatening your wife," he said.

"You don't? I would say the entire visit was a threat, with particular emphasis on his suggestion that Carrie had been involved with Greg Dillon, followed by his accusation of murder."

Finnegan was slowly shaking his round head from side to side while he shuffled through the pages of his notebook.

"I don't see any accusation here, Mr. Porter."

Ben consulted his own notes. "'It had to be you or your husband, any idiot could see that.' I'm quoting from my wife's recollection, and she doesn't recall things that didn't happen."

"Well, that's a wild statement, sure, but not really a threat. And you have to understand that the guy was angry. He's got a lot of problems. I can't tell you about them, of course." Finnegan's eyes glinted smugly behind his wire-rimmed glasses.

"Lieutenant, I recommend that you add one more problem to his list: Lock him up." Ben was breathing hard; he could feel his pulse racing. He swallowed noisily. "In fact, I demand it as a citizen in need of protection. Place Frank Lundy under arrest before you have another violent crime on your hands."

"In the first place we have no evidence against Lundy." Finnegan paused. "Well, maybe his mental state, I'll give you that. But he was home in bed when Dillon's murder occurred; he does not possess a gun, as far as we know, or a knife." Finnegan permitted himself a sly grin. "I guess you know who *does* own a knife, don't you? And you may have a damn good motive."

"Goddamn it, Finnegan, I thought I'd convinced you that there was nothing, absolutely nothing, going on with Carrie and Greg Dillon."

"Funny that so many people think there was."

Ben was on his feet, his whole body trembling with rage. "Do you know what you are, Finnegan? You're a short-sighted bully. You ought to be kicked out of this job, and I'm going to make it my top priority to see that you are!"

"And I'm going to slap you into a jail cell if you don't quiet down."

Finnegan had not so much as shifted his bulky form in his chair. He was like an imperturbable Buddha firmly set on his shrine.

Ben paced to the window, breathing deeply to calm himself. After a moment he turned and said, "Are you aware of the fact that Frank Lundy has been undergoing psychiatric treatment?"

Assuming an expression of weary condescension, Finnegan said, "You know, Mr. Porter, we're not as behind the times as you seem to think. Many people get psychiatric help these days; it doesn't mean they are any more threat to society than the rest of us. Possibly less."

"That is true, of course. If the patient is getting the right therapy."

"Exactly what are you implying by that remark?"

"I'm not sure, to tell you the truth." Ben found himself actually smiling at Finnegan, a first, as far as he could recall. The man looked totally baffled, and Ben reflected that if he accomplished nothing else at least he was ruining Finnegan's Sunday.

This had also occurred to Finnegan, who consulted his watch and said, "If you are finished, Mr. Porter, it is Sunday morning..."

Again Ben smiled at Finnegan, at the same time striding back to his chair, where he seated himself comfortably.

"I won't be finished here until you give me some assurance that your department will provide protection for my wife and family—the most obvious method being to place Frank Lundy under arrest. Pending investigation, or whatever you call it. I'm not saying the man is a murderer, only that he is very disturbed and may take some rash action."

"You're pretty anxious to tell me how to run the police department. Well, I happen to think you could use some advice yourself, and here it is: Keep your wife at home where she belongs, Mr. Porter, and you'll have a lot less problems."

"Fewer problems."

"Whatever. Any guy who lets his wife sashay off to some office every day while he hangs around the house and paints pictures is asking for trouble. This whole mess could be blamed on that one fact."

"Of course. Why haven't I seen that? Greg Dillon might be alive today if Carrie had stayed out of the publishing business. I know she'll be glad to give up her work when I point that out to her."

For an instant Finnegan looked pleasantly surprised. Then his small blue eyes narrowed suspiciously. "You're a real smartass, Porter. Now how about getting out of here so I can enjoy what's left of my day off?"

"First I'd like to ask you another question about providing protection for the citizens who pay your salary. Why is it necessary for Jenny Dillon to hire a bodyguard for her son? Can't the police department lend her a man while they investigate a possible kidnapping threat?"

"Kidnapping threat? What the hell are you talking about, Porter?"

"She didn't report it to you? Jenny is missing the latest photograph of her son, Cabby; one that she is certain was on the dresser in her bedroom. She's convinced that it was taken by someone who is planning to kidnap him."

"She must be crazy."

"Well, she might be feeling slightly paranoid just now, granted. Having her husband murdered in cold blood could have that effect. Even so, it would be smart to take precautions, don't you think?"

"I don't know how I can be expected to take precautions if I haven't been asked to. I'm not a mind reader."

"Clearly. Or you might have guessed what I was implying when I questioned Frank Lundy's therapy."

"Come on, Porter. I refuse to sit here on a nice Sunday morning and play games with you. What about Lundy's therapy? Assuming that it's relevant to this case, which I doubt."

"Suppose you're upset enough about something to go to a psychiatrist. He's supposed to treat you in a way that makes you feel better, right? And possibly behave better, straighten out your life?"

"Sure, that's what they get paid for."

"But suppose the psychiatrist—let's call him the therapist—gets you more upset instead of less? Maybe because he's figured out the problem wrong, maybe because he's inept, or maybe deliberately, because he wants to make you act in a particular way." Ben paused to study Finnegan's rosy face, which had deepened in hue as he listened. "Have you considered such a possibility, Finnegan?"

Shifting his weight to one bulky haunch, Finnegan tugged a handkerchief out of his trouser pocket and, first removing his wire-rimmed spectacles, wiped a film of perspiration from his face. Keeping his eyes fixed on Ben Porter, as if he feared he might seize the opportunity to escape, he then bunched the handkerchief and returned it to the pocket, freeing his hand with some difficulty.

"I'll tell you why I haven't considered that possibility. First, I never heard it suggested until about two minutes ago. Second, I've been around long enough to recognize bullshit, which is what that theory is. Third . . . no, wait a minute."

Ben had gotten to his feet and was halfway to the door before Finnegan managed to pull himself out of his revolving desk chair.

"Third, the only reason to dish out that kind of bullshit is desperation. You must be desperate, Porter, to invent a story like that, and you're crazy if you think I'm going to waste time on it."

By now Ben had reached the door, but as he was about to seize the knob there was a brisk knock on the other side and Vince Muzzio pushed open the door and stepped into the office.

"The Lundys are gone," he said. "Left town this morning when Riley thought they were at Mass."

Finnegan, standing behind the desk, shifted his glare from Ben Porter to Muzzio. He said slowly and distinctly, "Riley *thought* they were at Mass?"

"He followed them from the apartment to St. John's..."

"I don't suppose he bothered to go inside the church?"

"Yes, he went in, but he sat in the back so they wouldn't see him."

"And then forgot about them? Carried away by the service, was he?"

Muzzio, experienced in gauging the severity of his boss's fits of ill humor, saw that the hour spent with Ben Porter had been seriously damaging.

He lowered his voice to a soothing croon and said, "Early Mass gets a crowd in the summer, you know, Tom. So Riley said he lost them when the service was over, but he didn't worry because he had his eye on their car—the red compact wagon they drove over in."

Muzzio paused, suddenly aware that Ben Porter was not entitled to hear his report. Reluctant, however, to remind Finnegan of Porter's presence, he continued. "Apparently, though, they had left another car—probably Maria Lundy's blue convertible—in back of the church the night before. They must have taken off in it."

"Or maybe they took a cab. Or a helicopter." Finnegan slowly lowered himself into his chair again, and gazed dejectedly at Ben. "I'd say Jenny Dillon is better off hiring her own bodyguard, what do you think?"

"Well, Lieutenant, let's face it. Your men don't get a lot of practice at this kind of thing. You're not running Scotland Yard, after all."

"Lucky thing." Finnegan looked sadly from Ben to Muzzio, then out the window at the tantalizing beauty of the sparkling day.

Ben cleared his throat and said softly to Muzzio, "I'd better be going."

Muzzio nodded solemnly, then muttered, "What's this about Jenny Dillon and a bodyguard?"

"He'll explain. It's probably nothing, but she's worried."

The two men regarded each other in silence for a moment then, with a nod in the direction of Finnegan, Ben said, "The poor fellow has had a bad morning already. Be kind to him, Vince."

But the door was closed, firmly, before he had finished speaking.

SEVENTEEN

GROGAN'S FISHING CAMP had added a bar and grill only that spring, and Ed Grogan was still undecided about whether or not it had been a good idea. While his wife, Molly, had a point when she said they would attract a better class of fisherman if they offered dinner and drinks as well as breakfast, Ed wasn't so sure he wanted a better class. The men he felt comfortable with were perfectly satisfied with the beef and mashed potato dinners served at Mike's Diner five miles west on Route 17, and their drinking requirements were equally simple: beer all day, which they took along to the streams in their own coolers, and whiskey or gin at night, usually drunk from pints they had brought from home.

Running a restaurant had never been an ambition of Ed's, a bar even less so. Where there was booze there were problems; even in your own house on a Saturday night, where at least you could choose the company. A public place like a fishing lodge was wide open, especially one situated on a state highway; but of course there was no question of moving. Grogan's father had started the place in the twenties, and by now it was one of the best-known camps in that part of the Catskills.

The establishment had grown, over the years, until the small frame cottages dotted over the hillside behind the Grogan homestead numbered twenty-five. Fishermen had always been able to supply their basic tackle needs from cabinets kept in the front parlor of the house, where one of the Grogans' four children was usually on hand to make sales and issue fishing licenses. The three boys could also supply expert advice on local fishing conditions, and the

eldest was earning notoriety for tying flies that were irresistible to the native brown trout.

Ginny Grogan enjoyed fishing almost as much as her
brothers, but her mother had insisted that she learn to
cook. In fact, one of Molly's strongest arguments for
adding a restaurant had been that it would keep Ginny
constructively occupied behind the scenes: an important
point now that she was seventeen and about to graduate.
Ginny had curling red-gold hair, an upturned nose, and the
kind of figure that had kept the boys trailing after her for
four years already; Molly wasn't sure how much longer she
could hold out—especially in a rural environment, where
entertainment and interesting jobs were equally hard to
find.

So Ed had finally consented to visit the bank, where he
obtained a mortgage with frightening ease, and now a raw-
looking new building almost as big as the house stood next
to it, and Ed was spending his evenings behind the bar instead of out on the stream where he belonged.

At least on Sunday nights he could close up early. Most
of the fishermen had left, not to be replaced until the following day, so no dinner was served and bar business was
usually slow. At the moment he had only three customers,
and if they were winding up, as it appeared from the way
they were swirling the ice around in their glasses and not
talking much, he might be out of there by eight.

Ed heard a car pull into the drive, and he squinted toward the door, mentally crossing his fingers. Sometimes
drivers stopped just to look at the map or ask directions.
But in a moment the door swung open, was held that way
by a guy waiting while his wife went through, and when she
did Ed caught his breath. He had to admit she was the
most gorgeous-looking woman he'd ever seen in his place.
He could tell that the three men sitting together thought
the same by the way they straightened up and fell silent
while they stared at her. He wasn't surprised when one of
them held up his glass and rattled the ice, asking for a refill, and of course the others followed suit.

Ed nodded, then gave his attention to the new arrivals, who were obviously expecting to settle in. The man wore the tentative expression of one who hopes for a welcome but isn't sure he'll get it and, sure enough, when he came closer Ed remembered him as a member of a fishing party that had stayed at the camp once the preceding spring. The woman asked the way to the ladies' room, and then flashed him such a glowing smile you might think he'd given her a present.

He was so busy watching her walk toward the back, where the rest rooms were, taking in the curve of her hips in her smooth white pants and the way her glossy black hair lifted from her shoulders as she moved, that he had to ask the man to repeat his name. It was Lundy, Frank Lundy, he said. He smiled at Ed too, but it was a tight, nervous smile, and Ed recalled the way he had sat with his friends in the evening, a little apart as if he were an observer, and not laughing at the jokes as hard as they did.

"My wife and I would like a cottage for a few days, if you have one available," he said. "I tried to phone, but your line was busy, and we left in kind of a hurry."

"We can take care of you all right. Let me make these drinks, then I'll have a look at the chart."

Frank Lundy didn't look like the type to have a wife like that, but it was none of Ed's business. He wouldn't mind spending a few days in a cottage with her any time.

She was on her way back, turning that beautiful face in his direction, and Ed suddenly found himself transformed into a genial host. "Have you had dinner?" he asked Lundy. "I think the kitchen is still open."

Lundy looked uncertainly toward his wife. "Well, I don't know..." he began. When she reached his side he said, "What do you think, Maria? Shall we have dinner here? Or a drink?"

"Let's have a drink while we make up our minds." She turned to Ed, who was stepping out from behind the bar to deliver the drinks he had made. "Or are you about to stop serving? It is Sunday night."

Again she turned on that smile that made him feel like a hero, and Ed stopped in his tracks. "No, no, take your time," he said, "we serve dinner till nine." He couldn't believe it was his own voice he heard, and he quickly added, "Of course, we're closed tomorrow night, Monday."

While he carried the tray of drinks to the three men Ed was aware of Frank Lundy seating his wife at a table, where he waited for Ed to take their order, then went in search of the men's room. Ed hadn't made it back to the bar before one of the men at the other table was on his feet, approaching Maria Lundy with a sappy smile.

"Excuse me," he said, "haven't I seen you performing somewhere? Forgive me if I'm wrong, but aren't you an actress? Or a singer?"

"In a small way." Ed could see by the way she shook her hair back that she was smiling up at the guy. "A *very* small way."

She laughed, a velvety, melodious lilt, and Ed hastily plopped a handful of ice into each of their glasses and grabbed his tray. By the time he got to her table the guy was leaning on it to look into her face, and Ed had to ask him to move so he could put down the drinks.

She was saying, "I sing sometimes at my cousin's club in Springfield, Connecticut—the Crazy Cat. Have you been there?"

Before he could answer Ed was glad to see Frank Lundy returning. When he reached the table his wife's new acquaintance was holding his hand out and introducing himself, wearing such a cordial, welcoming expression he might have been the host of the place.

His manner didn't cut much ice with Lundy, however, who gave him the briefest possible handshake, said curtly, "Frank Lundy," then pulled out a chair and sat down in it without asking the guy to join them.

Maybe he was her husband, Ed thought, except wouldn't he be used to other men trying to move in on him by now? Unless they were newlyweds; but somehow that didn't fit.

Mentally Ed ran down the list of vacant cottages. The nicest, in his opinion, was number 23. Molly had done a great job on the new curtains and spreads, made it too nice for the average fisherman, actually, but it would suit this lovely woman, maybe get her to stay longer.

Ed fell into a daydream in which Maria Lundy was turning down the pink and white bedspread on one of number 23's twin beds, taking her time to do it because she felt shy with him there. She was wearing a white satin nightgown...

"May we have a refill, please?"

The words were clipped. Reaching for the glasses behind the bar, Ed saw that Lundy's face was taut and he did not look at Ed as he waited, but first at the three guys, who were beginning to get noisy, and then at his wife. She had taken out her compact, the way women do when they're left alone, and seemed to be giving all her attention to her face; still she had to be aware of the effect her presence was having on the other three men.

"I'll take these over for you."

Ed started to put the fresh drinks on his tray, but Lundy reached for them impatiently, saying, "That's okay," and started for his table.

"Are you ready to look at a menu, Mr. Lundy?" Ed called after him. Not expecting any dinner business, Molly had let Ginny go out; she'd be spitting nails if he didn't get the Lundys out of there pretty soon.

"We still haven't decided," Lundy replied. "Give us another ten minutes, okay?"

He sat down and began muttering to his wife, and, although Ed couldn't hear what he said or what she said in return, he could tell by the stiffening of her posture that she was getting mad.

He began to rethink the question of which cottage to give them. If they were going to fight he didn't want to hear it, and number 23 was the closest to the house. Number 12 was the one for this possibly delicate situation; it was right on the edge of the woods, therefore the most private, and almost as nicely decorated as 23. Though yellow was not the color he would have chosen, everything matched: towels, curtains, bedspreads, even the wastebasket. The TV was the best one in the camp, so if Frank Lundy wanted to fish at all, leaving his wife on her own...

In his mind Ed Grogan started on another scenario, one in which Molly went marketing while Frank Lundy was fishing, and the TV in number 12 happened to go on the blink just as he was passing.

IT HAD BEEN Ben Porter's idea to track down Joe De-Lucca, the owner of the Crazy Cat, after he and Howard had decided it would be both futile and unkind to approach Maria Lundy's mother.

"The poor woman is probably a wreck already," was Howard's opinion. "That is, if Maria has been confiding in her."

"It's hard to imagine Maria keeping her mother updated on her most recent activities. Still, she must have given her some warning that she might be slightly involved in Greg's murder investigation—just to prepare her."

"But not a forwarding address when she decided to skip town." Ben peered out the car window to catch the name on a street sign. "Carter Street. Doesn't Tulip come in here pretty soon?"

"Wait a second, we're off the map." Howard unfolded another section of the Springfield street map and after studying it said, "Looks like three more blocks, then it should be on our right."

The Crazy Cat, not surprisingly, was closed on Sundays; but Howard and Ben had driven over to get the proprietor's name from the door, and then had the good luck to find him listed in the Springfield telephone directory. He was not at home when they called, however, but his wife expected him back around five o'clock. Without explaining their purpose, Howard had simply left word that he would drop around and hoped Joe could spare him a moment on a business matter.

"We're probably wasting the nicest Sunday afternoon of the summer on this goose chase," Ben said as he turned right onto Tulip Street, "but it's the only lead I can think of."

Number 422 was the third house on the left, and Ben swung into the narrow concrete driveway to turn around, then pulled up where a strip of flagstone path met the curb. They were in an old section of Springfield, walking distance from downtown, an area of middle-income respectability, where people kept their fifty-foot lawns neatly mowed and painted the trim on their frame houses themselves.

The DeLuccas' had been done that spring. Going up the walk Ben noticed how the white paint glistened in contrast to the pale yellow on the clapboards, though it too looked flawlessly fresh. A flight of five wooden steps led to a wide screened porch running across the front of the house, and when Ben pulled the door open he saw that it was furnished with a complete set of white-painted aluminum furniture with rainbow-striped vinyl-covered cushions. Beside the screened front door stood a white pot containing plastic flowers in tones of pink, green, and violet that exactly matched the cushions. The Crazy Cat must have had a good year.

Ben rang the doorbell; unnecessarily it turned out, for they could hear, over the sound of the dishwasher running in the kitchen, a man's firm tread approaching, and soon Joe DeLucca opened the screen door and stepped out onto the porch to join them.

He was a tall, DiMaggio type, whose narrow, impassive face did not change expression as he flicked a swift, measuring glance over his visitors.

"What can I do for you?" he asked.

"I'm Ben Porter." Ben held out his hand. "And this is Howard Keating."

With brisk nods the men shook hands, then Ben went on, "You may have heard of me from your cousin, Maria Lundy. She poses for me sometimes. I'm an artist." He paused, smiling. "I mean I'm a painter trying to be an artist."

"An important distinction," Howard put in. He too smiled at Joe DeLucca, but obviously the nightclub owner was getting a mistaken impression of their purpose.

"We don't go in for art at the Crazy Cat," he said. "If Maria gave you the idea I'd be interested."

"No, we're not here to sell you anything, Mr. De-Lucca." Ben was careful to avoid Howard's eyes. "I mentioned my acquaintance with Maria only to identify myself as a friend of hers—a long-standing friend, in fact. That is why Howard and I are here. We wondered if you could help us find her?"

"Find her? What are you talking about?"

Howard said, "Apparently Maria and Frank Lundy have gone away. Without telling anyone where. We are somewhat alarmed, you see, because of the investigation going on at the moment into the death of Gregory Dillon. I imagine you've heard about it."

"Sure I've heard about it, but what's the connection with Maria? She's entitled to go out of town if she wants to, like anyone else." Joe DeLucca peered suspiciously at Howard. "What are you getting at anyway?"

"May we sit down, Mr. DeLucca?" Ben said quietly. "This may take a little time, but please hear us out. We are not trying to pin anything on Maria. On the contrary, we are concerned about her safety."

He saw the faintest softening in the wary black eyes and an almost imperceptible relaxing of the stiff shoulders as their host led them to the sofa and chairs grouped in the center of the porch. They sat down and Joe DeLucca carefully adjusted his dark brown polyester trousers over his knees, then sat back and crossed his arms.

"Naturally I'm interested in Maria's safety," he said, "but if she's in some kind of danger—or you think she is—how come you don't go to the police?"

"The police know about it; in fact, we found out from them. They've been keeping an eye on the Lundys. I don't see any reason not to tell you that, because of course you must know that Maria was a good friend of Greg Dillon's.'' Ben braced himself for an outburst, but DeLucca merely raised his eyebrows thoughtfully.

"I'm puzzled about you two,'' he said. "About what you're after. Are you a couple of private detectives or what?''

Ben pulled out his wallet and extracted one of his business cards, which he handed to Joe DeLucca.

"I'm a publisher,'' he said, "and Howard is my lawyer and close friend. We've taken an interest in the case because we know the people involved and also because—I hesitate to tell you this because I'm afraid you'll get the wrong idea about my motives—the body was found on my premises; in my office, in fact, which is probably the reason I won't feel comfortable...''

"Or even safe.''

"You're right, Howard. I won't feel safe and neither will my wife, who works with me, until Greg Dillon's murderer has been caught.''

"You're on the spot, I see that.'' Again Joe DeLucca's cool measuring glance moved between his visitors. He sighed, then he said, "I warned Maria she was headed for big trouble, but she thought she had everything under control. Of course, with her looks...'' A faint, thin smile appeared on his face. "By the time she was twelve you knew she'd be trouble to somebody, someday. I told Frank that more than once.''

"Well, the point is, we thought you might have some idea where they might go.''

"So you could do what?''

"Find them. Make sure they're okay. Try to get them to come back.''

"It doesn't look good, does it? Skipping town when you're under suspicion.'' For a moment DeLucca's dark face was stern with disapproval, then he regretted his words. "Not that either Maria or Frank would be capable of killing, you understand. I can swear to that, having known Maria all my life and Frank for at least five years.''

"I'm inclined to agree with you about that, but you see, when they remove themselves from police scrutiny they're also removing themselves from police protection, and there is reason to believe that Greg's killer is not finished. His wife has received veiled threats..."

"Very veiled, Ben, you must admit."

"That's true. She may have imagined the whole thing. Still, if we could find Maria and persuade her to come back I would feel a lot better."

"I'm trying to think where they might go, and the problem is they never go anywhere. Puerto Rico on their honeymoon, I remember that, but that was four years ago, at least."

"More like three, I think."

"Okay, three. Since then they've stayed close to home, and if you want my opinion that's part of the problem. Maria gets bored, with no kids and Frank working all the time. A girl like her..." Joe shook his head gravely. "She needs some trips, some fun; that's why she sings in the club, which she also has no business doing. Frank's a smart guy, but he sure is dumb about that."

"He has a lot of company."

"Well, sure, women are tough to figure out." Joe glanced upward, where the thump of running feet indicated the presence of at least one small child. He leaned forward and said in a confidential tone, "My wife has the two kids, the house to take care of—not a dinky apartment—and I take her on two trips each and every year. We just got back from a week in Atlantic City. What a spot!"

"You're a good provider, Joe."

"What?" Pushing aside memories of boardwalks and casinos, Joe returned to the subject of Frank Lundy. "When I finally persuade Frank to take a break does he come up with anything like that? Hell no, he goes along on a fishing trip—the same bunch of us go to the Catskills every spring—and he doesn't know the first thing about fishing; doesn't even enjoy it. Then I guess he figures he's had his vacation, never mind Maria's."

"So he did go away that one time. Where do you stay? Do you camp out?"

"No, we stay at Grogan's Fishing Camp. Have for years. But I can't see Frank taking Maria there. It's strictly a man's place, nothing but fishing."

"Still, it might be worth a look, or a phone call. Can you tell me how to get there?"

Joe DeLucca hesitated; he studied the fingernails on his right hand while he tried to make up his mind. "I don't know if I should, but if you really think Maria might be in danger..." The sounds from upstairs, which now included two high, excited voices, seemed to propel him to his feet.

Saying, "I have the route marked on my New York road map; I'll get it out of the car." Joe DeLucca strode across the porch, pulled open the screen door, and started down the steps.

His visitors watched him go, then Ben glanced at his watch.

"It's too late to start up there tonight," he said, "especially with fresh tuna steaks for dinner. Marinated in lime juice and ginger." He slid back in his chair and stared up at the ceiling, recalling the ingredients. "And coriander. Then quickly grilled. You're coming to dinner, aren't you, Howard?"

"Well, Carrie asked me, but I was just there, you know, and..."

"I think you'd better. We have a lot to discuss—including who goes to the Catskills tomorrow, you or me."

"Or Carrie?"

"Not Carrie, emphatically not." Ben sat upright to make his point. "Please try to remember, Howard; woman's place is in the office."

EIGHTEEN

Monday, June 30 Morning

IN THE EARLY MORNING darkness Maria reached for Greg, and when his arms folded tenderly about her she felt as if her heart might burst with joy. In her sleep-muddled mind she knew it was strange that he was there in her bed, but it did not matter. The extraordinary happiness stayed with her while they made love with a gentle passion she had almost forgotten, then she fell asleep in his arms.

Hours later the aroma of hot coffee woke her again, and she opened her eyes to see Frank sitting in a chair, watching her. The room was dim; he had not opened the lined chintz draperies that shut out the light. She smiled at him drowsily, but instead of smiling in return or coming over to give her a kiss, he got up and pulled the curtains open, instantly flooding the room with sunlight.

"Hi," she said, "did you bring me some coffee too?"

He did not answer at once, but walked over to the bed carrying his coffee cup, then stood looking down at her wearing an expression she could not read. His face looked whiter than usual, the gray eyes were opaque, yet they seemed oddly brilliant, perhaps because of his concentration: He was staring at her as if he had been ordered to memorize every feature of her face.

She felt self-conscious lying there while he studied her, and she pushed herself up and shook her tangled hair back over her shoulders. Then she realized she was naked and, catching sight of her nightgown lying crumpled on the floor close beside the bed, she suddenly recalled her earlier waking, in the darkness.

For a fraction of a second she thought Frank must have caught her in bed with Greg; then reality took over. Her lover had been her husband, of course; she had only dreamed of Greg. But then why was Frank glowering at her? What had happened to his tender, loving mood? Had she—God forbid—murmured Greg's name in Frank's ear?

She said, "Excuse me," and reached past Frank's legs to pick up her nightgown. Pulling it on, she tried desperately to remember every detail of the predawn lovemaking, but her mind was fuzzy and she realized that she must have had too much to drink the night before. As if to confirm the diagnosis, her head began to ache piercingly. She had no recollection of coming to bed, or of having dinner. And there must be more she had forgotten or Frank would not be staring at her in that strange way.

Maria swung her legs out of the bed, but Frank did not step back. He stood so close that her knees brushed his trousers, and she had to tilt her head back to look into his face.

Cautiously she took his free hand and lightly shook it back and forth, saying, "Hey, did you bring me some coffee too?"

"I ought to throw this in your face."

She saw then that his hand was gripping the coffee mug so tightly that the knuckles were white and that his whole arm was trembling, almost uncontrollably, it appeared. Maria sank back and seized a pillow for protection, but she saw at once that Frank was as horrified by his behavior as she was.

He swung away from the bed, nearly staggering in his haste, and shakily placed the mug on top of the TV set. Then he leaned against the set while he drew a handkerchief out of his trouser pocket and mopped the perspiration from his pale face.

Without looking at her, he said stiffly, "I haven't hit you yet and I hope I never do, but by God, that was a close one."

"But why, Frank? What are you so angry about? I thought..."

"You thought you could get away with it, right? Act like a whore right under my nose. Oh, Frank won't care;

Frank's used to it—is that the way you think? Frank put up with Greg Dillon, he'll let me do what I want."

He had turned to face her again, fixing her with the slaty glare she had met when she opened her eyes a few moments earlier, only now he was panting harshly and gripping the corner of the television set as if it were a life-line.

"I don't know what you're talking about, Frank, but I hope you're not going to rake up all that business about Greg. I thought we had agreed to put it behind us. That's the only way..."

"You think you can do whatever you like as long as you say you're sorry, am I right? That seems to be the pattern."

He suddenly pushed himself away with such force that the TV set rocked back and bumped the wall. He strode to the bed, his hands clenched into fists at his sides and, bending forward until his face was on a level with Maria's, he began firing words at her.

"I've been a horse's ass all this time, but last night I got the message and I got it good. There's no trusting you, not even when I'm in the same room. Any guy who makes a play can get you—even a bunch of shoe clerks like last night. Even they looked good to you, and you couldn't be bothered to hide it. I had to practically drag you out of that restaurant. If you hadn't passed out I wouldn't have dared go to sleep—you would have slipped out and gone after them."

He stopped, out of breath, and when he saw that her face had turned white and her eyes were wide with shock, his thin lips curved in a trembling smile.

Maria's lips too were shaking as she said, "Frank, I can't believe this. Please tell me what I did. I don't remember anything awful."

"Of course not, you were drunk. A drunken nymphomaniac, that's what I've got for a wife. Great. I'm real proud."

"I must have had too much, I agree, but surely I didn't do anything so terrible. Those men were perfectly nice, but

I wasn't interested in them, Frank; I was just being polite.''

"Polite! That's a new name for it. You were like a bitch
in heat.''

"Frank!"

Again he looked faintly pleased by her reaction. "Am I
getting through to you—finally? I've been the world's
biggest sucker, that's clear, trying to understand, trying to
forgive, when what you needed all along was a swift kick
in the teeth.''

He drew himself up sanctimoniously. "But I'm not that
kind, and you know it. In fact, I see now you've been taking advantage of the fact that I'm too much of a gentle-
man to knock you around. Well, don't count on it any
longer, Maria, do you hear what I'm saying?''

"Frank, I think you need help, I really do.'' She was on
her knees on the bed clutching a corner of the sheet in her
clenched hands. "Dear, why don't you call that doctor
you've been seeing, that psychologist you told me about?
He could help you, I know he could.''

Frank laughed, an explosive, humorless bark. "I've
been listening to that bum long enough. We're going to
start doing things my way and see what kind of results we
get. For starters, you're not leaving this cabin. Not till I
figure what to do with you; I don't care how long it takes.''

"Come on, Frank, you can't lock me up in here. You
wouldn't.''

"Can't I? You think not? Well, here's the key to the
room, see it?'' He held up the key on its black plastic tag
marked with a fluorescent number 12. "This is *my* key,
Maria, and this one would have been yours.'' He dangled
the second room key before her eyes. "But guess what?
You don't have one. And I can lock the door from the
outside when I go out, which will be soon.''

Seeing her glance frantically at the chintz-curtained
window, he walked over to it and, as if he were proud of
his workmanship, pointed to the metal lock. "While you
were sleeping off the booze I had plenty of time to jam this
up so you'll never budge it. Anyway, you'd be taking a hell

of a chance because I'm not going very far. I'll have my eye on this place every minute, and—something you didn't know—I've got a gun. I don't want to use it, but, as you may have noticed, I'm very, very upset.''

"Frank, I don't believe this..."

"Make yourself comfortable, that's what I suggest, and maybe after breakfast I'll feel better. I hope so, I really do.''

He strode to the door, opened it and stepped out. She heard the key turn in the lock, then the crunch of his footsteps on the gravel road.

WALKING DOWN THE HILL to the restaurant, Frank Lundy was too preoccupied to notice the beauty of his surroundings. Under a flawless blue sky everything was in motion: The leaves on their nodding branches danced in the sun like glinting coins, and the wheat carpeting the nearby slopes shimmered silkily in the playful breeze. Even the wet blades of grass that Frank's feet trampled sprang lustily upright again when he passed.

Nearing the restaurant building, Frank might have sniffed the fresh scent of new lumber mingled with the aroma of bacon cooking; but he had not noticed that earlier when he came for coffee, and he did not notice it now, at nine o'clock.

All he could think about was the big question: Should he or should he not really buy a gun? He'd said it, now he might as well do it. But the idea scared him silly. What if he actually hurt Maria? The thought set him trembling uncontrollably; he'd have to deal with it later, after he had something to eat. He wasn't hungry, but he'd better eat because of the shaking, and he supposed he should get something for Maria. Not that he gave a damn, but he couldn't let her starve to death. Or he didn't think he could.

He pushed open the screen door and went in, and was at once relieved to see that at breakfast the place looked very different from the nightmare scene he remembered. No sign of the smartass drunks who had been practically slobbering over Maria, or of that know-it-all bartender, who was apparently the proprietor. He probably thought Frank was the world's greatest wimp; in fact, he'd probably told the rest of the staff the whole story: how he sat there with a sickly smile on his face, watching, not doing a damn thing, while his wife acted like a tramp with three total strangers.

At the nearest table set for four Frank pulled out a chair, glancing defiantly around the room. If anyone thought he was ashamed to show his face that morning they just happened to be dead wrong.

But only one table was occupied, and that by a gray-haired professional type who was engrossed in a crossword puzzle he was doing in what looked like the magazine section of Sunday's *New York Times*. He must have brought it with him, Frank figured as he sat down; he hadn't seen any newspapers for sale when he had registered in the main house the night before. They did have a pay telephone, he had noticed that, though it wasn't important, since there were phones in all the rooms. Recalling what he had done with the one in cottage number 12, he smiled, then stifled it when he saw the waitress approaching his table.

She was a pretty young thing, about seventeen, he guessed, with curly red hair and a sassy shape which her skintight jeans emphasized. The proprietor's daughter? He imagined so, because what other cute young girl would be working here at this hour? Also, she asked for his order with the same kind of cocky grin he'd seen on the bartender. They were related all right.

He ordered fried eggs, bacon, whole wheat toast, black coffee; then, with a little chuckle, asked if it might be possible to get something to take to the cottage.

"My wife is sleeping in this morning," he said, fixing an indulgent smile on his face. "Her beauty sleep, she calls it—not that she needs it."

The girl nodded understandingly while he peered at her closely to see if she had already heard about his wife's beauty. Her dad could have told her earlier that morning about their lovely new guest and her gutless husband.

"What would you like to take her?" the girl was asking. "Some fruit, maybe? And a sweet roll? Then it won't matter if she doesn't wake up for a while."

"Good thinking. What did you say your name was?" Frank was grinning too hard, he could feel it.

"Ginny. Ginny Grogan." She was smiling expectantly, as if it should be some kind of a thrill to discover you had a genuine member of the Grogan family waiting on you.

"Well, say, this is a great place your family runs." Frank sounded fatuous, even to himself, and he saw the crossword puzzler glance up with a half-smile, then quickly look away. "How about that coffee, Ginny," Frank went on, careful to lower his voice.

"Yes sir, I'll get it right away. I just brewed a fresh pot."

Again he sensed the inference that she was doing him a big favor. Boy, these farmers thought they were hot stuff, deigning to share their bounty with a poor city slicker. When, if they only knew the complexity of the people they were dealing with...

Frank felt himself smiling again; then he made his face solemn, mindful of the crossword puzzler, who he knew had been covertly watching him ever since he came in. He sat frowning, in fact, at the place mat, which had a scrawly green design on a white background. He wondered if he could get a look at the date on that fellow's Sunday *Times Magazine*. Frank would bet it was weeks old; he had probably done the puzzle over and over, using it as a cover while he watched.

Ginny brought his coffee in a white mug that had the same green design on it as the paper place mat. He would have asked for a cup and saucer, but he didn't want to while that man was there; coffee took forever to cool down in a mug.

When had he told Maria about Garvin Thorpe?

Frank sat back, holding his coffee mug, frowning into it now instead of at the place mat. Searching way back, he did remember telling the Doc—as he always thought of him, never mind how chummy he tried to get—that he would level with Maria about him; but he couldn't recall actually doing so.

He wondered if Thorpe had been trying to reach him. It seemed likely that he would, at least if he were as concerned about him as he professed to be. On the other hand, in their last conversation Frank had made it pretty clear that he was fed up. He straightened in his chair, feeling good as he remembered. Thorpe could tell the police anything he liked. They would spot him as a nut, just as Frank finally had.

His eggs arrived, cooked the way he liked them, quickly turned over so they were firm but still tender; the bacon was crisp and dry, the toast crunchy. A perfect breakfast. He gave Ginny a big smile when she cleared away his plate.

"That was great," he said. "Now if you'll tell me where I can buy a morning paper..."

While Ginny was giving him directions to the village of Banister, five miles to the east, Frank saw the "professor" fold his magazine section and get to his feet. He searched his pocket for change, left a tip on the table, then walked out, giving Frank a nod as he passed his table.

Frank, pretending to be listening closely to Ginny's instructions, was actually stifling a wave of merriment. His lips twitched as he thought of the skinny, gray-haired guy jumping into his car and speeding to the news store in Banister. You must be new at this job—the words sang in Frank's head—because any ten-year-old would be too smart to go to Banister now.

Of course if he did he could buy a gun. All the more reason to put off any trip to Banister until he was sure, really certain, he could handle it.

Ginny had placed a white cardboard box on the table for Frank to take to Maria. He asked for a cup of coffee, which Ginny brought in a Styrofoam cup with a lid, then, promising to see her again at lunchtime, he took the box and the cup and started back to the cottage.

He had gone perhaps twenty paces beyond the main house, which stood across the lawn from the restaurant, when he stopped and looked back at the comfortable frame building. The wide veranda with its row of pine rocking chairs seemed to beckon to him. Wouldn't it be great to spend the morning sitting there, just rocking and chewing the fat with anybody who happened along?

The pay telephone was just inside the door, he remembered, in a booth for privacy. He could place a call to Garvin Thorpe and if the doctor wasn't in he could just sit there and try it again. Maybe leave the number? Not the one in the booth, because someone might come to the cottage to get him, even though he had told them Maria was resting and didn't want to be disturbed. He would have to give the situation more thought.

As Frank turned and once more headed for cottage number 12 at the edge of the woods he was almost overcome by another surge of gleefulness. That "professor" fellow must be halfway to Banister by now. How satisfying it was to think of him wasting the whole morning hanging around the news store. Better yet, there might be two news stores and he'd be running back and forth. Frank came close to chuckling out loud at the thought of it.

When he reached the door of the cottage he stopped to listen. It was totally quiet; Maria must have gone back to sleep. He frowned at the box in his hand. He couldn't starve her, but if she gained energy from the food she might get obstreperous and start screaming for help. Quick as a flash he thought of the answer to that: Garvin Thorpe had prescribed sleeping capsules for him, and he had had the foresight to take them out of his toilet kit before locking Maria in—just in case she got suicidal.

Hoping she hadn't heard his approach, he tiptoed around to the tree-sheltered side of the cottage, pulled a pill bottle out of his pocket and emptied the contents of one capsule into Maria's coffee. Then he returned to the front and inserted his key in the lock.

The next time he bought coffee for her he would order decaffeinated.

NINETEEN

BEN PORTER PARKED his Mustang in front of the Mountain View Motel, then carefully folded the road map with Joe DeLucca's notations and tucked it into the glove compartment. If by some wild coincidence Frank or Maria Lundy should happen along he wouldn't want the evidence that Joe had directed him here lying on the front seat. Without it he could undoubtedly invent some plausible reason for visiting Banister that wouldn't involve them.

The reason would be fishing, he saw that the minute he stepped into the lobby of the simple one-story building. Instead of being painted red like the outside, the interior walls were of unfinished wood and hung with photographs of smiling fishermen displaying their catches, all of trout, either one or two large rainbows or six or eight small browns strung together.

The room clerk obviously functioned as fishing adviser and tackle salesman as well. The guest register occupied only a small area on the top of a glass case filled with boxes of flies, leaders in their plastic envelopes, spools of line, and a selection of snippers, tweezers, and other implements necessary for fly fishing, a sport very different from the spin fishing to which Ben was accustomed.

No one was around, so he hit the bell that weighted down the open pages of the guest register, then stood staring at the date printed in heavy black letters: Monday, June 30. The day was significant to him for some reason; he couldn't think why.

Giving up on it, Ben ambled into the room that opened off the lobby, where more fishing paraphernalia was displayed: rods and reels, nets, creels, and a variety of boots, hats, fishing vests, and waterproof trousers. The walls were hung with colored prints of fishermen standing in sparkling streams, their fishing rods arced by the weight of freshly hooked trout. Ben pictured himself wading in a sun-dappled brook, imagined the sudden sharp tug of a fish taking the fly he had cast to it with such skill, such precision... Smiling to himself, he selected a slender graphite rod from the rack. He balanced it in his hand, then tried a tentative cast just as a stooped, grizzle-haired man appeared in the doorway.

"Nice, isn't it?" he said, grinning approvingly at Ben's choice.

Ben nodded. He had indeed been impressed by the rod's light weight and springy flexibility. "What do you get for one of these?" he asked.

"That one..." The man approached slowly, supporting himself on a knobby malacca cane. With long, gnarled fingers he fumbled at the price tag attached to the rod, then announced, "This one's two-fifty. Of course, you picked my top rod. You can do a lot better."

"I hope so." Ben grinned. "I'm new at fly fishing. Never tried it, in fact, but I've always wanted to and this looks like a golden opportunity."

"Well then, you don't want to buy a lot of fancy equipment. Wait'll you get hooked." Cocking his head, the man, the proprietor of the place, apparently, smiled cozily at Ben, his bright blue eyes twinkling at his own joke. "I can fix you up with rentals if you're just experimenting; all but the line and the flies, of course."

"And I'll need a lot of good advice."

"No problem about that." Again the blue eyes twinkled. "Most anybody you see around here will be glad to give you a hand. Of course you won't find any two of them agreeing on anything."

Ben laughed. Then he said, "I've never seen one of these before. It's for bug protection, I suppose." He had taken a khaki hat from the shelf and was intrigued by the circle

of dark green netting that fell from the brim when he unsnapped it.

The proprietor reached for the hat and popped it onto
his head. The netting, weighted by a rim of fabric, fell to
his shoulders, completely obscuring his face and neck.

"They used to come in handy, but with the sprays we've
got nobody wants them any more. This is the last one I
have, and I'm not ordering anymore."

"I'll take it."

The subject of a disguise had come up the evening before, but had been quickly dismissed as unnecessarily
melodramatic. "You are *not* to get that close," Carrie had
ordered. The hat, however, was too good to pass up and if
never used for anything else would be perfect for a cos-
tume party.

The proprietor was frowning. "I hate to see you load
yourself up with stuff you don't need. I have to charge
$8.95 for that hat, even on sale."

"I know it's frivolous, but I just can't live without that
hat," Ben replied. "Now let's get serious about this. First
of all, do you have a vacancy?"

AN HOUR LATER, when Ben made his way down a narrow
corridor to his room, he was carrying not only his suitcase
but a pair of waterproof waders, a rod, net, and creel; and
his new friend was stumping along behind him with boxes
of flies, a can of insect repellent, and a paperback book on
fly fishing.

Ben unlocked the door, and the two men edged their way
into the room and dropped their burdens on the bed.

"Nice," Ben said, looking around the room, which appeared to have everything he needed. He switched on the
reading lamp attached to the headboard of one of the twin
beds, nodded approvingly, then glanced into the tiny refrigerator that stood in one corner.

"That's a new wrinkle," the proprietor said proudly.
"Just installed this morning." He hobbled over to show
Ben the paper and pencil attached to the machine with a

small chain. "You just write down what you use and turn it in when you leave. Honor system."

"How about joining me in a drink right now?" Ben suggested. "It's been a long, dry day."

"Well..." After a moment's hesitation the cane was shifted from right hand to left, the right extended for a handshake. "Bolton's the name, Tom Bolton. Don't mind if I do."

"Ben Porter." The two men shook hands, then Ben gestured to the room's one upholstered chair, a maple-armed model with orange and brown daisies printed on its cretonne cushions. "Make yourself comfortable, Tom. What will it be? Scotch?"

"That's fine, but I'll have to make it a quick one." He tapped his watch. "It's five-thirty. The fishermen will be coming in and they usually need some equipment."

"How about dinner? Do you serve meals?"

"Just breakfast. And we pack box lunches to take out. Dinner you get down the road at Mike's or one of the places here in Banister." Ben handed him his drink, and Tom said, "Cheers," then drank it down in one long, slow swallow.

He wiped his knuckles across his mouth, then set the glass on the refrigerator, saying, "Thanks, I needed that."

"Thank you for your help with the gear." Ben followed him to the door and held it open. "I suppose early morning's the best time, right?"

"Sure, the earlier the better. Then you want to come in for a while at midday when it warms up. Go back out late in the afternoon; that's when they bite."

Tom Bolton started down the corridor, then paused and turned to say, "Don't forget to sign the register when you go out, okay? We never got to it."

"I'll do that," Ben said. "See you shortly."

He stayed in the doorway watching the proprietor make his halting way to the lobby and thinking again about the date on the open page of the guest register. Monday, June 30.

He went back into the room and closed the door. He planned to call Carrie to tell her where he was; maybe she would remember. With his hand on the telephone it struck him.

The repair-ready postcard he had retrieved from Greg Dillon's mailbox. Monday, June 30, was the day Sullivan's Electronics opened up following their vacation. He would ask Carrie to go over there first thing on Tuesday. If she didn't immediately claim the appliance Greg had sent to be fixed someone else just might notice that it was missing, and that would never do—not if the "appliance" turned out to be what Ben devoutly hoped it was.

With a sudden sense of urgency, he dialed his home number.

IT WAS LATE AFTERNOON before Frank Lundy finally made up his mind to call Garvin Thorpe. By then he had spent several hours sitting on the porch of the main house, and had noticed that he could not overhear anything that was being said in the phone booth just inside the door unless its door was left ajar.

Still, the stuff he talked to the doctor about was extremely private, and after he had dialed Thorpe's number Frank peered uneasily through the glass door, hoping no one would come around while he was talking. When, after four rings, the answering device clicked on, inviting him to leave a message, Frank nearly gasped with relief. He hung up quickly, thinking, the hell with it; he couldn't go through that kind of agony again, no matter how much he needed help.

He needed help? The words hadn't sounded in his brain until that moment, but suddenly he knew it was true. And he must want to be helped pretty badly to stand sweating in that phone booth waiting to hear the voice that had become so important to him.

He pushed the glass door open and walked out to the porch. He was too keyed up to sit down again in one of the rockers, so he paced up and down the wide wooden floor, wondering why he had not left a message for Thorpe to call

him. Well, of course he could not sit there twenty-four
hours a day, and what if Thorpe returned the call and told
somebody he was his doctor? Wouldn't take long to figure out what kind of doctor, when there he was at a fishing camp, obviously in good health, physically.

So he would have to leave the number of the phone in his
cottage, and hope Maria would continue sleeping the way
she had for most of the day—thanks to Dr. Thorpe's magic
capsules. Each time he went to the cottage he would get the
telephone from the trunk of his car, then return it when he
left to get meals. But he couldn't be seen toting the instrument around; he would carry it in . . . what?

His head had begun to ache, and as he tried to think he
felt his face grow damp with perspiration once more. This
was some strain he was under; he needed to talk to Dr.
Thorpe soon. Should he tell Thorpe he was thinking of
buying a gun? Well, no, better not; he'd just get the doctor stirred up over nothing. On the other hand, if he decided to do it he didn't want any interference.

He went back to the telephone problem. He could carry
it in a fishing creel or a knapsack. But even the real fishermen didn't have those things with them all the time. He
could be reading a book. He remembered reading stories
where people hollowed out books in order to conceal guns,
but he would need a very large book for a telephone.

Suddenly a picture sprang into his mind of that phony
professor with his crossword puzzle. That was the ticket!
It took some people days to do the Sunday *Times* crossword; if the news store had one left he could roll the magazine section around the phone easily—at least until he
thought of some other place to keep the instrument when
he had to be out, some spot nearer the cottage.

Heading for the car in order to drive to Banister and buy
a newspaper, only a newspaper, Frank felt his spirits lift.
There might be a way out of this dilemma yet.

IN THE DIM ROOM Maria Lundy tried to open her eyes. It
was very difficult, she could not imagine why. Her lids felt
as if they had weights holding them down. Fuzzily she

thought about touching them to find out, but that was too much trouble.

She dozed again, and the next time she woke she sensed a change—not in her leaden condition, but in the room. She thought about trying to open her eyes, or maybe move one hand, but some wariness kept her still. Then she heard Frank's voice. He was talking on the telephone. Its ringing must have awakened her.

He was saying, "That's all right. I've changed my mind. I'll come in to the office when I get back."

There was a pause, then he said, "I didn't know that."

Another pause, briefer, then, "No, of course I'm not frightened of anything. I just wanted a little advice, but never mind..."

Maria held her breath, straining to catch every nuance of his voice in hopes that she could discover who he was talking to.

He said, "I suppose she has, but we can't go on like this. You've got to help me decide what to do."

A silence, then, "I must be. This morning, for the first time ever, I came close to hitting her."

After the next pause he gave a sharp, humorless chuckle. "She's under control right now, and I plan to keep her that way."

There was a longer pause, and when Frank spoke his voice was full of doubt.

"I don't think Maria would hurt me. I never..."

After a brief silence he said, still sounding dubious, "A psychopath? You really think so?"

When he next spoke the doubt had been replaced by anger. "Is *that* what's going on? By God, it's a good thing I called you."

His next words were, "You mean there's more that I don't know? Well, tell me, for God's sake."

Maria heard real anguish in his voice as he pleaded, after another pause, "No, don't hang up. Tell me..."

But in a moment the telephone was slowly replaced, and the room was silent except for the sound of Frank's labored breathing.

TWENTY

Tuesday, July 1 Morning

AFTER STUDYING the small area map Tom Bolton had given him Ben Porter decided to set out on a stretch of the river about a mile south of Grogan's Fishing Camp. The streams were owned by the state and could be fished by anyone with a license, so there was no problem about trespassing. However, Ben wanted a spot that offered concealment, as well as being within easy walking distance of Grogan's, and after he pulled off the road—wincing as thick branches scraped his car—he climbed out and walked back to the pavement to check whether the license plate could be seen from there.

Finding that the blue and white marker was completely hidden by the foliage, Ben strode back to get his gear. Frank Lundy, if he happened along, might see the car, but would have no reason to connect it with a possible pursuer, however paranoid his frame of mind.

Ben took off his loafers and pulled on the rubber wading boots, fastening the straps through his belt, as Tom had instructed. He put on the fishing vest, placing his boxes of flies and his map in the pockets, slung the light canvas creel over his shoulder, and carefully drew the slender fly rod from the car. Tom had threaded the line through the guides, then had tied on a fly and shown Ben how to replace it when he needed to. He had also given him a rudimentary casting lesson, and Ben had felt chagrined at his own clumsiness in handling the heavy fly line.

"It's different, ain't it?" Tom had taken the rod to demonstrate the technique that would send the line out far and accurately. "You're throwing line now," he said, "not a heavy plug like you do with spinning gear. You'll get the knack if you keep practicing.''

Feeling like an astronaut in the heavy boots, Ben made his way to the edge of the river and peered dubiously at the swirling eddies and small, rushing cascades created by its rocky bed. The water looked very deep, and he was pleasantly surprised when he stepped in to find that it reached only eight or nine inches above his ankles.

He waded out to the center, and made his first tentative cast, which looked nothing at all like Tom Bolton's. For an hour he practiced, gradually gaining the feel of it and the timing needed to shoot the line to a chosen target. Then he hooked his back cast on a high tree branch, and after carefully retrieving the fly began moving upstream in the direction of Grogan's Camp.

An hour later Ben was thoroughly enjoying his new sport, though he had seen no sign of a fish. He felt as carefree as a child as he waded through the sparkling water, stopping frequently to cast, and now and then actually placing the fly where he meant to. He figured he had reached the vicinity of Grogan's Camp, however; so he reeled in his line, made his way to the riverbank, and clambered up the slope to the road.

There he faced a rolling wheat field that stretched as far as he could see. He fished the map out of his pocket, and, after locating himself as best he could, turned to the right and began trudging along the road. An instant later he heard a car approaching, and quickly stepped into the shadows to watch it pass. It was a black pickup truck with a pretty, red-haired girl at the wheel, and Ben was delighted to make out the words Grogan's Fishing Camp lettered on the door of the cab.

He started out once more and soon rounded a curve in the road from where he could see a cluster of farmhouses and a row of cabins climbing the hill behind them. A cloud of dust marked the progress of the pickup truck, which had disappeared between the buildings.

Ben looked at his watch. It was only eleven o'clock, too early for lunch, but he would think of some excuse for visiting Grogan's. Feeling a little foolish, he took off his hat to make sure he knew how to release the netting so that it would fall down to cover his face. If he saw either of the Lundys he would have to move quickly.

A SUDDEN SHARP SOUND WOKE Frank Lundy, and he sat up alertly in his chair and peered over at the bed, but Maria was still sleeping, or so it appeared. He got to his feet and walked quietly to the window to look out through a gap in the curtains. The tray of piled-up dishes had been taken away from beside the door; the noise of it must have wakened him.

He had been careless, dozing off like that when it was so near time to give Maria another capsule. He consulted his watch and saw that he had another half-hour. Then he looked down at the telephone on the floor beside the chair, willing it to ring.

He had left a message at least two hours earlier. Suppose it hadn't gone through for some reason; what would he do?

Maria stirred, moaning faintly, and he tiptoed to the bed and stared down at her. God, she was beautiful, even now, without makeup and with her hair in a tangle on the pillow. The paleness of her skin and the faint blue shadowing around her eyes and in the hollows of her cheeks brought out the incredible symmetry of her face. She looked noble and pure, as if she were possessed of saintly wisdom. He wished he could talk to her, ask her what to do. He missed her. He had never felt so alone.

Frank felt tears pricking at his eyelids. He couldn't stand any more of this, no man could. He would wake her up and take his chances.

He was reaching out to grasp her shoulder when the shrill ring of the telephone pierced the silence, making him tremble violently.

He plunged across the room and snatched up the phone. "Why the hell did it take you so long," he whispered into it hoarsely.

The pause that followed was brief; then Frank said, "The rest of them can wait. This is an emergency."

His next words were apparently in reply to a question. "No, but something may happen any minute. I think I'm going crazy."

A silence, then, "I have been patient, haven't I? Damned patient."

When he spoke after the next silence it was in a tone of dawning comprehension.

"You're saying I've overdone it, is that it? You think I've given her the impression that I'm too weak to make her stay in line."

Listening to the answer, Frank nodded in agreement. "I do feel stronger—I don't see how you know that."

Still slowly nodding his head, he said after the next pause, "I can do anything I want to."

Then, "That's right. And one way or another I'm going to get that across to her."

Without waiting for any comment Frank replaced the telephone and turned to gaze at the motionless figure of his wife.

His head felt fuzzy. There was a throbbing in his temples. He tried to reconstruct the conversation, but all that came through was one word: *weak*.

He wouldn't look weak with a gun in his hand. His lips twitched as he pictured Maria's face when she saw it. She'd know then that he meant business.

Suddenly he couldn't wait to hit the road to Banister just one more time.

"IT'S KIND OF embarrassing to run out of flies before lunch, I suppose, but I'm new at this."

In the front room of the main house Ben was talking to George Grogan, the eldest of Ed's boys and the one he was training to some day take over the management of the business.

Although he could not imagine the state of being new at fly fishing, George smiled understandingly and began taking trays of flies out of the glass case so Ben could examine them. Then, watching his new customer select the largest and gaudiest of the feathery lures, George spoke up.

"If you don't mind, sir, I'd like to recommend a few they're more likely to take." He grinned at Ben. He seemed like a guy who wouldn't mind a little advice, unlike some of the pompous world travelers they got in there.

"By all means. I'd appreciate that." After glancing quickly around the room, Ben pulled off his hat and ran his fingers through his tousled brown hair. "I suppose I was picking the ones that looked good to me, not the fish."

"That's natural, I guess. Trouble is, it doesn't catch fish." With a surprisingly delicate touch for a big man, George was picking out the tiniest of the flies, some no more impressive than a piece of lint one might brush off a lapel.

"You think I'll be able to tie those on?" Ben asked doubtfully. "I can hardly see them."

George laughed. "We'll have some instruction on that." He tossed his head in the direction of the front door. "Here comes the expert now, my dad. He'll give you a lesson."

The screen door banged shut and Ben turned to see a tall, ruddy-faced man in well-worn jeans ambling up to him. He held out his hand in greeting.

"Hi, I'm Ben Porter," he said. "Your son is giving me some badly needed assistance."

Grogan shook hands, his palm as hard as a hoof against Ben's. "George knows all the tricks," he said. "You staying with us?"

Ben shook his head. "No, I'm in Banister at the Mountain View. You probably know Tom Bolton."

"Known Tom all my life. How's his arthritis these days?" As he spoke Ed Grogan moved behind the glass case and swiveled the open guest register around to face him. He bent over the open pages, frowning as he ran his finger down the list of names and addresses.

George, meanwhile, was counting the flies he had selected and placing them in small plastic boxes for Ben to take with him.

"That's $14.89, plus tax." He pulled out a chart, fig-ured the total on a scrap of paper, and shoved it across the counter.

Ben dug out his wallet. "Kind of an expensive sport, isn't it?" he said, and saw George smile, though his fa-ther seemed too engrossed in his perusal of the register to have heard him.

"You know what they say. 'God doesn't count the time you spend fishing.' So I guess it's worth it." George handed Ben's change across the counter. Then he turned to his father.

"I told Mr. Porter you were the guy who could teach him to tie on those little flies. How about it?"

"Sure. Glad to. Let's go outside where the light's bet-ter." But it was clear that Ed Grogan had other things on his mind.

The two men walked out to the porch, then down the steps to the wide lawn that separated the main house from the restaurant.

Four or five cars were parked on the gravel drive that served both buildings and, as he had on the way in, Ben swiftly surveyed the lineup searching for Maria Lundy's blue convertible.

"Is that your only parking area, Mr. Grogan?" he asked.

The question seemed to annoy Ed Grogan. "No, natu-rally we have a road running directly to the cottages. For unloading. And each cottage has a parking space right be-side it."

Ben turned to study the hillside behind them, and Ed Grogan followed his gaze.

"Of course they're most all out fishing this time of day," he said. "All but..." He stopped, and Ben saw that Grogan too had noticed the rear of a dark blue car pro-truding from a space slightly behind the last cottage, the one closest to the woods.

Ben said easily, "Well, it's almost noon, and I under-stand midday isn't the best time for fishing."

"True enough, but that guy hasn't been near the stream since he got here. Unless he goes in the middle of the night, in which case he knows something the rest of us don't."

Ed's brow was furrowed with perplexity; he could not seem to wrench his eyes away from that one cottage.

"You must get some people who don't fish, just want a vacation in the country."

The idea of not fishing appeared to confound Ed. "There isn't another blessed thing to do around here, you can see that. Why do you think I haven't put in a pool or anything? This is a fishing camp, Mr. Porter, and usually booked solid. Those people, the Lundys, just happened to come when I had a cancellation."

"And you haven't seen them since their arrival?"

"Oh, I've seen him. He comes down to the restaurant for meals, and usually he takes something up to the cottage for his wife. Told me she's under the weather, but she sure looked good when they got here."

"Maybe they're honeymooners." Ben suggested with a smile.

Now he had Grogan's attention. "That could be the answer," he said, sounding eager to believe it. "She is the most gorgeous woman I ever saw. Black hair, you know? And built. And a face like . . . well, she ought to be in the movies. Makes most of them look like dogs." He paused. "I didn't get the idea they were newlyweds, though."

"Maybe they're not wed at all, did you think of that? They may be pressed for time."

But Grogan was shaking his head, and frowning again. "I'll tell you why I think they've been married a while. They came in two nights ago around dinner time—which isn't much of a deal around here on Sunday night—so they were having some drinks, figuring what to do, when one of the other guys in the bar tried to get cozy. I wouldn't say he exactly made a pass at this guy's wife, but he was sort of fresh, you know? And she got a little bombed—enough so she seemed to enjoy having this guy make a play for her. And the husband got sore."

"Oh? You're right, that doesn't sound like honeymoon behavior. Ideally, that is."

Grogan gave a snort. "'Ideally,' I like that. Well, the upshot was, the husband finally ordered some food, thinking it would sober her up, I guess; but then they had another drink and that did it. He starts giving her hell, but she couldn't care less. She goes right on laughing and joking with the guys at the other table—there were three of them in all—and I could see there was going to be trouble. So I went out to the kitchen to hurry up their dinner—though Molly was already burned up about having to cook on Sunday night—and when I got back he was pulling her out the door."

"He got rough, did he?"

"Not really, or I'd have stepped in, of course. I won't stand for that stuff in my place—restaurant or cabins—if I know about it."

"You can't always know, though, can you? It's quite a responsibility."

"You're damn right it is." Grogan turned to look at the cottage on the hill again, this time glaring angrily. He hitched up his jeans restlessly, as if he were preparing to spring into action; then he almost snatched the rod Ben was holding and said, "Well, let's get that fly tied on."

Ben watched as Ed Grogan tied the tiny fly to the cob-web-thin leader his son had added to the end of his line.

"I don't know how you do that," he marveled. "I can't even see that fine line."

"Hold it up against something dark, like those bushes."

Grogan turned once more, and immediately became distracted by some activity going on at the farthest cottage. "There. He just came out; did you see him?"

Ben nodded. "Yes. He seems to be getting into his car. Listen, Ed, I'd better get back to the river. Thanks a lot for your help."

While he spoke he unsnapped the mosquito netting that rimmed his hat, allowing it to fall and obscure his face. Ignoring Ed Grogan's astonishment, he gave a friendly wave of his hand and began hurrying across the lawn toward the gravel driveway, keeping close to the hedge so he would not be conspicuous.

He was standing in the shadows a few feet from the drive when Maria Lundy's old blue Plymouth convertible came down the hill with her husband, Frank, at the wheel. As the car approached Ben stepped farther back among the branches; but this was an unnecessary move as it turned out.

For Frank Lundy was grimly peering straight ahead, and he did not shift his gaze until he reached the main road and swung the car to the right, in the direction of Banister.

TWENTY-ONE

Tuesday, July 1 Afternoon

VINCE MUZZIO PRESSED the Dillons' doorbell and heard the sound of chimes coming from the back of the house. Through the screen door he could see that the wide center hall extended to the back, where another screen door opened onto the terrace. He liked that; he filed the idea in his head against the day he and Celeste might start building on the lot they had bought at the edge of town.

A figure came hurrying down the staircase that led to the second floor and in a moment Jenny Dillon was opening the door for him, looking, he saw, as distraught as she had sounded on the phone.

She managed a quick, anxious smile as she invited him in, then peered cautiously up and down the walk before closing the door and latching it securely. After that she stood hesitating in the hall as if she could not remember why he had come.

Muzzio said, "Shall we sit down somewhere, Mrs. Dillon, so you can tell me what the trouble is?"

"Yes, of course. I have it right in here, in the den. The letter, I mean."

The anxious smile flickered again as she started for a room off the hall to the right, and Muzzio felt suddenly compassionate.

He said, to distract her, "I like the way your house is laid out. It's nice and cool, isn't it?"

"Oh yes, it is." They were in the den by now, a square room with pine-paneled walls, and she glanced around as if surprised to see how attractive it was. "Yes, it's very..."

She hurried to the desk that stood before a high, chintz-draperied window and opened the center drawer to take out a rumpled sheet of paper that she thrust toward Muzzio.

"I told you that picture of Cabby was stolen, not lost. Now I guess you'll believe me."

A pencil drawing of a child filled two-thirds of the page, and it was obvious that it had been copied from a photograph. The angle of the head and the precise outlining of hair, shirt collar, and shoulders could only have been traced, for the inner detailing of the features was crude and unskilled.

As if to verify the source, the child's striped shirt and the digital watch on one wrist had been depicted with exaggerated care. To Muzzio the primitive rendering of the face was, in comparison, quite horrifying.

The message printed in black ink at the top of the page carried its own horror: "No bodyguard can protect Gregory Dillon's son from his heritage of evil."

Vince Muzzio saw that Jenny Dillon's lips were moving as she silently spelled out the words. He felt her sway against him, and he placed a steadying hand on her arm.

"Let's sit down, Mrs. Dillon," he said quietly, and keeping a firm grip of her arm he led her to the nearest chair.

"What does it mean?" she breathed. She sat clutching the carved mahogany arms of the chair while she bent forward to search Muzzio's face. "Is it a kidnapping threat or not? I don't know what to think!"

"We'll have to get this analyzed first of all," Muzzio replied. "Maybe we can trace it somehow. But I think it's the work of a crank, that's all."

"A crank? I don't understand."

"There's been a fair amount of publicity about your husband's murder, Mrs. Dillon, and that often leads to this sort of thing. Violent crimes trigger something in sick minds—make the nuts even nuttier. They want to be part of it, I guess."

"How horrible. And how cruel, to torture people who are suffering already."

"Sure, it's both of those things. But what I don't see here is a kidnap threat. I hope you'll put that notion out of your mind."

Jenny smiled thinly. "I would like nothing better than to do that, Lieutenant Muzzio. But first I need to know how the sender of this letter got his hands on Cabby's photograph. Have you an answer to that?"

Muzzio coughed. He had skipped over that troublesome detail, and it was a puzzler.

"I want you to give me a list of everyone who works for you: cleaning people, yard men, even baby-sitters—anyone with access to the house. We'll check them out; see if we unearth any disturbed personalities."

"You won't. At least I don't think you will." Jenny bent closer and whispered, "I think Greg's killer is behind this. Who else would talk about a 'heritage of evil'? Some fanatic must have been watching Greg; he saw the women coming and going at all hours, the parties—maybe he even disapproved of the nude paintings—and decided to punish him. I think it's the answer, Lieutenant!"

"Could be. In fact, Lieutenant Finnegan has suggested that theory. But it doesn't bring us any closer to a solution, I'm afraid. Unless you know someone who…"

"I can't think who it would be, but I'm going to work on it, I can tell you that." Jenny's brown eyes were alight with excitement. "When you got here I was making a list of all the people who might have seen Greg on a regular basis: the nearby shopkeepers, for instance, or any of the older townspeople with time to kill. I'm going to dig into this myself, Lieutenant, because I have to. My son's safety is at stake."

"Look, Mrs. Dillon, I know you're upset and worried. Any woman would be after what you've been through. But you must realize the police department is better equipped to investigate this thing than you are. I strongly suggest that you leave it to us."

Jenny rose to her feet. "I could have waited for you to solve Greg's murder as long as I had to; but when it comes to protecting my child I have no patience. None, do you understand?''

Muzzio stood up and took her hand. ''Mrs. Dillon, we have kids too. You can count on us to clear this up just as fast as we can.'' She tried to pull her hand away, but he held tight. ''Please don't go poking around, okay? You may get closer than you should to the answers, and that could be real dangerous.''

''Have you uncovered any leads, Lieutenant? In the week since my husband's murder?''

As Jenny spoke she drew away from him, and Muzzio let her go.

He said slowly, ''We have some leads, yes. Nothing definitive yet, but...''

He was alarmed to see her throw back her head and laugh as if she had just seen the point of a wonderful joke. ''Let's see what I can come up with in the next week, how's that? You may be in for a surprise—you and whoever is mistakenly thinking a nice lady like Jenny Dillon would never go looking for trouble.''

She paused and her face took on an expression of implacable determination. She whispered huskily, ''I'm going to find the person who is trying to destroy my family; I don't care how dangerous it is. The only way you can stop me is to find him first yourself.''

VINCE MUZZIO SPENT the remainder of the afternoon worrying about Jenny Dillon. Ever since he had first met her, right after her husband's murder, she had occupied a special place in his regard. Even in the first throes of shock she had maintained her dignity, and, amazingly, had displayed a gracious concern for all the people who filed in and out of her house in those trying days. He recalled how she made a pot of tea for her mother at the same time she kept hot coffee coming for the police and other officials, and how she had comforted the older woman when she broke down, as if she were the one to have suffered the greater loss.

That's a real lady, he had thought at the time, and her demeanor at the funeral and during the long periods of questioning had confirmed his evaluation.

He hated to see such a woman lose her grip, as it appeared had happened. There had been a look in her eyes that frightened him; she seemed almost demented. Muzzio knew, as everyone did, how mothers will fight for their children, but this was going too far. She wasn't just a tigress protecting her cub, she was—he hated to use the word—a *crazed* tigress, and he didn't have the first idea what to do about her.

No use asking Finnegan; he could imagine what he would say: Put her under twenty-four hour surveillance. That would be all she needed to push her over the brink.

Muzzio picked up his car telephone to call headquarters. It was after five, and unless something had come up he might as well head home. There was nothing special, he was told; the usual list of minor traffic accidents and false burglary alarms, plus a complaint from Dr. Garvin Thorpe that some kids had driven across his lawn in the night. The kind of dumb vandalism that always went on in the summer when school was out.

Muzzio replaced the mike and slowed down, peering out the window for street signs. He was only a few blocks from Thorpe's house; might as well drive past and see how bad it was. The psychiatrist or psychologist—whatever he was—was a close friend of the Dillons. The vandalism might have something to do with the case, especially if Jenny's theory about a fanatic had any validity.

Right now she was acting like a fanatic herself. She wouldn't have . . . No, it was too crazy; still, Vince tried to recall Finnegan's questioning of Jenny. She had been fully aware of her husband's flagrant infidelities, he remembered that, and he had respected her calm acceptance.

Now that he'd seen another side of her, however, that serene understanding didn't quite ring true. A woman who displayed such ferocity when her child was threatened was hardly the type to take her husband's faithlessness calmly. He knew how Celeste would feel; she'd want to kill him.

Oh God, Vince hated the path his thoughts were taking.

He turned onto Thorpe's street and crept along looking for a lawn with tire marks gouged into it.

He wondered, if he saw the doctor's car in the drive, whether he would have the nerve to drop in and ask a few questions about Jenny's state of mind. The problem was, although Thorpe was the only psychiatrist around, he was Jenny's good friend and unlikely to have an unbiased opinion.

Nonetheless, Vince could feel him out and, if nothing else, maybe get him to talk Jenny out of snooping around to find the person who was threatening her child. Thorpe spent a lot of time with her, Vince knew that; surely he would have some influence.

He had reached the house. There was the damaged lawn and beside it the hedged-in parking lot for Thorpe's patients. Muzzio swung into the drive and parked beside the doctor's car.

Wednesday, July 2 4:00 A.M.

MARIA LUNDY LAY very still in the dark room. She knew she dared not move, but she could not remember why. She was thirsty, very thirsty. She licked her lips and found they tasted surprisingly of applesauce. She tried again; there was no question about it.

She turned her head slowly and carefully and opened her eyes for a fraction of a second. She was alone in the bed. And the motion had made her aware of a slight pain in her jaw. Dimly she remembered something then: a struggle, and Frank's angry panting as he tried to force a spoon between her lips. He had been determined to feed her applesauce, but why? And why had she resisted even when he hurt her face trying to force her mouth open?

He was drugging her. Or trying to. Some instinct had made her stop drinking the coffee he had brought, and although she was still helpless with drowsiness her mind was slowly beginning to function—well enough, at least, to tell her to refuse any more food or drink.

She wondered if he was there in the room, perhaps asleep in a chair. She held her breath, listening, straining her ears for a sound, however faint. If he had gone out she could get out of the bed and slip away. She did not move as she listened. If he had gone out she could get up and pull on some clothes, or even her robe, which she had hung on the back of the bathroom door.

No, better not. In a minute she would very quietly sit up, then if nothing happened she would slither out of bed and grope her way to the door. If she found the room was empty should she stop and dress? No. He might come back before she got away. Just go. Leave in the crumpled night-gown she had on; it was the only sure way.

She became aware of the smell of whiskey. She listened and caught, she was certain, a faint, gurgling snore. Frank must have been drinking when he fell asleep in his chair. Her heart sank. Now the situation was even more unpredictable.

The one thing she suddenly knew with conviction was that she had to go to the bathroom. It was risky, but if Frank had gotten drunk enough to pass out he probably wouldn't hear a thing.

Lifting the sheet so there would be no rustling, Maria wormed herself to the edge of the bed and slowly sat upright. At once she felt dizzy, and she waited for her head to clear before daring to swing her legs over the side. Then she placed her feet carefully on the floor, welcoming the normalcy of the rug's scratchy texture. She pulled herself up, waited again for the dizziness to pass; then, feeling like an exhausted swimmer reaching the shore, she staggered the few steps to the bathroom, pulled the door open, and went in.

She did not dare turn on the light, so she fumbled groggily about and managed to drink a glass of water and rinse off her face in the darkness. Then she took a deep breath, mentally sent up a prayer for safe passage through the bedroom to freedom, and slowly and silently opened the bathroom door.

Instantly she heard a muffled, snarling cry as a form exploded out of the blackness and hurled her onto the bed. He fell on top of her, and before she could scream his fingers closed on her throat. She could feel his body shuddering; he was sobbing with rage.

"You bitch!" He panted the words into her ear. "Trying to get away from me. But I'll never let you, never . . ." He tightened his grip on her throat.

Behind her closed eyes Maria saw whirling pinwheels of light. "Holy Mother, help me," she prayed; but the pinwheels were blending into one huge spinning sun. She felt consciousness slipping away.

Suddenly he let go of her neck and seized her shoulders instead. He began to shake her viciously, causing her head to snap forward and back until she felt her neck would break. Abruptly he stopped and slapped her hard across the mouth.

She fell heavily back among the pillows, and he gasped. Then she felt the touch of his hands again, but gently, cautiously, as he lifted her into his arms and smoothed her hair back from her forehead.

"Forgive me, forgive me, my darling." He was weeping; she could feel his tears on her cheek. "I could never hurt you. I want to punish you, but I can't; I love you too much."

She stirred, trying to push herself free, and to her surprise he let her go. But he was sobbing, snuffling like a child, as he climbed off the bed. He knelt beside it, clasping his hands as if to pray, but it was to her he was praying, beseeching her to forgive him, to forget what a miserable, cowardly fool he was, to help him make a new start; he would go anywhere, do anything, become anything she wanted, if only she would promise never to leave him.

Maria pulled herself up. The soft gray light of morning was filling the room, and she could quite clearly see her husband's wet, distorted face. All her fear was gone, and she felt nothing but contempt for this drunken fool and his maudlin blubbering.

She said, "Pull yourself together, Frank. You've been drugging me—I don't even know for how long—and you just tried to strangle me. I can't stay with you any longer; it's too dangerous. Now stop this carrying on and take me home."

He fell back on his heels, still looking up at her piteously. He said, "You'll go home with me, then? That's all I want—the chance to make a new start. Everything will be different, I promise."

"Yes, it will be different because we won't be together anymore." She had gotten out of bed and was turning on the lamps. "I'm going to take a shower and get dressed, and I wish you would get me some coffee, and some for yourself." She turned and looked at him appraisingly. "You'd better tidy up first; you're a mess."

When he still did not move from his position beside the bed she shrugged and turned away to begin searching the dresser drawers for fresh underwear. With her clothes over her arm she walked past him and disappeared into the bathroom. After a moment she heard the door to the room open and close, then the sound of the car starting up.

In the shower Maria felt like an invalid up for the first time after a debilitating illness. The splashing water and clouds of steam confused her, and more than once she stopped and held onto the shower curtain till a wave of dizziness passed. Still, she scrubbed herself and shampooed her hair determinedly, as if getting her body clean might erase the effects of the preceding hideous days.

When she stepped out of the tub she opened the bathroom door a crack to let out the steam. She listened for sounds from the bedroom; then she remembered that it was still very early. No doubt the restaurant was closed, and Frank had driven into town to find some breakfast for them.

She dried herself and her hair, then applied makeup with her usual care. She felt almost normal as she pushed through the bathroom door to the bedroom; she was not thinking about Frank, but about which shirt and pants to put on for the drive home.

So at first she did not take in the implications of the sight that awaited her: her husband sitting stiffly in a straight chair while he aimed a gun at her that he held with both hands, steadying his wrists on his crossed knees. His face was white and covered with a sheen of perspiration, his eyes as opaque as slate.

He said, "Sit down, Maria. Right there on the floor."

Slowly she sank to the carpet, where she sat leaning against the wall. Some instinct made her rest her open hands on her thighs, palms upward, perhaps to symbolize her helplessness. She did not smile or speak, however, but met his eyes with grave composure.

"I have to get you out of my life somehow," he said, his voice quavering, "or you'll destroy me."

"I'll be glad to get out of your life, Frank. Just put down that gun and let me walk out of here. I promise you'll never have to see me again."

Before she had finished he was slowly shaking his head. He said, "Do you think I could stand to have you marry someone else? Have children with him?"

Again she heard the quaver in his voice, but the gun in his hands remained immobile. She had never seen him able to hold his hands so steady.

She forced herself to look up from the gun and into his eyes. She said, "You won't do it, Frank. You don't really want to. You love me too much."

"Too much is right." He laughed harshly. Then he turned his left wrist slightly and stole a glance at his watch. He said, "You have until eight o'clock, at most."

She noticed then that he had placed the telephone on the floor beside his chair. Was he waiting to kill her until after he had received an important business call? The surrealism of it made her head spin; she seemed to have moved into some Alice in Wonderland world where madness ruled.

She tried to keep her voice steady as she said, "You're expecting a call, aren't you? From one of your clients?"

"I don't have to account to you for my telephone calls. Or anything else, for that matter."

Choosing her words carefully, she said, "I'm sure your clients miss you, Frank; you're so good at your work. Hadn't we better go home now so you can get caught up?"

She smiled coaxingly, and raised herself to her knees. If she could distract him long enough to get to her feet maybe she could grab the gun.

He seized her wrist and hurled her back so violently that her head struck the wall.

"Forget it, Maria. You're not going home. Maybe I'm not either; I haven't decided."

He glanced at the instrument on the floor, and she fancied she saw his pale face turn even whiter. When he looked back at her his face was like a tragic mask. She could see the bones of his skull sharply outlined beneath the waxily glistening skin.

He said, "I suggest you spend the next few hours making your peace with God. He is the only friend you have left."

TWENTY-TWO

Wednesday, July 2 5:00 A.M.

A FAINT BREEZE STIRRED the heavy branches of the fir trees, allowing the pale light of the night sky to fall on Ben Porter's face. He groaned and attempted to turn over, but the thick sleeping bag confined his legs. He kicked at it vainly, trying not to come fully awake, but it was too late.

Cursing, he pushed himself upright and sat blinking sourly at the forest setting he had chosen for the poorest night's rest he could remember. Something had been stabbing into his spine; he twisted around and lifted the sleeping bag to look underneath. There it was, a network of firm, woody roots too well hidden in the grass to be visible in the dark. And he had forgotten to bring a pillow, so his neck ached fiercely, in tune with the rest of his body.

He wriggled free of the bag, then rolled it up, vainly trying to return it to the compact bundle it had been when he bought it. Then he cautiously peeked over the top of the bushes that cut off his view of Grogan's Fishing Camp and concealed him as well from anyone looking up the hill. Because the tall trees kept out the sun, he had had to go perilously near the edge of the woods to find the bushy growth he needed for a hiding place. He was startled now to find himself only a few hundred feet from the last cottage, the one he had stationed himself to watch. It hadn't seemed so close in the thick darkness before the moon rose.

Ben crouched down, hugging the sleeping bag, while he tried to decide what to do next. He longed for coffee; on the other hand it was too early for anyone to be stirring— an excellent time to risk a look through the Lundys' window, providing, which was unlikely, they had left the curtain open.

He studied the course he would have to take. Between him and the cottage the ground was open, except for two slim birch trees and a low pile of rocks. Not exactly adequate shelter in case Frank and Maria took a notion to walk out and have a look at the coming sunrise.

But they were hardly the type, after all—a nightclub singer and an accountant. Under normal circumstances neither one of them would go near a place like Grogan's, and for that reason Ben didn't share Ed Grogan's consternation over Maria's nonappearance. She was probably quite happy having meals brought to her in the cottage while she watched TV and worked on her hair and nails.

He tucked the sleeping bag beneath a bush, then began crawling on hands and knees down the slight grade toward the shadowy grove of birch trees. He quickly reached it and stopped to peer between the slim trunks at the cottage, which was now only about a hundred feet away. He heard no sound and could see no change in the state of the only window visible to him. The curtain was drawn, as he had expected and for which at the moment he was thankful. Suppose Frank Lundy suddenly pulled it open and looked out? Picturing the expression on that serious, bookkeeperish face at the sight of a prospective client creeping out of the woods on his hands and knees, Ben choked back his laughter. Finding an explanation would require all the creativity he could summon up.

He wriggled along the ground toward the rock pile, remembering war movies with infantrymen inching across the battleground, their faces blackened for camouflage. He was doing it exactly the same way except for the dirty face. He stopped, and again fighting an urge to laugh, unsnapped the netting from his hat brim so that it fell around his face. Would Carrie believe this? Never.

When he reached the back of the cottage he stood up, pressing himself against the red-painted wood siding as he edged along the wall to the window, which he saw was tightly closed. He listened, holding his breath, straining to hear the slightest sound from within.

There was nothing, not even the creak of a bedspring or the rumble of Frank Lundy's snoring.

Ben lifted the netting from his face and pushed back his sleeve for a look at his watch. It was only twenty after five; any person sane enough to sleep in a bed instead of a lumpy sleeping bag was good for another hour at least. Plenty of time for him to drive back to the Mountain View and get cleaned up.

He crouched, slid away from the cottage, and began making his way back up the slope as silently and cautiously as he had approached.

CARRIE PORTER WAS also moving with silent caution as she tiptoed across the upstairs hall in her bare feet, praying that this time Brooke had fallen asleep to stay. The child had picked up an ear infection, probably at the club pool, and had wakened Carrie three times from what had already been a restless sleep.

All the while she sponged her daughter's face with cool water, administered aspirin, and rocked the perspiring little body in her arms Carrie was mentally preoccupied with the question of Ben. She had tried to call him at three the previous afternoon, immediately after returning to the office from Sullivan's Electronics. She had tried again before leaving for home, then had made at least six attempts during the evening. Finally she had called the front desk of the Mountain View Motel, but the manager had not seen Ben since morning, and could only suggest that she keep trying his room directly.

Now her anxiety was giving way to resentment. He could have checked in; he must know she would worry; he was on the track of a possibly psychotic murderer, after all. Supposing he had gotten too close and the Lundys, one or both, had caught him out? Ben was not a detective, experienced in shadowing criminals. She could not imagine why she had allowed him to get so involved in what was not a game, as he seemed to consider it, but a deadly serious murder investigation.

Back in her own room at last, Carrie started to climb into bed, then went to the bathroom for an aspirin instead. Her head was throbbing, and she would have to wait at least two hours before trying the Mountain View again.

At the bedside she hesitated, then knelt and carefully pulled a cardboard carton out from beneath the bed. Without turning on a light, she carried it to the small desk that stood beneath one window, placed it on a chair, and folded back the panels covering the contents. She bent to take something out of the box, then straightened instead and drew the curtains closed.

She felt her heart beat faster as she reached into the box again, and this time removed an object about twelve inches square, which she carefully placed in the center of the desk top.

It was a telephone answering machine, the one that had been installed in Greg Dillon's cottage studio. Sullivan's Electronics had put the machine in working order only a day or two after Greg brought it in; then, being unable to reach him, had sent their usual repair-ready notice in the mail and gone away on vacation.

In Mr. Sullivan's presence Carrie felt she hardly dared open the compartment that held the recording tape. What if he realized the importance of any messages that tape might contain? Would he not insist on turning it over to the police?

But apparently Mr. Sullivan was not a reader of detective stories, for he watched benignly while Carrie fumbled with the plastic cover, then volunteered the answer to the question she had been wondering how to ask.

"That's the same tape he brought in," he said. "I would have given him a new one, but it's hardly worn at all."

"Fine," Carrie breathed. "Mrs. Dillon will be glad to have this back, I know. How much do I owe you?"

She paid the bill, requesting a receipt in case of any official questions that might be asked, then watched impatiently while Mr. Sullivan tried fitting the machine into various odd cartons until he found one that pleased him.

"Good idea to keep a machine like this covered if you're not using it for a while," he said as he lowered it into the box with maddening deliberation.

She nearly snatched it out of his hands and hurried out the door. The tape might reveal nothing—probably would not, she told herself, if Greg's messages were as mundane as the ones she and Ben received.

Still her head hummed with excitement as she drove home to call Ben. She would of course await his return to play the tape, she could not say why exactly; that was simply the way she and Ben did things.

The long, frustrating night had changed her viewpoint, however. Ben was having an adventure he apparently couldn't be bothered to tell her about; she would reward herself with adventure of another kind.

She knelt and unplugged a floor lamp from the wall socket, then connected the cord of Greg's answering machine.

She got up and, first closing her bedroom door so the sound would not wake the children, checked to make sure the tape was in position and pressed the playback button.

7:00 A.M.

BEN PORTER WAS WAITING in his car when Ginny Grogan walked across from the house to open the restaurant for breakfast. She invited him in to wait for the coffee maker to get going and the stove to heat up, and he hadn't been there five minutes before the place began filling up with fishermen, early as it was.

Nobody talked very much, just nodded to one another and exchanged a few comments about the previous day's catch. There was an easy dignity about most of the men, and Ben sensed an unspoken appreciation of nature and solitude that he himself had felt while he waded the rocky stream.

Sipping his coffee, Ben reviewed his tactics in regard to the Lundys. His morning excursion had given him a hint of the humiliation he would feel if either Maria or Frank discovered him skulking around their cottage. Instead, he decided to approach them openly and somewhat honestly as a concerned acquaintance who had been dismayed to stumble upon them at Grogan's when he had private information that the police were searching for them.

It would be in their own interests to return to Springfield at once, he would point out; not because they were under suspicion, of course, but simply because of appearances.

He felt so much better after working it out, and then tucking away an order of Ginny's blueberry pancakes, that he decided to put in a call to Carrie. A look at his watch, then at the location of the phone booth, changed his mind, however.

The rear vestibule, where the telephone was located, had no windows; he would not be able to see cars passing the restaurant, and if the Lundys were traveling on from Grogan's they might be setting out at just about that time.

So Ben paid his bill, got back into his car, and drove up the hill to cottage number 12. He parked in a narrow clearing fifty yards from the cottage and walked quietly over to the door; *not* skulking, he told himself, merely being considerate in case the Lundys were still asleep.

When he reached the door he could hear a man's voice inside, briefly speaking, pausing, speaking again, obviously on the telephone. Ben could make out few words—the windows were closed and the curtains drawn—but he thought he detected a rising urgency in the cadence of the voice; and at one point he clearly heard Lundy exclaim, "No, goddamn it!"

Ben felt his pulse speed up. He quietly stepped around to the tree-shadowed side of the cottage and flattened himself against the wall, listening to the voice as it rose and fell in increasing agitation.

Where was Maria while this disturbing conversation was taking place? He heard no voice but Frank's, and the man was clearly in great distress. Shouldn't Maria be interrupting, or making some sound of sympathy or concern?

There was a crash, then an exclamation he could not make out. Frank had dropped the telephone.

Silence fell. In cottage number 12 there was an absence of sound so total that Ben held his breath, certain his breathing could be heard through the wall.

A gunshot shattered the silence, the sound so loud in his ears Ben thought he had been hit. He jumped away from the side of the cottage, dazed, his ears ringing. For a second he gaped at the clapboard wall of the cottage, wondering why it remained intact. Then he heard a gasping cry from within, and he stumbled to the door and began to bang it with his fist, shouting, "Maria! Frank Lundy! Open the door!"

The door swung open, and Maria gazed at him with huge shocked eyes, then slowly stepped back so that he could enter.

In the dim room her body shimmered, pale and luminous. Ben saw that she was wearing only a white satin bra and panties. Her dark eyes were locked on his as though she might fall if she looked away. Her right hand held a small pistol.

Gently Ben took the gun from her, dropped it into his pocket, and led her to a nearby chair. She sat down compliantly, still keeping her eyes fixed on his face.

Then Ben slowly turned and saw what he knew he must see: the figure of Frank Lundy slumped in a straight chair in the center of the room, his face and the front of his shirt covered with blood.

On the floor beside Frank's chair an ivory-colored princess telephone began to ring.

Ben looked from the instrument to Maria, but her white face did not change expression. Stepping gingerly to Frank's side, Ben picked up the telephone and said, "Hello," then after a pause, "No, this is a friend. Who is calling?"

After hearing the reply he said, "I can't talk to you right now. There has been an accident."

He could feel his pulse throbbing as he stared at Frank's bloody chest, willing it to rise and fall, however slightly.

In response to the next agitated query he said, ''I don't know yet. That's why I have to get help here immediately.''

He hung up briefly, then dialed the operator and asked for the police.

TWENTY-THREE

Wednesday, July 2 Morning

STANDING AT THE DESK in her walnut-paneled study, Jenny Dillon dialed Garvin Thorpe's office number for the third time in ten minutes, and for the third time was rewarded with a busy signal. For a moment she listened, staring into the mirror above the fireplace, where her huge, tormented eyes gleamed darkly in the pale oval of her face.

Then she could stand no more of it, and she slammed the phone into its cradle and almost ran out of the room and down the hall to the garage. If Garvin's phone was busy he couldn't be with a patient; she had better get to his office before one arrived.

In the car she was calmer, realizing that when Garvin heard her idea he would no doubt cancel his next appointment anyway. She actually managed a smile as she paused at a stop sign; her idea was so simple, so obvious, really, yet no one else had thought of it. She would need Garvin's support, though, to face up to Finnegan. She simply could not talk to that man. He always looked at her so sternly, with his fat, red face looking ready to burst under the strain of concealing his disapproval. Obviously he thought she had been a brainless, and probably immoral, fool to put up with Greg Dillon all those years. As if he could have any conception of the quality of a man like Greg. Her eyes brimmed with sudden tears, and she impatiently wiped them away so she could see to turn into the Thorpes' driveway.

It was empty, she was glad to see, and she hurried to the office entrance and, finding the inner door standing ajar, pressed the bell once, then pulled the screen door open and stepped inside.

There she hesitated. This was Garvin's turf, after all, and the door to his consulting room was closed. She tiptoed over to listen; if he were still on the phone she, of course, would wait until he was finished.

She heard nothing, so she tapped lightly on the door, then slowly opened it, saying, "Garvin? I hope you don't mind, but your line has been busy and I..."

"Jenny! What are you doing here?" He half-rose from his chair behind the desk, looking first astonished and then alarmed. "Has something happened? Is Cabby all right?"

He quickly moved around the desk to take her hands while she said, "No, nothing's wrong—at least nothing new. It's just that I can't stand waiting while the police fool around in their dumb, procedural way. I'm going to find out who's threatening Cabby myself."

Garvin began to shake his head, but Jenny rushed on. "I have to, Garvin, I just have to, and before you try to talk me out of it, listen to my plan. I'm going to go to Lieutenant Finnegan and demand the return of Greg's paintings. Here's where I need your help, because I get paralyzed when I try to talk to that man. But everything of Greg's is mine, isn't it? So how can they keep his work locked up for so long?"

"Jenny, you know the police think the paintings may somehow provide a clue to Greg's killer. I don't think they can be forced to release them until the case is solved."

While he was speaking Garvin drew Jenny to the sofa that stood before the window. He seated himself, then patted the cushions beside him, but she stayed on her feet looking down at him.

"I've been thinking about that," she said slowly, "and as I recall, there were no restrictions on the paintings until after the fire in Greg's studio. I remember Lieutenant Muzzio suggesting that I keep the studio locked until I had time to sort everything out, but I was perfectly free to do what I liked with the pictures. Then all of a sudden they were off-limits. But I want to see them, Garvin. If I study those paintings I just know I'll get some ideas about who might be persecuting me."

"Do you think you'll also come up with the identity of Greg's murderer?" Garvin was smiling indulgently, but he stole a quick glance at his watch as he spoke.

"Why is that such an amusing idea, may I ask? I'm not a child, Garvin, or an idiot, so please don't treat me like one."

Immediately he was on his feet. "I'm sorry, Jenny, if I sounded patronizing. It's just that..." He paused, trying to formulate his thoughts while Jenny watched grimly.

She said, "Garvin, this morning Cabby was acting like himself for the first time since Greg's death. He ate all his breakfast and talked about Brooke Porter's birthday party and he really seemed happy and normal. And then that bodyguard arrived to walk him to school and he changed right before my eyes." Jenny's lips were trembling as she forced herself to continue. "The man is perfectly nice; he's young, and he's really very sweet with Cabby; but when he came in the door it was as if all the horror came with him. Cabby got very quiet and serious, and he looked at me as if to ask, how long do I have to live like this? And I, I just..."

Jenny stumbled to the sofa and sank onto it, sobbing with her face in her hands.

"Dear Jenny, it's terrible for you, I know." Garvin was beside her, trying to pull her to him, but she resisted and stubbornly turned her head away while she groped for a handkerchief in her skirt pocket.

"No, I'm through being babied," she said as she wiped her eyes. "You've been wonderful to me, Garvin, but I have leaned on you too much—just as I've counted too much on the police to solve this horrible crime." She sat up very straight and looked at him levelly. "I'm a mature, intelligent woman and I am going to take matters into my own hands. With you or without you, I am going to Lieutenant Finnegan and demand to see Greg's paintings."

"Jenny, I want you to be careful," Garvin began. He paused to listen to the sound of a car pulling into the driveway, and he seemed distracted as he went on, "There are paintings of Greg's you haven't seen, ever, and for a good reason, I gather.''

Wheels crunched on the gravel, and Garvin got to his feet and peered out the window.

"It's Enid," he muttered, and once again glanced at his watch.

Jenny stood up and seized his arm. "What do you mean there are paintings I haven't seen? What's so surprising about that? Greg never did show me all his work; what about it?''

"Jenny, I hate to do this, but can we talk some more later? There's something I have to attend to, I'm afraid." Garvin bent close to study her reaction, and although she felt tortured by curiosity, she managed a reassuring smile.

"Of course, Garvin. I shouldn't have burst in here and upset your schedule. Just try to call me later in the day, won't you? Before I do something silly?''

Instinctively she had assumed the helpless manner to which men responded best, even to the quaver in her voice, and she was not surprised to see a tender warmth appear in Garvin's eyes.

"Thank you for being so understanding," he said huskily, then gently kissed her cheek and watched her walk through the reception room and out the front door.

As she crossed the driveway to her car, Jenny's head was whirling with speculation. For the first time in their lives Garvin Thorpe had wanted to be rid of her. And at a time of crisis, when she had greatly needed his help.

She drove through town slowly, reconstructing their interview in her mind, recalling that, while he had not agreed with her decision to confront Finnegan, he had given her all his attention until the moment he heard Enid returning home.

That was it, of course. Enid was jealous of the time he was spending with Jenny. And what wife wouldn't be? Especially when she knew that Jenny had been his first choice and when his solicitude over the past week suggested that he still cared for her.

Thinking of Enid's unhappiness, Jenny was filled with remorse. She would hate to be the cause of another emotional upset for her friend, so she would manage without Garvin from now on, much as she would miss his support. She drew a deep breath and turned the car in the direction of the police station.

THE TWO NURSES on duty at the Banister Medical Clinic took charge of Frank Lundy with a calm efficiency that astonished Ben. They were waiting outside the rear door when the police ambulance pulled in. As soon as the attendants had carried Frank's stretcher into the clinic, the nurses had checked his pulse and blood pressure and had removed the bloody bandage to take a quick look at the wound.

Ben was careful to look away. He had seen all he could stand when the police officers applied first aid after making the startling announcement that Frank was not dead at all, but wounded, and perhaps not as seriously as the copious bleeding seemed to indicate.

When the gauze was lifted from his face, Ben heard a quick intake of breath from the young policeman who stood beside him. "Boy, she fixed him good," he whispered.

Instead of penetrating Frank's skull, the bullet had channeled across the top of his cheekbone and continued on through his left ear. Now, in addition to bearing two ugly wounds, his face had become grotesquely swollen, his eyes mere slits in the distended purple skin. Ben was glad Maria had stayed behind with Ed and Molly Grogan.

"Those nurses are amazing," Ben muttered, watching them wheel Frank into a treatment room and deftly transfer him to the examining table.

"We get a lot of gunshot injuries in the hunting season," the cop replied. "They know what they're doing, especially these two."

"I suppose you also have a top plastic surgeon in Banister?"

The young man grinned. "As a matter of fact, the vet's pretty good at patching up ears—dogs' ears anyway. But I don't suppose this guy wants to go home looking like a retriever."

"Might be an improvement at this point."

Ben looked around the sparsely furnished waiting room. "I have to make some phone calls," he said, "but first, what about the legalities in a case like this? I don't suppose you can treat this as a hunting accident?"

"Hardly. There's no question his wife shot him, probably with intent to kill. I don't know what the sheriff will want to do, though. Probably get rid of them if he can."

"I can help with that; take them back to Connecticut, where this incident will have a bearing on a certain murder case."

"In separate cars, wouldn't you say?"

"That would make for a smoother trip, yes. Now, where's a pay phone? My lawyer can help us figure it out."

IT TOOK THE REST of the morning to arrange the transfer of Maria and Frank Lundy from New York State to Connecticut. Ben would take Frank back in his car, it was decided, while a state policeman escorted Maria in her own convertible, with the young Banister cop following.

Ben restlessly prowled the dusty corridors of the Chase County courthouse while negotiations went on between the sheriff and Howard Keating and Tom Finnegan in Springfield. He was in a fever of impatience to talk to Carrie, but the only two pay phones in the courthouse were out of order, and since the sheriff seemed to need his constant reassurance that Maria would not try to escape or attack her escort on the trip to Connecticut, he dared not leave.

Finally, at noon, a small motorcade headed for Grogan's Fishing Camp, where in the spare room of the main house Maria sat awaiting the next episode of the bizarre drama in which she found herself starring.

She might actually have been a movie star, she thought, the way Ed and Molly Grogan treated her. They kept tiptoeing in with anxious smiles to make sure she was comfortable, not too hot or cold or hungry.

"There's a draft from that window," Ed observed on what must have been his fifth visit. He marched over and firmly closed it, and although Maria had been enjoying the way the fresh breeze made the organdy curtains billow into the room, just like the ones in her childhood home, she thanked him. She mustered a smile, in fact, as she almost always could in the presence of a man like Ed, no matter how terrible she felt.

Not that she felt all that terrible. If anyone had pinned her down she'd have had to say that her dominant emotion was gratitude for being alive. Guilt was far from her thoughts. Frank had been reduced to a cipher: He was the man who might have killed her but hadn't, and since she hadn't killed him either they were even.

The score was settled with a finality that was almost amusing. No ambiguity in this case. Everything was over, her marriage, her love affair, her career, such as it was. Those were the factors that had shaped her as a person; now she seemed to have no shape. She felt light, weightless; she felt, she realized with amazement, free.

It was baffling, also shocking, to feel so buoyant and carefree when everyone would expect her to be either wringing her hands in remorse or trembling in dread of the prosecution she would have to face. She hoped her lightheartedness didn't show, and when she heard Grogan's footsteps in the hall Maria deliberately made her face solemn.

When he had closed the window he came over to the easy chair where she was sitting and stood gazing down at her almost wistfully.

"I'm real sorry your visit to Grogan's turned out like it did," he said. "If you need me to testify or anything, I'll be glad to say you didn't make any trouble; it was him, your husband, who was acting crazy." She started to speak, and he raised his hand to silence her. "I know you don't want to talk about it, not now anyway. Just remember, when this gets settled you'll always be welcome back at Grogan's.'' He mumbled the final words, looking away from her, his already ruddy face the color of a brick.

Before Maria could reply, the first car rolled into the driveway and Ed turned and left the room.

"NOW WAIT, CARRIE. See if I guessed it right. Was it Greg Dillon's answering machine you picked up at Sullivan's?''

"How did you know that?''

"Never mind, I'll tell you later. Here's the important question: Did they leave any of Greg's messages on the tape?''

"I think I'll let you wonder for a while. Just the way you let me squirm all day yesterday. Didn't it occur to you that I might worry if I didn't hear from you?''

"I'm sorry, Carrie; it was out of my hands. You'll understand that when I have time to explain. Now tell me who you heard on that tape.''

"Just Margaret Thatcher asking if Greg would paint her in the nude. And one or two others.''

"Damn it, Carrie . . .''

"See you later, darling. Drive carefully.''

With a crash Ben replaced the pay telephone in Grogan's lobby and strode out the door to where Frank Lundy waited in the car.

TWENTY-FOUR

Thursday, July 3 9:00 A.M.

HOWARD KEATING PROPPED four folding chairs against the wall, then tried the front door handle of the Porter Publishing Company. The knob did not turn, nor did the door swing inward when he gave it a push. Carrie must have gotten a locksmith at last.

He had returned to his car and was taking two more chairs out of the trunk when Ben Porter's Mustang drew up. Ben climbed out saying, "Wait, I'll give you a hand."

"Not needed, thanks," Howard replied. "Is everything set?"

"I think so, though dear old Constable Finnegan is still threatening to back out. He's feeling solicitous about the Lundys. Isn't sure they should be subjected to any stress in their precarious condition."

"He has a point, Ben." Howard watched his friend extract a folded wooden easel from the back seat of the convertible and prop it against the car. "Why the easel?" he added while Ben dove back to wrestle with a large paper-wrapped package. "Don't tell me you got Finnegan to..."

"No such luck." Ben backed toward the sidewalk, careful not to tear the paper on the flat object he was pulling out of the car. "Finnegan held firm on the Greg Dillon nudes. He's a man of character, you know."

"Well, that looks like a painting to me. What are you up to, anyway? I can't okay any funny business; especially any tricks you've thought of to trap the Lundys. They're under the protection of the law now, both of them."

"Please don't worry, Howard. I can't confide in you completely, I'm afraid, but I assure you I have no plans to intimidate either one of the Lundys. I'm not a cruel person, after all, and they've been through the wringer.''

"They certainly have." Howard picked up the folding chairs, hooked his other arm through the easel, and started up the walk.

Ben followed, carrying the large, flat package as well as a smaller cardboard carton. On the porch he rested the first against his hip while he pulled his keys from his pocket and opened the door.

"I thought Carrie would get here before us," he said. "Maybe she thought Jenny needed a little more encouragement."

"You were very persuasive last night; eloquent, I might even say, thanks to two martinis."

"Three."

"But in the cold light of morning I'll be surprised if most of those people don't back out of this."

"When I promised a sensational revelation? And told each of them I couldn't possibly bring it off without his help? Come on, Howard, you know human nature better than that."

He led the way into his office, the second room on the right, where he opened the easel and stood it in front of the window behind the desk. While Howard brought in the chairs Ben placed the wrapped painting on the easel, then began pushing furniture around to clear the center of the room.

"Coffee," he muttered, "Let's see: three of us, two Lundys, one Dillon, two Thorpes..."

"Two Thorpes? Enid's coming too?"

"To observe. Carrie convinced her it would be worth her while as a psychological experiment. Now where was I? Eight, plus Finnegan and Muzzio makes ten."

"Right." Howard was unfolding the chairs and placing them in two rows. "Where will you sit? Behind the desk?"

"Um, yes, and let's put Finnegan and Muzzio near the doors, just in case. There's one for each."

"Ben, I really have to caution you..."

"And I'll want this little treasure close to hand, but where the others can't see it." Ben had opened the carton and removed the answering machine Carrie had retrieved from Sullivan's Electronics. He carried it behind the desk, where he pulled out one of the lower drawers and placed the machine on top of its contents; then he plugged it into a wall socket. He straightened and said to Howard, "Can you see the thing from the front of the desk? Any of it?"

Howard shook his head. "What are you going to do, record the meeting?"

"Not exactly. That's part of the surprise." He bent to check the tape in the machine, then faced Howard again and said, "If anything goes wrong—if I have a heart attack or something—I'm counting on you to take this out of my pocket and keep it in a safe place."

He extracted a tiny tape cassette from his blazer pocket and held it up for Howard to see, then slipped it back.

Howard said, "What about the painting? Shall I unwrap it now?"

"No, no, Howard; mustn't touch." Ben considered the location of the easel with its mysterious, paper-covered burden, then stepped over to the window behind it and drew the tailored cotton draperies closed. He carefully moved the easel behind the closed curtains. He walked around to the front of the desk and studied his arrangement of the chair, the answering machine, and the completely concealed easel, then he glanced at his watch. "Quarter to ten. I wish Carrie would get here."

"I'll start the coffee," Howard said, heading for the door.

Ben followed him into the hall, but as they reached the kitchen the front door opened, and Carrie came striding in, her blond hair flying, her face flushed with excitement.

"It's nearly ten, guys," she said breathlessly. "They'll be here any minute."

She darted into her office to unload her usual armful of papers and manuscripts, then quickly popped out again. "What about my doors, Ben? Should I lock them in case..." She stopped, grinning at the men while she caught her breath. "This is too much for me, I'm hyperventilating."

Ben went to her and put his arm around her shoulders. "Carrie, maybe you should go home. We don't know what may happen, after all. What about it, darling? Just to relieve my mind?"

Slowly her smile faded while she studied Ben's face, seeing the struggle there between concern for her safety and the excited anticipation he could not conceal.

"Maybe I should," she began; then there was the sound of footsteps on the wooden floor of the porch, followed by the chime of the doorbell, and Carrie clutched Ben's hand.

"Too late," she breathed, "they're here!"

She quickly kissed his cheek, then hurried down the hall to open the door.

TWENTY-FIVE

Thursday, July 3 10:00 A.M.

JENNY DILLON WAS the first to arrive, wearing a white linen skirt with a thin, red cotton blouse and a wide, brass-buckled leather belt. Her brown eyes widened with apprehension as she stepped through the door; this was her first visit to the site of Greg's murder and, looking around the dingy hallway, her face turned noticeably pale. Ben, immediately aware of her emotion, tucked his hand under her arm and guided her into his office while Carrie hurried to the kitchen for coffee.

"I don't know whether I can face the Lundys," Jenny said grimly as Ben seated her, "if they're the ones who are threatening Cabby."

"Jenny, I'm hoping that after today you'll have no more worries on that score. Please try to get through it; that's the only way you'll ever be sure."

She stiffened suddenly, gazing past his shoulder, and Ben turned to see Frank Lundy standing in the doorway, his swollen eyes peering over the gauze bandage that covered his wounds. Behind him stood Vince Muzzio, and as Ben went to greet them he saw Maria Lundy coming through the outer door, followed by the burly figure of Lieutenant Finnegan.

Maria wore a pale blue silk dress and white sling pumps. She stumbled slightly as she stepped into the hall, and Finnegan quickly seized her elbow, wearing an expression of grave concern. He kept a tight hold on her arm as they walked toward Ben's office.

They reached the door just as Frank Lundy was taking a seat next to Muzzio, and Maria hastily drew back.

"You didn't tell me Frank would be here," she said to
Ben. "I don't want to see him. You told me I wouldn't
have to," she continued, addressing Finnegan. Her voice
shook so that they could barely make out her words. "I
won't do it, I can't stand it."

Ignoring Finnegan's accusing scowl, Ben said, "Excuse
me, Lieutenant," and stepped between them, forcing the
police officer to drop Maria's arm.

Taking her hand, Ben led her a few paces away, then said
to her softly, "Maria, we have gone through some of this
together, so I think I understand how you feel. Please trust
me when I tell you that if you cooperate for just a few
minutes, you'll be finished with the whole ugly mess."

She stared at him dumbly. She would not acquiesce, but
she did not pull away, and after a moment Ben said quietly to Finnegan, "Let her wait until everyone is here, then
give her a seat near the door, will you?"

Finnegan said nothing, but took his place at Maria's
side, saying, "We can leave if it's too much for you, Mrs.
Lundy. You're under no obligation to do this...to Mr.
Porter, you know."

"I'll try to get through it if you promise to keep Frank
away from me." She spoke in a faint whisper, and Finnegan bent his head close to hear, then looked up at Ben and
nodded sharply.

"Okay," he said, "but you do anything more to upset
Mrs. Lundy and I'm getting her out of here."

"I understand, Lieutenant. Thank you for your help."

Ben left them, feeling shaken by the tenuous nature of
his arrangements. He glanced nervously at his watch, then
toward the outside door. If the Thorpes did not arrive soon
it would be impossible to keep the others from leaving.

Fixing a reassuring smile on his face, he peered through
the doorway at the waiting group. "Five minutes," he said,
"then we'll be all set."

No one smiled back. Jenny Dillon looked down and began searching her bag for a handkerchief. Howard Keating did not move from his position in front of the desk, but
Ben saw him shake his head ever so slightly. Frank Lundy

shifted in his chair and glanced suspiciously around the room. Even Carrie's expression was bleak; clearly she felt dubious about Ben's ability to keep these tense people assembled.

Unable to keep still, Ben paced to the outside door, and found Enid and Garvin Thorpe climbing the steps to the porch, Enid wearing the black linen sheath and heavy silver jewelry that suited her so well.

Garvin shook Ben's hand, saying, "Sorry, Ben. I hope we're not too late."

"I think you're just in time," Ben replied. Then he ushered them through the door and along the hall to his office.

STANDING BEHIND HIS DESK, Ben looked slowly around the room. As soon as Garvin and Enid Thorpe were seated Finnegan had led Maria to a chair placed just inside the door from the hall. Frank Lundy had watched his wife's arrival in obvious consternation, but when he started to get to his feet in order to approach her Muzzio had pulled him back.

"Thank you for coming here today," Ben began. "I'm sure you know you were invited to help clear up the mystery surrounding the murder of Greg Dillon here on these premises a little over a week ago."

He paused, and Carrie from her place at the back of the room saw the stillness that gripped each seated figure.

"I think you'll be interested to hear that the police are no nearer a solution today than they were a week ago."

Carrie heard nothing so overt as a sigh of relief, but she saw a crossing of legs and general relaxing of posture; she fancied she heard everyone start to breathe again.

"In my own efforts I have come upon a bit of evidence that may be useful. I need your help, however, before I can determine its importance. Please listen closely now, and see if you can identify any of the voices you hear."

Ben bent to press a button on the answering machine in the desk drawer and immediately there was the sound of a beep, then a woman's voice saying, "Greg, this is Alice

Stewart. I can't remember whether my next sitting is Thursday or Friday. Please call me as soon as possible."

Jenny Dillon gasped. Her face had turned a sickly gray-white. "Where did you get that?" she breathed; then stopped as another beep sounded and the next voice poured into the room.

It was Maria's. Though she did not give her name, there was no mistaking the musical cadences as she said, "I meant what I said to you, Greg. I'm coming over tonight to get my things, probably around eight o'clock. Please don't be there. I don't want to see you."

There was an explosive sound from Frank Lundy, and again Muzzio seized his arm, this time keeping a grip on it.

In a moment they heard another beep, followed by a man's voice saying, "This is George, Mr. Dillon. That molding you ordered came in, but I need to know which painting it's for. Please call me."

During this speech Ben slowly drew the cord of the draperies behind him until they were fully opened. There, framed between them as dramatically as an auctioneer's display, stood the easel with its strange and somehow shocking burden: the flat rectangle wrapped in brown paper that Ben had guarded so carefully.

There was a restless stirring, a soft exclamation from Jenny Dillon, then, after another beep, they heard the sound of a woman's clear, strong voice on Greg Dillon's message tape. "Greg, you're such a rascal. I know you lied about this afternoon. I can read you so well..."

"Turn off the machine, Ben. Right now, do you hear me?"

Eerily, it was the same clear voice, but alive in the room with them. For Enid Thorpe had risen to her feet. She was standing very still and pointing something at Ben—a small pistol. Carrie felt her heart stop beating.

For what seemed long minutes the recorded voice continued: "...I'll forgive you once more, my darling. It seems I have no choice..." Then the machine snapped off, and Enid spoke again, her tone as cool and conversational as before.

"I'll kill you if you unwrap that painting, Ben."

Ben stood perfectly still and straight, his eyes boring into Enid's with what Carrie was horrified to recognize as challenge. Then, very slowly and deliberately, he began ripping the paper from the painting on the easel.

Muzzio was on his feet, attempting to lunge past Garvin Thorpe to grab the gun; but Garvin said, "It's all right, Lieutenant."

Wearing an expression of unutterable sadness, he rose and gently pulled the pistol out of his wife's hands.

"I think you'll find this is the gun that killed Greg Dillon," he said. He handed the pistol to Muzzio an instant before Enid collapsed into his arms.

TWENTY-SIX

Thursday, July 3 Evening

"IF I LOOK ten years older it's your fault, Ben Porter."

In the midst of cutting a bite of poached salmon, Ben looked up at his wife, who sat across the slate-topped table, half in shadow. She smiled at him, her teeth gleaming white, her eyes glinting like sapphires in the soft, flickering light cast by the tall glass hurricane candles.

Ben put down his fork and reached across to cover Carrie's hand with his. He grinned at Howard Keating who was seated next to her. "I'd say she was at least twenty-five, wouldn't you, Howard?"

He turned back to Carrie and for a moment they studied each other through the dimness, as if seeking assurance that neither had been changed by the events of the day.

Carrie slid her hand free and reached for her wine glass.

"That was the longest moment of my life this morning: waiting for you to go stubbornly ahead, as I knew you would, and uncover the painting." The crystal glass sparkled as she lifted it to her lips. "I pictured the shot, the ambulance ride, the scene in the hospital room. By the time Garvin grabbed the gun I think I had picked out my dress for the funeral." She smiled at Ben apologetically. "Just to calm my nerves, you understand, darling."

"Of course. Whereas I felt no fear because I knew that in an instant you would hurl yourself on Enid, give her a karate chop you learned at the movies, and get the pistol away from her without even mussing your hair."

"And perhaps you were also feeling courageous because Garvin had told you he took the bullets out of the gun?"

"He didn't tell me that until later, Carrie. You heard him yourself, when we were congratulating him on his control."

"He handled the whole thing amazingly," Howard put in. "He must have realized it was essential to get Enid to go to the meeting. She could have explained the telephone message somehow, so I don't think there's a chance she would have cracked if you hadn't confronted her with that painting."

"No one has ever reacted so strongly to my work before. But of course my nudes are pretty shocking."

"Oh, was that a nude? How do you tell?" Howard looked genuinely curious.

Carrie said, "You should supply a guide to your paintings, Ben. A sort of glossary of body parts and facial features. They'd probably sell better if people could understand how naughty they are."

"You two are abysmally ignorant about abstract art. Never mind, I'll give you some more salmon anyway."

Ben pushed back his chair and got to his feet. All day the air had been a thick, unmoving curtain of heat that one longed to push aside. Even the smallest leaves on the trees had been too limp and discouraged to tremble.

Now suddenly a white flash of lightning shook the sky, giving a ghostly presence to the three who had chosen to eat their dinner on the deck.

"Thank God for Lanigan's," Ben said, returning to the table with a platter of cold poached salmon and a dish of green mayonnaise to go with it. "Cold meals always require a lot of hot cooking."

"It would be better if you had made it though, Ben; we all know that."

"That's right, keep the compliments coming if you want to stay out of the kitchen." Ben served himself a spoonful of sauce and tasted it appraisingly. "More tarragon and chives would help. I believe I'll . . ."

He was pushing back his chair again, but Carrie stopped him. "You've accomplished enough today. Take it easy."

"I agree," said Howard. "Anyway, I still have a lot of unanswered questions about Greg's murder. Clearly, Enid was having an affair with him, and had allowed him to do a nude painting of her. That was what she expected to see when you unveiled the picture on the easel."

"Enid Thorpe lolling on Greg's sofa in carnal abandon. Sorry, my imagination isn't up to it." Carrie reached for the salad bowl on a small table beside her. "Then she must have set the fire at the studio, hoping to destroy the picture."

"Possibly she did destroy it. We still haven't been allowed to see what they salvaged, you know."

"I don't think I want to," Carrie said. "Enid is a fabulous woman, attractive, superintelligent. I can see how she might have an affair with Greg, but why in the world would she let him paint her in the nude?"

"Well, in a way that deviation was what got my attention." Ben leaned forward, eager to make his point. "When you described the envy you sensed when Enid talked about Jenny I thought about them all in college together, with Enid not so sure of herself then, not so good-looking, and Jenny getting all the guys. Knowing Jenny could have Garvin too if she wanted him. And then Jenny marrying Greg and having a son. I suppose Enid would like to have children, wouldn't she? All women have the need, haven't they?"

"Oh, I think so. It's pretty basic."

"I remembered reading somewhere that having a person's portrait done is a way of demonstrating possession of the subject. That goes for the husband paying for the picture and also the artist who paints it. Well, I turned that around." Ben sat back, smiling expectantly at Howard and Carrie.

"What do you mean?" Howard asked.

"I think he means that the subject could be said to possess the artist. Is that the idea, Ben?"

Ben nodded at his wife approvingly. "Right. For a time at least. While the painting is being done the subject has the artist's total attention. And of course nudity adds a dimension of intimacy."

"Enid must have figured that all out psychologically. She probably thought she was totally ensnaring Greg. I can picture her congratulating herself on being so much smarter than all those other women who hadn't a chance of holding him. She couldn't have known they had done the same thing."

"And then she found out about Maria." A breeze had come up, portending rain, causing the candles to flicker in their low glass chimneys. In the changing light Carrie's face was sorrowful. "It must have been an awful discovery for her, when she was possibly getting more and more sure of herself."

"Could she have thought Greg was really in love with her? Would a smart woman like Enid be so deluded?"

"Garvin was helpful on that score after you left, Howard. Apparently he had gotten suspicious enough to question Enid pretty closely the night before last and she confessed to being obsessed with Greg. That's the way she put it, 'obsessed.' He got the impression that she was the aggressor, not Greg."

"I wonder what made Garvin suspicious?"

"Remember my telling you about the phone call I answered right after Maria shot Frank? How it was Enid saying she was calling for Garvin? Well, the real reason she was calling was to continue the so-called therapy that she, Enid, had been administering to poor, mixed-up Frank." Ben paused, glancing from Carrie's uncomprehending face to Howard's. "Frank had called the house to talk to Garvin and since he wasn't in, had left Grogan's number with her."

"Are you saying that Enid was counseling Frank on the telephone? Why would he stand for that?"

"You have to understand his desperation. He was scared stiff that he was about to flip and do something harmful to Maria, and Enid apparently understood that. She has a great gift of empathy, Garvin explained to me, which would have been very useful in her work."

Carrie said slowly, "I suppose she explained to Frank that she too was a psychotherapist, well qualified to advise him, especially in an emergency situation."

"She might have claimed that Garvin shared his cases with her, maybe said she often acted as his assistant." Howard's face was filled with wonder. "The woman has incredible nerve."

"But, Ben, how did you or Garvin figure out what Enid was doing?"

"Garvin overheard her end of a telephone conversation and realized, with horror, need I say, that she was talking to Frank Lundy. Of course he made her explain what she thought she was doing." Ben paused for a sip of his wine. "Just trying to help, she told him. The poor man had sounded so upset when he called, and Garvin wasn't around, and she knew what to do." Again Ben paused, this time for dramatic emphasis. "She knew what to do all right, which was to goad the guy, knowing how unstable he was, getting him more and more furious at Maria until he would shoot her, or try to. Either one would accomplish her purpose."

"Her purpose being to make Frank appear to be Greg's murderer, of course."

"Yes, as a function of his ungovernable passions, which he would demonstrate by shooting his wife."

"And if he should happen to kill Maria his defense might be that *she* had murdered Greg and was about to turn on him."

"Which she did. The latter, I mean."

"Either way, Enid would be in the clear."

"Imagine the agony she caused that poor, sick man." In the flickering candlelight Carrie's eyes were soft with pity. "I can't believe Enid could be capable of such cruelty. I don't want to believe it."

"Obviously Enid is very neurotic, Carrie. You know she's had problems in the past. Garvin hinted that the last few years have been hellish."

They sat in silence watching the candles, which had burned down to wicks fizzling in their pools of melted wax.

One went out, then the other and, as if signaled by the darkness, huge, loudly spattering drops of rain began to splash on the table and on the deck around them.

All three leapt up, reaching for salad bowl, fish platter, bread basket, plates, and napkins. Ben pushed open the sliding screen door, and they hurried into the kitchen and set everything on the counter. Then Carrie ran upstairs to close windows, pausing at the foot of the stairs to call to the men, "Not another word till I get back!"

AN HOUR LATER dinner had been cleaned up and Ben was pouring nightcaps: Scotch for himself and Howard, vodka for Carrie. They smiled at each other as they sank wearily into the soft chairs around the kitchen fireplace.

"Why are we doing this, will you tell me that?" Carrie suppressed a yawn and lay back in her chair, her eyes half-closed.

"Just a few loose ends to tie up, then I'll take myself off."

"You have a fine legal mind, Howard, that's clear," Ben said. "Even if you don't know enough to go to bed when you're done in. Not to mention your hosts."

Howard ignored him. "Now here's the way I'm putting it together. On the night of the murder Garvin goes over to see Jenny, leaving Enid supposedly working in her study. But Enid goes out. Why?"

"Judging from her telephone message, she'd been trying to get together with Greg and he was being evasive. Suppose she called him again as soon as Garvin left and again he put her off—perhaps rudely this time."

Carrie sat up in her chair. "That's quite possible, because he knew Maria was coming to get her things and he hoped to talk her out of it."

"Then Frank Lundy comes to the door and leaves the package containing a gun." Howard looked at Ben. "How does she know it's a gun, by the way?"

"I asked Garvin about that, and he said Frank told her. She knew Frank was disturbed; Garvin had warned her to be careful, so she was taking no chances."

Carrie picked up the thread, "So when Frank leaves she is lonely—there's Garvin with perfect Jenny again—and she's full of rage and frustration over Greg..."

"And for the first time she has the means to punish him: Frank's pistol."

"But Howard, Enid is an intelligent, civilized woman."

"Also very sick. Anyway, I'm not saying she took one look at the gun and decided to use it. More likely, she went out for a walk, hoping to see what Greg was up to."

"And took the gun along for safekeeping?"

"Who knows her reasoning at that point?"

"All right, then say she gets to Greg's studio just as Maria is pulling out."

"After that she sees Greg leave—for his trip to the drugstore—and she follows him and accosts him when he comes out. When he sees how emotional she is he gets her away from the store; they walk down the street to where it's dark and quiet..."

Carrie said, "To the Porter Publishing Company, in short, closed up for the night."

"And out in front—or maybe on the porch—they argue and he gets fed up enough to tell her he doesn't give a damn about her, and she shoots him." Ben swallowed what was left of his drink.

"They had to be on our porch. She never could have dragged him up the steps."

"She panics then of course, pushes on the door, and, like magic, it opens up." Howard spoke slowly, working it out. "So she drags Greg inside, then on into Ben's office with some idea of delaying discovery, and there she sees Ben's fishing knife and inspiration strikes; she plants it in Greg's chest to confuse the issue."

There was silence. The rain had stopped, Ben realized, and he got up and opened the glass door to the deck. He stood sniffing the night air, cool and fresh now, after the cleansing rain.

"Looks like the heat wave is over," he said. "We'll sleep well tonight." He turned and looked pointedly at Howard. "When we get a chance."

Howard pushed himself up from his chair, jingling the ice in his glass. "One more question: Was it Enid, do you think, who threatened Cabby? And if so, why?"

"I don't understand that myself," Ben replied.

"I think I do." It was Carrie's turn to pull herself to her feet. "Enid wasn't thinking straight, let's face it. She must have been horrified at what she'd done and scared stiff of getting caught. And while she's suffering all that guilt and tension entirely on her own, unable to get comfort from anyone, her old friend Jenny, the one who should be paralyzed with grief, is totally monopolizing Garvin. For all Enid knows, Jenny might get him for her next husband; he's always been crazy about her. And in addition Jenny has a son. Greg's son. It's too much. Even if she has no real intention of harming the child, Enid can't deny herself the pleasure of making Jenny suffer."

"And Cabby is the only means she has left."

"All right, that does it." Howard made his good-byes and departed, and within fifteen minutes the house was dark, with both Porters in bed and on the edge of sleep.

"Oh, I knew there was something," Carrie said fuzzily from her pillow. "Sorry, darling, but this has been bothering me. How did you know the appliance being fixed at Sullivan's was Greg's answering machine?"

"I wondered when you would get around to that." Ben propped himself on one elbow and said, "Remember when I did a sketch of Greg's studio after the fire? Mostly because Jenny wanted it?"

"Yes, did you give it to her?"

"Not yet. But while I was putting in the color I recalled something about the desk. It was beautiful wood, walnut or something like that, but it had been standing in the sun for a long time, and the color of the wood had faded—except for a dark square beside the phone. The usual position for an answering machine."

"You're a genius."

"No, just a well-trained househusband."

"But why wouldn't you tell me when I asked you?"

"Well you see, in my position I have to guard every remaining vestige of masculinity."

"I wouldn't use the word *vestige*, Ben."

"We'll see about that tomorrow night. Now go to
sleep."

MURDER
WITHOUT RESERVATION

A TONY AND PAT PRATT MYSTERY

BERNIE LEE

With only three more major sequences left to shoot,
the picture looked like a successful wrap. But that was
before somebody shot the horse and the drug dealer,
before Tony went crashing through white-water
rapids to save a terrified boy from drowning, before
the runaway grass fire and way before somebody
dumped a pair of deadly rattlesnakes in the Pratts'
bedroom....

Available at your favorite retail outlet in May, or reserve your copy for April shipping by sending your name, address, zip or postal code, along with a check or money order for $3.99 (please do not send cash), plus 75¢ postage and handling ($1.00 in Canada) for each book ordered, payable to Worldwide Mystery to:

In the U.S.

Worldwide Mystery
3010 Walden Ave.
P.O. Box 1325
Buffalo, NY 14269-1325

In Canada

Worldwide Mystery
P.O. Box 609
Fort Erie, Ontario
L2A 5X3

Please specify book title with your order.
Canadian residents add applicable federal and provincial taxes.

RES

 WORLDWIDE LIBRARY®

POISON PEN

A CHARLOTTE KENT MYSTERY

MARY KITTREDGE

Struggling each month to fill the pages of her new magazine for writers, Charlotte Kemp finds herself up the proverbial creek when she discovers her biggest, and very nearly only, contributor, Wesley Bell, sitting dead in her office swivel chair.

Then Charlotte discovers the hard way that she's at the top of somebody's must-kill list—an ending she'd like to skip entirely . . . if possible.

A DEB RALSTON MYSTERY
DEFICIT ENDING
LEE MARTIN

Ready or not, Ralston is back from maternity leave, haunted by the look of a young teller who is taken hostage and later killed— the first in a string of victims.

Deb Ralston is soon hot on the tail of the murderers and heading straight into deadly danger.